Anouar Benmalek

THE CHILD OF AN
ANCIENT PEOPLE

TRANSLATED FROM THE FRENCH BY
Andrew Riemer

VINTAGE

Published by Vintage 2004

2 4 6 8 10 9 7 5 3 1

Copyright © Librairie Arthème Fayard, 2000
English translation copyright © Andrew Riemer, 2003

Anouar Benmalek has asserted his right under the Copyright,
Designs and Patents Act, 1988 to be identified as the author
of this work

First published in Great Britain in 2003 by
The Harvill Press

First published by Pauvert, an imprint of Librairie Arthème
Fayard, in 2000 with the title *L'Enfant du peuple ancien*

Vintage
Random House, 20 Vauxhall Bridge Road,
London SW1V 2SA

Random House Australia (Pty) Limited
20 Alfred Street, Milsons Point, Sydney
New South Wales 2061, Australia

Random House New Zealand Limited
18 Poland Road, Glenfield,
Auckland 10, New Zealand

Random House (Pty) Limited
Endulini, 5A Jubilee Road, Parktown 2193,
South Africa

The Random House Group Limited Reg. No. 954009
www.randomhouse.co.uk/vintage

A CIP catalogue record for this book
is available from the British Library

ISBN 0 09 945369 X

Papers used by Random House are natural, recyclable
products made from wood grown in sustainable forests.
The manufacturing processes conform to the environ-
mental regulations of the country of origin

Printed and bound in Denmark by
AIT Nørhaven A/S, Viborg

To Truganini, who died on 8 May 1876, the last representative of the Aborigines of Tasmania, a people wiped off the surface of the earth by a perfect genocide: its victims forgotten, the murderers free of blame.

Then bring me back the days of dreaming,
When I myself was yet unformed,
When song welled up in me, and teeming
The tuneful fancies in me swarmed

Goethe *Faust*
(Translated by Philip Wayne)

PROLOGUE

Queensland, North-East Australia, December 1918

From the window, I am examining the garden with attention. It is strewn with cane tables and chairs. A crowd is milling around. My eyes search eagerly for the arrival of my family, my son, back alive from hell, Margaret, his courageous and headstrong wife, his daughter Joan – my granddaughter – whom I adore. Then I look for Tridarir, my constant shadow, the human being who was, at one time, our only reason for living. Our greatest failure too. The taciturn Aborigine is not there, he has vanished for the day. Or perhaps, as is his way sometimes, he has gone, for a month or more, on one of his strange wanderings in the desert, from which he returns filthy with dust, almost dead from hunger, and in even greater despair.

I should be happy. Yet I feel a fool among fools. At the very moment when the Reverend Key motions to me, with a broad smile, that I should join them, nothing matters for me as much as this body stretched out on the bed at the back of the room. My wife's body. Emaciated. I thirst for life. Such thirst. For her and for me.

It's a fine day. A salty scent of spring. As if the Pacific Ocean, instead of being hundreds of kilometres away, had squarely invited itself to visit us.

I am so old now. I look at my wrinkled hands, at the lines running all over them. I am filled with resentment that they have become so weak, so ugly. My God, what is the meaning of this insane desire to go on living in such a decrepit body? I look behind me. The bedcover has been thrown back. My wife has not stirred. Despite the gloom, I can make out the base of her breasts. Formerly, when my eyes used to light on her bosom, my heart, my tongue, my sex would grow numb with lust. And I loved that lassitude of desire above everything else. Now, as soon as my fingers stroke the scaly skin on her neck, I am filled with an overpowering sense of compassion. For my companion too, my wounded vixen, these years have passed too quickly. And no-one teaches us how to grow old.

To think that half a century ago (but has it been as long as that, five decades more furtive than a heartbeat?) I was a prince of the blood, nephew of the Emir Abd El Kader, that I came close to becoming, in my turn, a servant of the Muslims' God and after that one of their leaders! At present, in the evening of my life, I am known as Harry, and I am just back from a tedious sermon in the Anglican church of Allisson, a small town in an outrageous land, lost between mountains and the bush.

Outside, the noise of the party. To celebrate our son's homecoming, safe and sound, we have invited all our neighbours. Save for the Kellys, whose son, accused of turning his back on the enemy, faced the firing squad of the Anzacs, the expeditionary force raised by New Zealand and Australia. We have great regard for the Kellys, particularly because their eldest son was a friend of the family. We gave the matter much thought, without reaching a humane resolution: to invite them was to expose them to contempt and, worse, to ridicule; not to invite them was to drive them further into their misery. My son Joseph – whom I call Yousef in my heart of hearts – is carrying on like a madman. From where I am, I can hear him bawling:

"Australia, perhaps it is the arsehole of the world, but oh! how I love that arsehole!"

He is tight already, as are probably all the men who were recently demobbed. They have earned the right to get drunk. They have just come home after four years of war in Europe and the Orient. There is a kind of brutishness in the air, a wild joy at being among those who have survived an immense massacre, mingled with a despairing but

2

unconfessed sorrow for their complicity in a crime. Yesterday, as we were making the final preparations for the party, Joseph-Yousef said to me in a peculiar voice:

"You know, Dad, what we went through at Gallipoli was so horrible. The Turks and us, we tore out each other's guts like madmen. I found out that I could cut someone's throat or drive a bayonet into his belly as easily as this!"

Standing at the table, he dug his knife into the loaf. He who had left for war "as strong as a rutting kangaroo", as he boasted, has grown much thinner. That was the first time since he came back that he spoke to me about *over there*. He did it again, digging his knife around in the bread:

"A mob of butchers and butchered, that's what we'd become . . . Me as much as the others . . . A bit of booze to make you forget the fear and the stinking corpses of the blokes who'd been your mates, three or four hours of sleep snatched here or there, women you paid for or, more often, raped, and our officers lecturing us on patriotism, honour and all that stuff. And everywhere they led us, we followed them like sheep, those officers who treated everyone, soldiers and civilians, like animals. A blowfly was worth more than we were . . ."

He cleared his throat. His voice was filled with resentment. Never had he spoken to me so coarsely. He has grown older than me, he with his thirty years and I overtaking him by close to fifty.

"At least we can be sure that we've hit rock-bottom. After this another war won't be possible, that's for sure!"

Then a sigh, a little scornful:

"You were lucky, Dad, you never knew war. I'm getting on your nerves with all this complaining."

We were in the cellar. He shifted the barrel of beer, the beer which I brew right here, and of which – I a Muslim! – am so proud. He poured me a glass:

"You're going to see, we'll build a wall around Australia, we'll get rid of all the bloody warmongers, and we might as well send the Chinks and Niggers packing too. We'll be on our own, and we'll make this beautiful Australia of ours grow. This is going to be a paradise, I tell you!"

3

His voice was shaking with unusual excitement. I said nothing in reply. Even after so many years of pretending, the same anxiety took hold of me again. I could not stop myself from taking stock of the features of the man face to face with me: fortunately he resembles his mother so much . . . I clasped my idiot of a son against me – the only child we had, and so late in life – and I thought, with a pang in my heart: If only you could guess at how much cruelty He who reclines in Heaven keeps in store! Go back to your wife and little girl. We never have enough time for those we love.

Here is the bookcase, the piece of furniture I treasure most in this house at the end of the world. There are a good many books there, some in French, most of them in English. Paradoxically, I am the one who buys and reads works in French. My wife Elizabeth, although French is one of her mother tongues, prefers English. I believe she has never forgiven France for all the evil it had done to her. For my part, I had no choice: in this corner of the world, the only language in which I talk – rarely – about my own country is French. The more time passes, the more natural does this language become for me. People are generally born with one mother tongue. In my case, I am not far from acquiring another, though when dying . . .

I have put the Bible back in the compartment reserved for it, next to the sole book in Arabic I still possess, which has miraculously stayed with me through all these years. I fondle the gazelle-skin binding. It is a volume of verse, the *Book of Songs*, dear to my heart because it is the only keepsake left to me of my former existence. The printer in Damascus – I found the book in his neighbourhood – had the curious conceit of illuminating it like a Koran. The instinct to make sure that my hands are clean before leafing through it has stayed with me. Did the printer wish by this, perhaps, to make subtle fun of his compatriots' bigotry? As for me, I have not believed in God for a long time now, whether the Christians' or, otherwise, the Muslims'. Could a "real" God be so capricious in his dealings with his creatures? I still pray to Him though – and in three languages – a little through habit, equally perhaps to show some indulgence towards Him who was an ardent companion of my childhood.

Elizabeth has murmured, in English:

"Please close the curtains."

Her voice is very weak. Beads of perspiration stick to a lock of hair falling over her face. With difficulty, she pushes it aside. She tries to make a joke:

"What are you reading, Harry? The Song of Songs?"

She is speaking to me in French. It is always in French that she addresses me when she is in a teasing mood. Never in public. She presses her hands against the bedding, wanting to sit up. Her smile is lost in a frown. She shuts her eyes again. She manages to say – and her good humour is a torment:

"Come on, caress me. Put your hand there . . ."

It is an old pleasantry between us, this Song of Songs, which reaches back to the period of our life when, in order to perfect our disguise, I took to studying the Bible. I leafed through those hundreds of pages in which one prophet followed hard on the heels of another, where complicated genealogies gave birth in my mind to the most idle questions: so whom did Cain marry after he was hunted out of his parents' house? His sister? How old was he? And I, who from the beginning of my adolescence could recite without faltering a garnering from the 114 surae of the Koran, I recalled with ironic melancholy that the Book of Islam evaded just as assiduously that kind of precision.

And then my eyes lit with amazement on the blazing exhortations of the Song of Songs. At first I thought that someone had played a joke on me by selling me a dubious version of the Bible. I spent a whole morning reading and rereading those verses where the fair maiden's breasts "are like two young roes that are twins", where the beloved melts in delight in his lover's garden "where I have eaten my honeycomb with my honey, drunk my wine with my milk . . ." And I thought, disturbed: Ah Solomon! Right royal king though you are, face to face with your lover you were like all men. Your woman's cunt and her tits, that's what was paradise for you!

5

I was at my table, the book in my hand. Through the window, I caught sight of Elizabeth at the bottom of the garden. She was working in the vegetable patch next to the little farmyard we had in those days. I grew so stiff, unable to control myself any longer, that I rushed outside. Tridarir pretended not to notice how completely red in the face I had gone. The Aborigine, the only friend that I really have in this land, the antipodes to mine, was saddling a horse, and pretending that he had to do something to protect the fruit trees from being gnawed by cattle. I grabbed Elizabeth's hand and, almost without a word, I dragged her into the shed where I made love to her feverishly. When I told her what had happened to me, she burst out laughing, half shocked, half amused:

"The Bible as aphrodisiac, only a ninny like you could think of that."

Behind me in the room, Elizabeth is asleep. From time to time she grows delirious. Her lips murmur unintelligible fragments of speech. The doctor was very pessimistic.

"There's nothing to be done, it's old age," he flung at me with an air of indifference, as if he meant that she had lived too long.

I closed the door behind the doctor, my heart filled with hatred for this person who found it normal for a human being to die.

At present, Joseph knows nothing of this. He believes that his mother has taken to her bed with a simple cold. I did not want to spoil the joy of his homecoming. Elizabeth pretends to be unaware of the seriousness of her condition and talks to me about her plans for the coming winter.

I kiss her on the nose. She calls this our emu-kiss. I fight back a tear, sitting on a chair right beside the bed. There is a stabbing pain in my back and I am tormented by a strong need to piss. My hand is prisoner to my slumbering wife's.

A moment ago, I whispered lewd things in her ear. She started to laugh:

"I'll stay alive as long as I'm happy to behave disgracefully with you. Get into bed with me, and take my clothes off. Like before," she sighed, but she lost consciousness once more. I felt my heart stop. I wiped her face with a damp towel. She opened her eyes wide:

6

"What is happening to me?"

"Nothing my little bird, nothing."

Sobs, like stalking jackals, lurk at the back of my throat. Throughout my life, I have loved two women only. And each time fiercely, that is to say at the risk of my life. I do not know what happened to the first. I am now watching the second as she is dying. And it is my existence that is slowly departing with her.

The old woman on the bed tries to stir. She mutters something which her companion cannot understand. The man in the chair leans down to the invalid's mouth. Her speech is halting, laboured. Saliva dribbles from her lips.

"Mustn't tell anyone, Kader . . . Especially Joseph, promise me . . . Look after our Tridarir . . . Kader, where are you? Kader?"

His heart is beating faster. Good God, so many years have gone by since she called him by that name!

"But I am here, Elizabeth."

Then, taking hold of himself, his lips pressed close to his companion's face:

"I am here, Lislei. Don't be afraid, I am here. We two have been in hiding for so long . . . How could I leave you, my Lislei?"

PART ONE

1

High plateau, the south of Algeria, the month of Rajab in the year 1288 after the Hegira (April 1871)

The ostrich is no more than forty paces away. He could fire already, but his galloping mount is leaping around so much that he is afraid of missing his target. And besides, he has hardly any illusions about his skill as a marksman. The horse, despite its fatigue, increases its pace. It sensed that the huge bird was slowing down little by little. They have been rushing like mad for too long. At this rate, the ostrich is going to collapse, its tiny heart choked by the incredible exertion. This is, for the man, his first ostrich hunt; he is astonished by the contrast between the animal's grotesque lop-sided gait and the speed of its course.

"Blasted bird," he mutters, filled with admiration, "you certainly are the offspring of a camel and a stork!"

At present, he can almost touch the magnificent silky, swaying white feathers, the very object of a chase that seems to him more and more inane. The cock, reeling from exhaustion, can no longer manage to weave around. Besides, that would be of little use; beyond the pond next to the pink laurels, there extends, in front of the hunter and his prey, the unpitying flatness of the plain, spiked with thorny bushes and tufts of Spanish grass.

The ostrich comes to an abrupt halt. It hesitates, trying to conceal its rear behind a ridiculously small bush. The horseman is hard put to control the chestnut steed rearing in fright. The ostrich turns towards them. It raises a leg, lowers it and scratches the ground. Is it going to leap at them? The two talons on its elongated claws look as if they could disembowel a wild beast.

He makes his mount circle around the animal, keeping a respectful distance all the while. This is the perfect moment for firing, but he cannot make up his mind. A hoarse sound, interrupted by a series of splutters, emerges from the bird's beak. The large eyes above its obscene-looking neck stare at the pursuers through eyelashes which strike him as almost feminine. Does the fowl know that this two-headed monster is about to take its life? Is the frenzied jerking of the eyes in their sockets void of all expression a kind of supplication, perhaps? The man realises that for the ostrich he has cornered he must represent the Ozrin of feathered creatures, or another equally merciless deity.

"Great ass-arsed cockerel," he shouts, "you were about to rut; as for me, not only am I frustrating you, but I am here to teach you the filthy secret of what it is to die!"

He would like to savour his witticism. It is a fine day, and he has managed to thwart the females' ruses to protect their male – in full mating cry. He recognised them, despite the dust, thanks to their black plumage bordered with white on wings and neck. With its slender sex hanging between its legs and its first panic-stricken jerks, the bird brought to mind a lover, taken by surprise, fleeing without his undergarments. The man laughed and felt an odd sense of fraternity with the hapless male robbed of its delightful intimacy.

"You, at least, have managed to make love once or twice before dying. As for me, with the one I love there's nothing but gazing at her shoulders. I cannot make any sense of this. All I want is dallying, caressing and making love with this wretched Nour. And I've done none of that. Perhaps I never shall, what do you think?"

The heat of the chase has made the hunter forget, for the moment, the anxiety which has been tormenting him for several weeks, an anxiety shared, in all likelihood, by all the tribes, allies or enemies, from the coast of Kabylie to the Chaambas desert. Will they too be obliged to take part in this new war? How many of them will lose their lives? And he himself, his family, Nour, will they manage to escape if the place where their tents are pitched is laid waste?

The bird falters, then sinks heavily on its breast. A wave-like motion ripples along its neck from bottom to top, as if it were going to vomit. It is probably in its death throes: red-stained froth seeps from the slits in its beak.

"Damn" – the hunter is getting annoyed – "you are not going to start weeping?"

Its blood vessels must have burst. The bird blinks furiously, trying to throw off death as if it were a persistent mosquito.

The hunter's ardour has cooled. This creature, striving desperately not to sink into nothingness, has become far too human for him. The panting bundle of feathers reminds him of a baby whimpering because he is too exhausted to wail. The man is ashamed of his cowardice, he knows he will not pull the trigger. Disheartened, he muses: And with me, will my soul depart in an equally ridiculous fashion through the holes in my nose?

He spurs his horse, which, taken by surprise, shows resistance: the thoroughbred, although a grass-grazer, has found a liking for the game, not understanding that it could come to an end without a death-blow. The horseman gives the reins a fierce tug and turns his mount around. When he reaches the crest, he catches sight of the dust raised by Hassan's horse. He will have to submit himself to his raillery: he was the one to discover where the ostriches were, and he will not hide his fury when he sees his cousin coming back empty-handed!

His cousin is already hailing him from the foot of the hill. The rider clears his throat, then spits the dust out of his mouth. He shrugs, disgusted with himself:

"You're out of luck, ostrich. I am much more afraid of how this idiot cousin of mine will mock me than of your curses!"

He strikes the horse with his crop; the animals neighs in pain. When he finds the ostrich again, it is not dead. It is on its feet, but tottering. The man dismounts: he strides ostentatiously towards the bird, hoping that it will still have time to escape. But its eyes are shut and it does not react to the hunter's approach. Its neck is stained red by the foam seeping from its beak. The man would almost like to prop up the animal, which had narrowly missed crashing against a rock.

"A hyena would have chomped away at you anyway, little brother."

As the shot rings out, Hassan is already at his side. The animal's legs are still twitching. With a disagreeable smile at the corner of his mouth, Hassan exclaims:

"I couldn't understand at first why you were coming towards me. But the important thing is, Kader, that you've finally got it, your redoubtable chicken . . ."

Kader shrugs. He gazes at the mass of feathers half entangled in thorny scrub. In spite of himself, he had aimed correctly: the head, though it was hit point-blank, has not been damaged: only the right eye is missing. The cousin, astride his horse, adds, with a click of the tongue like an insult:

"I hope that you will show less hesitation in front of the French soldiers. They won't miss you, you can be sure."

Kader, in the grip of a vague feeling that he needs to vomit, makes no reply. He does not know whether this is caused by the death of the ostrich or the prospect of having to go to war soon.

"Do you really believe that we are going to make war, Hassan?"

The young man on horseback curls his lips, annoyed by his companion's sudden ill-humour. His heart is also heavy with apprehension, and he is filled with resentment because his cousin has shattered their tacit pact of heroism. He dismounts, holding two long strands of rope. He hands one to Kader. In a cutting voice, he grumbles:

"To the north, there's war already. I don't see how we can avoid it. Still less you and I! Perhaps you've forgotten, but remember: we are the eldest son in each of our families *and* the sons of chiefs . . ."

"You trust El Mokrani?"

"Yes . . . in so far as we have no other choice. The important thing is that he has managed to stir up all the northern tribes against the Christians. No-one else could have achieved that."

Hassan has started binding the ostrich's legs. The knot slips. He ties it again, then, in a flash of anger, kicks the dead animal.

"Kader, I know that you are going to tell me again that El Mokrani was appointed bashagha after he helped the Duke of Orleans defeat your kinsman, the Emir Abd El Kader in the campaign of the Iron Gates. But all that, it happened so long ago, before you and I were even born."

Kader, his eyes lowered, snorts contemptuously:

"Son of a noble family, I remind you that our mothers are sisters. And the Emir, if he is *my* kinsman, he is also *yours*!"

Hassan turns to his cousin. He is shaking with exasperation:

"He might have betrayed the Emir thirty years ago, but now he's a hero. There is famine everywhere. El Mokrani has gone into debt to feed the peasants in his district. Everything he owns has been put up as surety. In vain did he implore the French army – his allies what's more – to lower taxes and distribute food among those who no longer had anything to eat. They treated him with contempt. In the end, he decided that there was nothing left for him but to raise a rebellion. In any case, we no longer have the choice: people are starving in our villages and even God doesn't acknowledge us, despite our five daily prayers! At the least sign of discontent, the army just cuts down all the palms and all the olive trees, it arrests the agitators and raises taxes. If they are not paid, they confiscate our lands to make room for their Alsatians or their Maltese. Oh, they know well enough what they are doing, these accursed soldiers! Soon, we won't have anywhere but ravines and mountain peaks to hide our backsides . . ."

Hassan's voice has cracked. He pretends to be absorbed in trussing the bird. Then he gulps, overcome by a child-like sadness:

"We haven't lived through all this only to be treated like dogs."

Kader, with a lump in his throat, taps his cousin on the shoulder. The other, a strapping fellow, all muscles and tendons, lowers his head to hide his moist eyes. Kader remembers the two inseparable scallywags they were during their marvellous years in the oasis of Biskra. Hassan, his elder by two years, taught him how to climb as high as the crowns of date palms. They came to spend entire afternoons there, each perched at the top, exchanging secrets across huge fronds heavy with dates. Hassan said over and over again that, when he grew up, he would become a great traveller, the equal of Ibn Battuta, and go sailing in great ships in search of ambergris spawned by the ocean foam. "I don't want any more of this desert that dries you up, what I want is water — the sea, immense and endless!" he bawled, stuffing himself with green dates. He did not worry about the stomach ache that would follow, because, according to him, a future explorer had to make himself tough and train himself to eat anything. Once he waxed so lyrical that he slipped from his branch and came close to losing his life in a headlong fall. How many times did Kader envy his aunt's son for his intrepid nature: when he hurled gobs of spit at the legs of grown-ups he disliked and his knack of dreaming up the most glorious destinies for himself and his cousin . . .

His voice growing husky, Kader tries to jest:

"Give me the other rope, shepherd. You are going to see how you parcel up a fowl the size of this!"

They laugh, embarrassed because they are experiencing the same emotion. Hassan sighs:

"We'll never have a better opportunity. They have just been beaten by their worst enemies, the Prussians. Their country has been occupied, their army exhausted and, as if that weren't enough, the French have decided to disembowel each other in their capital. The story goes that they are eating rats and cats and that there have been thousands of deaths. Just think, they train their cannons on their own brothers. These Christians are madmen, believe me, son of my aunt."

He adjusts his tarboosh with fastidious care, then combs his fingers through his short beard. Always so careful of your person, Kader remarks in silence, with a pang of envy.

"Tomorrow we'll know everything. After the midday prayers in the market-place on Friday, the Elders will declare whether they will resolve to join El Mokrani. Until then, pull yourself together, and don't piss your-self in fear, poet."

"Idiot," Kader says, without managing to smile.

By the time they finish slinging the carcass of the ostrich between the saddles of the two horses, they are running with sweat. Their prize turns out to be so heavy that the horses have trouble remaining upright. Hassan tests the weight of the bird's thighs. He winks:

"For me the meat, for you the plumes: that's what we've agreed on, isn't it? What are you going to do with them? They are so delicate and beautiful that only a woman of taste can appreciate . . ."

Kader blushes at the thinly veiled sarcasm. Hassan bursts out laughing.

"Since you've become infatuated with that . . . that . . . what is she called, now? Nour, is that it? You think that no-one around you knows about it?"

Despite the handful of dust Kader has flung at his eyes, Hassan laughs even more uproariously.

"The women around here are terrors, you little prick, as you'll quickly realise. They'll tear your heart out and keep it for themselves."

"Tomorrow, you say?"

At last, the two exhausted horses, the blood-stained ostrich swinging lazily between them, reach the stony little path. The peculiar coupling makes its way along the narrow strip of water leading to the seguia. The palm grove with its countless green sails swaying gently in the setting sun spreads out in front of them. The two can already make out, at a short distance from the oasis, the multicoloured hills and dales of the tents of the tribes who have assembled from the four corners of the Sahara to consult with one another.

"Yes, tomorrow our fate will be sealed: to die quickly or to be snuffed out little by little."

"And you, my cousin, which do you prefer?"

"What do you imagine? To live, of course, and in a blaze! But do you think we have any choice left, Kader?"

He adds, a hand in front of his face:

"My God, I am as worn out as an old nag. This is not what I dreamt about when I was a lad . . ."

His voice is bitter and filled with rage. Kader is astonished at how exhausted his cousin looks. Coming back from the hunt had certainly taken a long time, but the rider guesses that his childhood companion has experienced a sudden urge not to go on feigning constant bravado and to reveal something of the anguish which is also goring him.

"Hassan, do you think there's any chance of victory?"

"None. To win a battle or two, to raze a few farms, to cut off the heads and purses of a dozen or so colonists to show that we are not slaves, yes. To chase them out of our land, no. Their cannons, their rifles are too powerful for us. What could we put up against them: starving warriors, peasants in tatters, a few clapped-out muskets, the interminable disputes among the tribes and many, many prayers, far less effective than goat-fart. Ah, but we are strong for religion! Go to the Imam, he'll even find out for you how many pebbles the Prophet recommended for wiping your arse."

Kader is suddenly overcome by rage against the inevitable:

"Are we then going to saddle, with our own hands, the black camel of death so that it may kneel in front of each of our tents? Is there no other way out? Perhaps those devils could be persuaded to change their mind? We have eloquent men amongst us, and with them there's only the blood-thirsty military."

Hassan's reaction is unexpected. His uncontrollable laughter almost makes him choke. His mount, taken by surprise, steps to one side. The ostrich's head slips out of the knots and bumps violently against the other horse's hoofs. Kader is almost thrown from the saddle. While struggling to control his terror-stricken horse, he hears Hassan shouting at him:

"By the houris of Paradise, cousin, your love for that Nour makes you as timid as a hare. Since when has a conqueror paid heed to the conquered? Have you ever heard of a mouse begging a cat for mercy?"

His voice burning with rage, Kader hurls insults at his companion:

"Blast your mouth, I forbid you to speak of Nour! And what's more, imbecile, gelded ass, help me instead of making speeches. This damned carcass is going to pitch me into the wadi!"

"Gelding yourself! Even a nag would refuse to obey someone as lily-livered as you are. When we overran Spain, did we pay any heed to the tears of the Spaniards we'd crushed ? We held them in thrall for seven centuries and left Andalusia only when bayonets were prodding our back-sides. No-one ever feels pity for someone on his knees, do you hear?"

Lips curled in disgust, Hassan observes his cousin's efforts to avoid sliding off his mount. Hands placed ostentatiously on the pommel of the saddle, he rails:

"Your family, just like mine, are the owners of slaves they had bought or abducted. Have you ever thought of them with compassion or to free them? That would seem absurd to you, worse, ridiculous!"

He reaches out to grasp the terrified chestnut's neck. He sighs, overcome by compassion for this younger cousin with soft and colourless features, which give him the look of a Christian, who has become a little too learned for his taste. The rumour runs around the tribe that, in exile, Kader had sought out the company of the French, even to the point of knowing how to speak their language. He denies it, of course, but the witnesses were precise. So, how can we not be suspicious of him? some muttered; if he became too familiar with our enemies' words, wouldn't he inevitably finish up not hating them enough and allowing them, perhaps, to get around him in one way or another at the crucial moment?

He, Hassan, loves him all the same, this shambling bean-pole, more than a brother, with whom he shared all the joys and sorrows of his childhood. What would he not give, oh God, to return to that sweetest of times when each morning was like a ripe orange ready to burst with surprise and joy? What would this listless Kader say if he knew that he, his cousin, hardened for combat as he insists he is, has been buffeted for some time by a panic which makes him go weak at the knees and clamps his guts?

"Pity and reason, those are the two things that are the first to fade in the heart of a man whom the chance of the moment has made a conqueror. If you were the stronger, perhaps you would be worse than they, Kader! God has lent us time, but He is a usurer, impatient when keeping His accounts. He has decided, once again, to call in the debt: our lives, and if that should not be enough to pay the interest He demands, the lives of our nearest too! So, don't prattle foolishly, my good cousin, go and recite a few verses to your beauty and prepare your soul to bite the dust . . ."

Kader has regained his seat on the saddle. He has grown pale. His horse is still pawing the ground, but a tug at the reins subdues its last, involuntary kicks. His cousin is looking him up and down with an air of reprobation. As if struck by what he has just seen, Kader feels a pang of anguish. He whispers sadly:

"Hassan, you've persuaded yourself that I am going to betray . . ."

2

Two years have already passed since Kader left Damascus for the south of Algeria. His father, Hajj Omar, was not able to endure exile any longer, even at the side of the Emir Abd El Kader. In Algeria, he had, over a long span of time, waged war at the side of his illustrious kinsman. At the time of his final battle on Algerian soil, Kader's father only just escaped capture by General Lamoricière's French troops. When the elderly vanquished Emir was deported to Constantinople, then to Damascus, Hajj Omar, who could no longer tolerate his clandestine life among the nomads of the southern Sahara, vowed a little too hastily to join him and to remain with him until his death. Over the long years, he did his best to keep his word, particularly because a large part of his tribal lands in Algeria had been confiscated for the benefit of European newcomers.

The child – who bore the same name as the Emir – was eleven years old when he discovered the Orient and twenty-three when he left it. He had not yet turned twelve when, once again, civil war flared up between the Druze and the Maronites of Mount Lebanon. The troubles quickly spread to the pashalic of Damascus, fanned in an underhand way by the Turks, who had a profound mistrust of Christians, suspecting them of collusion with the English, the French and the other enemies of the Ottoman Empire. A part of the Christian quarter of Damascus was sacked and burnt by rioters armed by the Pasha's police force. The old Emir, throughout the days of the massacre, strove like the devil to save the victims of the massacres, going as far as offering the protection of his bodyguard and his dwelling to hundreds of terrified Christians. As always,

Hajj Omar stood by the side of the Emir without hesitation. Over several weeks, his son saw him setting out at the risk of his own life to prevent Muslims from killing Christians. His puzzlement knew no bounds, the child did not understand why his own father was exerting himself so ardently to defend the co-religionists of those who had stripped them of all their goods in Algeria. He hated them, those *Rumis* who had made them flee from their oasis and their fine house, reducing them to outcasts without wealth or kin! Whereas even the trees in their garden were lovingly tended and enjoyed the privilege of having names! . . .

One evening, his father came home more than usually exhausted by a day spent trying to cajole the Turkish troops who had been enflamed by the prospect of plunder. An acrid smell of burning wafted up from the lower town. The son brought out the jug of water and, timidly, put to his father the question burning on his lips. The father's reply struck him like a whip:

"Do you believe, little ragamuffin, that the Emir would allow women and children to have their throats cut in front of his own eyes, even though they are Christians? He knows better than we what is good for our religion. We are not going to behave like jackals and rejoice at the misfortune of those in greater despair than we are just because we have been robbed of everything . . ."

Hajj Omar, noticing his eldest son's astonished face, adopted a milder tone:

"I know that you miss Biskra, my son. Your mother and I do too. This is not our home and we are poor. And that, that is more bitter than colocynth. But we are alive. In times such as these, that is one of destiny's greatest gifts. All losses are recoverable, save one: death."

His lined face grew dark with irony:

"Do you imagine that the Turks, just because they have the same religion as we do, love us all that much? In our family at least, no-one should harbour any illusions."

The child, confused, lowered his head. His father was referring to the story of a paternal great-grandfather who had behaved insolently towards the Bey of Constantine at the time when the Turks were occupying

Algeria. The family, warned in good time about the Bey's fury, fled in the dead of night and reached the oasis of Biskra, several days' journey by caravan from Constantine. Only the impertinent ancestor proved unable to join in their flight. Some time later, janissaries arrived to hand over to the family a large crate sent by the Ottoman authorities: it contained the intact body of that over-audacious grandfather, which had been stuffed . . .

That was how the son came to frequent the company of French shopkeepers. The father, Joseph Picard, a talkative and rotund native of the Auvergne, was a pastrycook who had fled from France with his large family on account of an obscure history of defaults and unpaid debts. Throughout what became for him "the wonderful Damascus years", the adolescent used to set out early each morning for the madrasa attached to the great mosque of the Umayyad; there he learnt, day after day, the finer points of interpreting the Koran and the more exacting subtleties of rhetoric and Arabic poetry. On his way home, whenever his slender means allowed him, he would stop at the Christian pastry shop to buy a fritter or some other sweetmeat. He had thought at first that he was dealing with an Armenian or a Maronite. When he learnt that the owner was a Frenchman, Kader stayed away from the pastry shop for several days. But curiosity, and the fact that the shop was the only one on his way home, made him once again push open the shop's tingling door. The owner had noted the deportment of this slender youth with so studious an air. He was made welcome, with amusement at first, then out of gratitude because the adolescent had boasted of his kinship with the Emir Abd El Kader, later from mere affection. The young Algerian entered into a boisterous intimacy with the man from the Auvergne, and came rapidly to be treated as a child of the family, so much so that the mother – who called him "my little Arab caliph" – decided to put aside an hour each day to teach him French. The couple had daughters only, and that probably rendered "the adoption" easier.

Two things, both absolutely new, soon wormed their way into the soul of the young man from the Sahara: that French idiom, initially so diverting yet complicated at the same time and . . . – the lessons always came to an end with a prodigious feast – the delicate silkiness of dark cocoa paste married to sugar and vanilla! For a long time, the two discoveries merged into one, and speaking French brought to him the irresistible longing for a mouthful of chocolate. He used to laugh when he caught sight of the plump shapes of the Picard couple: "It's not their fault, it's their language that makes them always hungry."

That was a difficult year for the young Kader, mingling shame with intense delight. Like an over-fortunate explorer, whom chance offered, one after another, two new continents, he had just discovered *two* languages!

The first, classical Arabic, which he learnt at the madrasa, revealed itself as very different from the rather rustic dialect of his native land. It was thrilling to hear, and the ardent rhythms of the Umayyad and Abbasid texts gave birth in his soul to an unquenchable thirst for galloping from one coast of Africa to the other, for the magnificence of Andalusia and for heroic deeds.

The second, the French language, could be, at certain times, precious and clear like droplets of mountain water, and, at others, voluptuous and libertine, oh how much so! as in those poems he memorised with greedy delectation and could not recite, even silently, without feeling that his face was turning crimson. But that language was also the language of the conquerors of his country! Several times Kader asked himself a question, which seemed foolish at first, but one he recognised as fundamental, and not merely where the French were concerned: how could one, at one and the same time, write such beautiful things and also kill people or hunt them out of their own homes without pity? He could only overcome the embarrassment of being much too interested in the language of his own people's enemies by telling himself over and over again that it was equally the language of those people from the Auvergne who had been hounded out by the laws of their country and who loved him, what is more, with such generosity.

Hajj Omar grumbled in public about this son who was always so thick with those common kneaders of dough. But when he learnt that the pastrycook's wife was devoting so much time to his son's education, he sent the Picards – on the sly, to be sure – a platter of couscous dressed with mutton and all manner of vegetables, accompanied by a splendid silver teapot, one of the very few objects of value he had not yet been obliged to sell.

In his heart, the elderly sheik was rather proud of this son who could babble away in Frankish gibberish. He defended himself against accusations of complacency – to the point of treason, according to certain of his intimate compatriots – by arguing that when the hour of liberty struck, his son would be better equipped to deflect the enemy's manifold ruses.

"Perhaps," sighed the patriarch, worn down by rebellion and exile, "this is the only means left to us to strive against it, against this accursed conqueror: to know it better in order, at length, to match its power and malice. Unless He who is enthroned in Heaven has resolved otherwise, and has prepared a lengthy punishment for us . . ."

As time went by, the man from the Auvergne and Hajj Omar developed if not friendship at least a reciprocal sympathy which rested on a shared sorrow, that of flight and exile from the soil where they grew up and where they had taken their first steps. When Kader turned nineteen, it was not unusual for the old chief of the tribe, on the pretext of looking for his son, to spend an hour or two chatting with the pastrycook, all the while sipping his Damascus coffee, which consisted almost entirely of grounds. When Kader appeared, on his way home from the theological institute, Hajj Omar made a show of complaining in order to exonerate himself from appearing to be on such friendly terms with a Christian: "Once more, you've kept your old father waiting, my scatter-brained son!" No-one was taken in by this feigned ill-humour: the father was puffing himself up with pride over this son about whom many good things were said at the theological institute. This Algerian lad had no equal, the head sheik of canon law had confided in him, in untangling a question of jurisprudence or designating the proper share to each beneficiary in a complicated inheritance. His familiarity with French, now acknowledged, was also going to facilitate, it was whispered, his recruitment into the diplomatic service of the pashalic of Damascus, and perhaps – who knows? – that of the seat of the Ottoman Empire, at Istanbul the Sublime!

Even Kader's mother eventually came to accept, without too many misgivings, that Kader spent so much time with the Picards. It must be said that she had convinced herself that the pastrycook's wife – "the great saucepot" as she called her unkindly at first – did not intend marrying Kader to one of her four daughters. On the morning of each of the great Muslim feasts she presented Kader with a platter of *cornes de gazelle* and *makrouds*. She had spent hours preparing them, conscious of the professional eye the "Other" would cast over them.

"Go," she urged him, with a smile which she tried to make look as if it were filled with bile, "go and give this to your Christian *aunt*, apostate of a son!"

Kader was amused by this and covered her with kisses. She pushed him away, exclaiming that this wasn't the way to behave when you were almost a cadi. The son set off merrily to deliver the cakes overflowing with honey to her whom he actually called "*Khalti*" Armande. Still under the supervision of the pastrycook's exacting wife who missed no opportunity to correct the rare mistakes he was still making, he could now speak almost fluent French.

"I would have liked to have been a teacher," she sighed, "instead of spending my life buried in flour and sugar. You are the only pupil fate has given me. So I'm not going to deprive myself! My girls, they think only of decking themselves out to catch a husband and to get away from this shop . . ."

"I have two families now and two languages," he came to think. He realised well enough that this created a clash of feelings in him which often left him confused to the point of anxiety: "I am filled with exultation and plunged into grief in Arabic, but I think of gracefulness and pleasure in French!" He had discovered that he encountered this duality just as much in his dreams. He dreamt only about his childhood or his parents, for example, in Arabic. If it was a matter of more sensual dreams, French took charge of rendering them more troubled, mingling nocturnal erections with visions of Syrian beauties whose kisses and breasts assumed, in a bizarre way, the taste of chocolate desserts . . .

He laughed -- and in a forced manner -- at his mother's behaviour when she was tidying the little cupboard which served as a bookcase: respectful and almost intimidated whenever she was dusting manuscripts and books composed in Arabic, disdainful towards everything that revealed Roman characters . . . She shoved those to the back of the cupboard in the hope that her son would no longer read them; she was afraid that by becoming too familiar with the writings of Christians, her eldest son would neglect his religion and would not easily accommodate himself to the tragic destiny which had been imposed on his country.

It must be said that "*Khalti*" Armande showed no greater good will towards everything that was on "the other side". Kader had taken pains to translate for her a few verses of Antar or Al-Mutanabbi, those princes of poets before whom all lovers of Arabic almost fell into a swoon. The pastrycook's wife listened to the end, but her set expression was worse than censure. One day she hissed at him, with an irritable grimace, that he was boring her stiff with that old-fashioned stuff:

"You, my boy, it's to Paris you should go to refine your taste and to learn something useful. You're wasting your time and your intelligence with these turban-heads of Damascus and their mouldy drivel about what's permitted and what isn't! Here, just look at this ridiculous tarboosh on your head . . ."

"But *Khalti*, Damascus is one of the most ancient cities in the world; it is even mentioned in your Genesis! . . ."

"And so? Then it needs an almighty scrubbing!"

The young man felt such bitterness at the lack of consideration she showed for everything that was Arab -- which lay, when all was said and done, at the "centre of his soul" -- that he did not set foot in her shop for three months. When he decided to return, the spell was broken.

Something had changed in the nephew of the Emir Abd El Kader, an exile and the son of an exile perhaps, but prince of the blood all the same. The pastrycook-teacher who, despite her fifteen years in Syria, had not deigned to learn more than the rudiments of Arabic necessary for the confectionery business, had misjudged her "little caliph's" ardour for the French language. The passion of Hajj Omar's son for everything to do with the literature and history of the Arabic Orient had only increased, perhaps in reaction against the miserable state to which his own family, formerly one of the most powerful in Algeria, had been reduced.

"Why can't I relish both, our lute and their clavecin?" he sighed, filled with resentment that his *aunt* sought to make him infatuated with her own language by scorning his mother tongue!

The rupture occurred during the year before their clandestine departure for the south of the Sahara. That day, Kader's father came home from the pastrycook's hardly able to contain his fury. He had spent a whole month on the Hajj, thereby accomplishing the great pilgrimage to Mecca for the first time in his life. He returned, elated by the experience, despite the enormous bandage around his forehead. Roaring with laughter, he recounted that it had happened during the ritual stoning of Satan at Mina, in the course of which innumerable stones were cast at the three stele representing the Devil: there were countless clumsy oafs among the crowd and a number of projectiles missed their targets. The day after his return to Damascus, Hajj Omar naturally went to the trouble of visiting his "infidel friend" . . .

It took Kader several days to disobey his father's enraged interdiction against ever again setting foot at the Picards'. Armande greeted him with the same warmth, but the young man needed only a few minutes to understand what had caused such terrible perturbation in the old sheik.

"We are going back to France," the pastrycook's wife confided in him, in a slightly edgy tone. "We can't go on living any longer so far from our own country . . ."

"Ah?" he exclaimed with astonishment, a pang in his heart because he was about to lose these Picards, who were so dear to him, "you no longer fear being arrested there?"

"No, on condition that we settle in Algeria. They will allot us a parcel of land, and if things go well . . ."

"But that's not France there!" he interrupted her, appalled that she could entertain such ridiculous notions.

"But it is. Over there's also ours now . . ."

"Look *Khalti*, it's ours, not yours!"

"What's got hold of you, you little fool? Algeria is French now, and will be for ever. And I can tell you that it's lucky, that Algeria of yours, to belong to us from now on . . ."

The young man and the woman in her apron had raised their voices. Her husband rushed to the rear of the premises and stared at them, astonished at the hostility of the confrontation. Kader, suddenly overwhelmed, lowered his eyes:

"If you leave and go back to Algeria, you'll simply be taking our place, that's all. You know that it's not right!"

He left the rear of the shop, struggling against the impulse to burst into tears; he would have liked to have revealed to these two people whom he loved so deeply the extent of their infamy, to have explained that exiles should not be able to betray other exiles in so cowardly a fashion. But sorrow overcame him, and he understood that their decision had been carefully considered: a card in the window advised that the establishment was for sale! Slamming the door in the faces of the petrified customers, he said again:

"You know that it's not right!"

Those were the last words of French he uttered for many long years: speaking French had become as painful for him as swallowing a fishbone: every word of that language seemed to him filled with sweetness, behind which treachery lurked. The Picards left for Algeria two months later, without his seeing them again or trying to do so. The following spring, Kader's father decided that they would also return to Algeria, even if they had to go on, he added, staring his interlocutors in the face, spending their live wandering among the sand hills of the Sahara to evade the soldiers who had made outlaws of them.

"We have family and kinsmen. They will help us and give us somewhere to hide," he insisted peremptorily.

No-one, not even Kader, who as a consequence lost any possibility of recruitment into the administration of the pashalic, tried to oppose the folly of the father's decision. Hajj Omar was in a perpetual rage, hissing between his teeth that he'd punch the snout of anyone who dared to maintain that he had less of a place in Biskra or in the Mitija than among these "mongrel shopkeepers"!

"Make haste, cousin. Everyone has assembled in the central square. The leader will soon give the order to depart!"

Kader glanced at Hassan in exasperation. The latter, cutting much too fine a figure in his white burnous, his mid-calf *seroual* and his boots of red leather, laughs nervously. All this seems like a poor farce, but they are really setting out for war! Is it as banal as this then, the day on which one could die? Kader muses. He busies himself with the rifle he has bought with his father's last savings. Hassan is better armed, he notices a little enviously, casting an eye over the brand new chassepot. Better dressed too. He pats, with sudden irritation, the little book bulging in the inner pocket of his kashabia: what silly childishness took hold of him at the last moment to burden himself with the *Book of Songs*? He would throw it away, right there, that collection of poems – or, yes, feed it to his horse – if he did not fear his cousin's mockery even more . . .

Nour's tent is in front of him. He had decided not to present the ostrich plumes to her. How everything, at present, seems to him to belong to another time! The meeting of the tribes had indeed taken place and the decision to join El Mokrani's campaign was sealed. The men raised their voices, exulting in their joy at taking part in the holy war against the Christians; the women trilled their ululations. No-one, however, was duped. Several spoke of devastated douars, of deaths by the thousands: for every Christian soldier killed, a hundred Muslims were massacred. The French are too strong, their cannons too powerful, their hearts pitiless: they did not hesitate smoking out the tribes of the Sbéhas and Ouled Raïs who had taken refuge in caves. Men, women, children, no-one was spared, despite shrieks of terror and cries for mercy.

Messengers arrived warning that a vast column of the French, made up of two battalions, was only a day's march away. Turmoil, close to panic, seized the assembly. Hastily, several detachments of volunteers were formed among young men of fighting age. Each brought along whatever he could for arms, then the most venerable of the elderly sages of the Sahara led the great prayer for the dead in the market-place. Not for those who had already died in battle. Those dust and God had already gathered to their bosoms. No, for the living assembled there in their thousands, young and trembling. Mothers sobbed, fathers feigned joy at their sons' courage when facing the ceremonies of death, but their hardened hearts wept quietly, without their being aware of it.

There. The time has come to go to war. Kader has saddled his horse, cleaned his rifle for the last time, checked his ammunition, and set out, despite his cousin's opposition, for Nour's tent.

He sees her now. He experiences a sense of immense futility. Like someone tormented by thirst who spills, of his own volition, the last drops of water remaining in his possession.

He says nothing. Because he would burst with rage. Or moan in despair. She too remains silent. She should have wept. Kader understands that there was only one worthwhile aim in his whole life: to love this woman. One of her glances is more precious to him than the wide world in all its freedom and dignity.

But the Imam has declared – and the whole world approved – that he, Kader, his cousin and the rest were already as good as dead, that their lives had been offered up for their country's glory and faith.

Yet Kader has never kissed her, Nour, nor caressed her, obviously. He never had the courage to do so. He experienced so often in his imagination, however, that extraordinary sensation of touching *for the first time* her face, her breasts, everything else . . . Is he going to die without swooning, breathless, in her arms? And all those deeds which he should have performed when the future was filled with numberless days – and has left undone? "My God, how Thou hast jested with us!" Kader's heart is beating furiously; he knows that what he is thinking is seeping out of him like water from a jar. He laughs gently, but with irritation: he recognised the scent of basil, thief of dreams. A pot of basil is incongruously enthroned in the middle of the tent. Never sleep in a place where there is a bush of basil, his mother advised him: it will steal you dreams and will waft its scent all over the oasis and, soon, all the world will share your most cherished secrets. He wants to say: it is the war that is the thief of dreams, Mother!

"Nour . . ."

She cuts him off, a joyless smile playing around her lips. She is wearing the silver necklace, embellished with guilloches, which he had arranged for a woman who lived nearby, who acted as an intermediary, to give her. Her long tresses are streaked with henna.

"What could I say to you in such a short time? You see, they are summoning you already!"

Outside, Hassan, in a rage, has raised his voice.

"Have you finished?"

The implication is insulting. Kader blushes with anger. He wants to go out and strike his cousin. But he cannot waste the few minutes left to him before their departure.

"Kader . . ."

The stifled supplication plummets between them like a stone.

Nour's eyes grow wider, she holds her breath. This is the first time that they have found themselves alone in an enclosed space. This is not at all how she envisaged it, this first time. Everything comes too late, she thinks. The man standing in front of her will probably never come back. Like fools, they played the traditional games of love, between fountain and flirtatious winks, wasting a precious opportunity, without understanding that war offers no-one a gift. For all that, how many times, in her immodest dreams, had she wished to be aroused by him, to taste his saliva, to smell his odour, to fondle his sex stiff with desire for her, his thighs . . . Then, yes, her heart and her vagina would have served some purpose! And now . . . She wants to howl. From afar resounds the monstrous noise of drums, accompanied by the shrill call of the zornas.

"Nour, when I return . . ."

"Don't speak foolishly, Kader, words will change nothing. You will not come back: you will be taken prisoner or you will be . . ."

She shuts her eyes. She stifles a sob. The clamour of the zornas has redoubled. A ray of light penetrates the roof of the tent and illuminates

32

the man and the woman. Nour's hands make a stabbing movement, which Kader does not at first understand.

Then fear seizes him by the throat; Nour has grasped the sides of her gown and pulled them up with a jerk.

"Come," she says in a mournful voice. "Even this I have no more time to offer you."

Kader senses a dry intoxication pressing around his head. Nour steps towards him, her belly uncovered. She grasps Kader's hand, places it against her pubis. She tries to bury the hand of the man she loves in the moist aperture of her vulva. Kader says nothing because he would weep if he spoke. Nour, for her part, is weeping, but with fury.

One last time she thrusts the man's hand between her legs and then pushes it away violently. She has let her gown drop; she is smoothing it with her hands. The man gazes at her, still stupefied. He does not know what to do with this fiercely burning hand, which is, nevertheless, his own.

Her voice is filled with hatred. He is behaving like a man condemned to death. He has not kissed this woman whom he holds dearer than the whole world, than his own honour, than the well-being of his family, than his country.

He makes for his horse. Hassan casts a scornful sidelong glance at him. As he whips his horse, Kader glimpses, through a gap between the tents, the brightly coloured patch of a distant carpet of poppies.

He has just enough time to be astonished by their joyous mockery:

"But how have you managed to strike root in so waterless a plain?"

He puts his hand to his nose, breathing in deeply his lover's scent. Suddenly stabbed by the absurdity of the situation he finds himself in, he allows a stifled laugh to escape his lips: these frail poppies – which he could trample without a thought – will they exercise their privilege to survive longer than he will?

3

La Rochelle, the Women's Prison, May 1872

"Run, Lislei, run, and hang on to the lassie."

In her sleep, Lislei is running faster than the soldiers in their red breeches. She is going to escape from them because, for goodness' sake, she knows Paris better than they, these swine who are more eager to chase after Parisians than Bismarck's Prussians. She gives a brutal yank to Camille's arm, the sweet Camille, her darling little niece. The child's arm is so chubby, so fragile that she feels that it would come off in her hand if she pulled it a little too hard . . . Camille is moaning, certainly, but she continues bounding along as furiously as her aunt. In her sleep, Lislei knows well enough that this could not be possible: her brother's daughter is only two years and a few weeks old and Thiers's damned soldiers are hurling themselves like devils after them and the other fugitives. Lislei struggles against her sense of how unreal all this is, because she knows that by itself that would be enough to rouse her from her sleep. Too quickly, too soon. At present she has nothing but this heavy sleep to protect her from the incomprehensible truth: to have failed in the promise she made to her brother, and to find herself imprisoned, for months now, in a fortress in La Rochelle, waiting for deportation for life to New Caledonia!

Then her dream changes. It is now her father and mother, drowned long ago in the Rhine of their native land, who know nothing about their children's misfortune. Pierre and she were still adolescents when their parents' boat capsized in a senseless mishap after it was struck by another vessel. Their father left nothing behind, the children had to fend for themselves, leaving Alsace for Paris in search of a means of survival. At first luck intervened. An English couple took them in, her as a maidservant and him as gardener and handyman. Despite their young servants' obvious lack of experience, the couple took a liking to them. After three years of service, Lislei could manage to talk with her employers in their own language. Then the English couple grew alarmed at the prospect of war and left the country . . .

Lislei, her heart battering away, shuts her eyes. The father and mother, smiles on their lips, inform her that they have been strolling around the village. Lislei guesses, however, that they are just back from the pretty cemetery submerged under twisted oaks, trees so venerable that the pastor, when he is drunk, claims that they knew Jesus Christ himself. Father and Mother had been contemplating – and, at that instant, this does not strike the young woman as absurd – their own gravestones. A shudder of fear suddenly takes hold of her because she is expecting her father to reproach her for not coming home sooner. And then no, her mother's face has grown so sad that that could not be it. Do they know that Pierre and his wife are dead? How is she going to explain to them that her brother would not listen to his elder sister's advice or reprimands and preferred to burn up his life, at his wife's side, among those crackpot communards? Ah, how much resentment she feels towards this brother she loves so dearly! They would have been able to leave Paris well before the siege or, at least, just after the surrender, when the Prussians had marched through the finest districts of the city! After all, it is not so terrible a shame to prefer life to a pointless death . . . And that woman, his wife, just as obsessed as he, who did not attempt to turn him away from his insane ideals, even though they had a little girl of tender age!

The old man takes her hand affectionately and, all of a sudden, Lislei sees herself transformed into a child of three or four years old. Her father lifts her, puts her on his shoulders and starts running. Her mother is almost leaping with joy, more lively in the dream than she ever was when alive. Lislei is puzzled by their wayward antics, but the child she has once more become bursts out laughing with relief, then suddenly, at the very midst of her slumber, she stops believing in it, and cries out in protest:

"Papa, I am not a little girl any more, I'm too heavy for you, stop, I beg you, I am going to hurt you!"

And the father, drunk with joy, replies:

"No, no, my girl, we haven't any time left. Oh, quick, glasses and a bottle of edelzwicker to celebrate this! How we've missed you, ah, if you knew how much you could make us miss you, you and your brother, since our accident! Tell me, when is he going to come home, that scoundrel? And his new little family? And our sweet Camille, so pretty that she's already bitten great chunks out of our hearts."

So they know then . . . Lislei feels tears trickling down her cheeks and on to her poor father's shoulders. Her mother, for her part, hides her face in her hands. The young woman wakes on her minute pallet, her face bathed in tears . . .

"My God, will it never end, this nightmare?" She shuts her eyes so that she need no longer see the nooks and crannies in a kind of shed where dozens of dark, prostrate shapes are asleep, some on the floor, mired in filth and despair.

Lislei's stomach is churning, but she sees once more a scene she cannot prevent herself from playing over in her mind, for the thousandth time since her imprisonment almost a year ago: the rumour, taken lightly at first, that the Versailles troops had broken through the defences of Porte de Saint-Ouen and were pushing towards the Madeleine, then the unthinkable: the impregnable Montmartre captured in a few hours because of negligence and treachery; a neighbour bringing little Camille with her because Marthe, Pierre's wife, had decided to join her husband on the barricades; the endless cannonade, and Thiers's soldiers putting to death with all their might anyone who looked more or less like a partisan of the Commune . . .

Earlier, another neighbour came to warn her that her landlord had denounced her as the local leader of the Commune's *comité de vigilance*. Despite her distress, Lislei smiled incredulously at the outrageousness of her landlord's accusation – to whom, it is true, she had "neglected" to hand over her rent since the beginning of the Prussians' siege. The neighbour shrugged:

"Then you'll be shot, my girl, if you stay here. The army pays 500 francs for a denunciation and its firing squads are not too fussy over details. Everyone hereabouts knows that your brother was on the barricades. For them, you or your brother, it's the same thing! Think about the little girl . . ."

Lislei fled across the streets of the blazing city. At first she made for the Hôtel de Ville, foolishly hoping to find help there, but the smoke made her retrace her steps. The Tuileries and the Palais de Justice were also on fire. She heard someone yelling that they were about to set Notre Dame alight. Corpses were piled on the cobblestones and people fleeing in carts did not hesitate, in front of her, to drive over the dismembered bodies of a man and a young girl in the uniform of the Garde Nationale. With Camille, she wandered all over the Paris of that accursed month of May, avoiding, by a miracle, cannon shells and the bursts of machine-gun fire from the barricades, which surged and died down with each new skirmish. She hid in courtyards and gateways, just managing to evade the patrols of one side or the other, cursing between her teeth now the Confederates, now the troops from Versailles, mad with fear and rage, her feet bleeding because she had been stepping over rubble mixed with slivers of glass from shattered windows. The little girl, for her part, took it all with a good heart and slept, her fists clenched, as she was carried by her aunt. She moaned now and then, asking for food, then fell asleep, exhausted.

At the end of the afternoon, panic overwhelmed Lislei. The bulk of the Versailles troops had reached the ruined block of tenements, not very far from the Ourcq canal, where she had found refuge. A man had been arrested a few metres from his cart, and killed on the spot with a bayonet-blow to his throat, because a passer-by had called out that he had seen him taking part in the execution of two priests from the nearby church. "We'll wipe them all out, these atheists," one of the officers bawled, cheered on by a small band of gawkers, some of whom had spat on the man's corpse.

She slid into an alleyway, climbed over an overturned omnibus and found herself in front of the canal. One barge was still at its moorings, others were drifting crosswise, bumping against one another. Most had been seriously damaged by the bombardments. One of them had gone under, only the poop was sticking out of the water. All the vessels seemed to have been abandoned. Leaping from deck to deck, Lislei made her way into one of the cabins. The little girl had woken up and was staring, her eyes filled with curiosity, at the compartment embellished with elaborate decorations, which had turned black from the smoke of the fires near the canal.

"Auntie, hungry . . ., Auntie, thirsty . . ."

She found her a morsel of bread and some cheese. The bread was stale and the cheese mouldy, but Camille ate heartily. Lislei rummaged in a cupboard and pulled out a tin milk-jug. Leaving the cabin, she plunged the receptacle into the water. She almost screamed when her hand touched a corpse floating next to the barge. The man was completely naked and most of his face was missing. Lislei smelled the liquid in the container: it was brown and stank of oil. She felt nausea overwhelming her. Camille had also come out on deck and was complaining even more insistently:

"Auntie, thirsty, Auntie, thirsty . . ."

Lislei shoved her into the cabin, begging her not to move again, and, vessel in hand, she crossed the canal from deck to deck as far as the shore.

This is how it all came to an end. A man in civilian clothes grabbed her by the hair. He sniffed the container, then started dragging the young woman towards a group of soldiers.

"Hey there, here's an incendiarist. She pongs all over from the paraffin in her pot!"

She tried to resist as indignant cries of "Oh, is she now?" cut short her protests. A sergeant struck her in the face, calling her a firebug, red scum, a good-for-nothing slut.

"You are in luck, kitty. Others would've already drilled you full of holes, despite your pretty gob!"

He gave her a violent kick. She rolled to the ground, striking the edge of the pavement. Brandishing his machine gun, the soldier sniggered sarcastically:

"Don't take much to make us change our mind!"

She got to her feet, her face stained with blood. As they were shoving her towards a group of prisoners, she screeched, on the edge of hysteria, that her niece was waiting for her in one of the barges, that she was only a baby, that she would soon die of hunger or drown!

"No, you can't do this! Look, she's only two! For pity's sake!"

One of the soldiers, losing his patience, grabbed her by the neck. His breath was heavy with wine. He menaced her with the sharply pointed blade of the bayonet on his rifle:

"Stop playing the fool, bitch. Pity? When you were on your way to set fire to decent folk in their houses? One more word and I'll spike you. I'll drag your guts out through your little pussy-hole and I'll tie them around your belly. None of us'd hesitate to give ourselves a little treat like that, don't doubt it even for a second if your life means anything to you!"

Lislei fell silent. The group of prisoners moved off again, surrounded by soldiers prodding them with their rifle butts. Blood was still trickling down Lislei's temple, sticking to her hair. Little by little, like a poisonous plant which had taken root in the innermost recesses of her heart, the extent of her misfortune rose in front of her in all its horror.

The order to wake up came early this morning. Never before had she felt such fear, for this is the great day: casting off for the end of the world, that Caledonia so far away that people say you can't see the same stars as in France. This is a second death, she thinks, but one so drawn out that only another death – that of the grave – could assuage it. She has thought of suicide, but she is too timid to do what is necessary. And then, there remains one hope. Not for her, but for Camille: one of the women prisoners managed to persuade her to entrust to her the few sous which the screws hadn't confiscated to pay someone on the outside who had undertaken to make the necessary inquiries. For four months, Lislei has been waiting for an answer ...

A sob slowly rises in her throat. Enraged, she stifles it: it's too easy to blubber all the time. At first, especially after the military tribunal passed its sentence, she wept a great deal: her father and mother were dead, her brother too. She did not count the death of her brother's wife, whom she came to hold responsible for Pierre's fate. And then there was dear little Camille, whom she had abandoned on a barge . . . No-one wanted to believe her, to listen to her. All were convinced that she was afraid because of what she had done, and that she had made up this story to soften the judges' hearts. They, it is true, did not hesitate condemning to death many women accused of being incendiarists. One woman of the Commune, who had insisted, loud and clear in front of the bench, that she was sorry she had not killed more of the soldiers under the command of the one she called the Fucker of Versailles, turned towards Lislei and spat at her with contempt:

"You gutless wonder, have some respect at least for your brother's memory!"

On one occasion, one of the prisoners – a prostitute she had met at the time of their transfer to the Chantiers prison – wanted to comfort her by saying that if Lislei's story was true, the little girl would have died long ago and that she had to resign herself to that. Lislei struck her and it ended in a brawl, with much clawing and hair-pulling. After raining blows on each other, the two women set about lamenting their fate, and each, with dishevelled hair and ripped skirt, tried to console her adversary. Lislei refused to join the group of Commune women. The one who seemed to be their leader did not insist, whispering that her life in prison and, later, after deportation, would become "very difficult".

"And you aren't, at least to my eyes, more than twenty-four or twenty-five, my girl . . ." she added with an unexpected air of compassion. "Prison time is different from what it is on the outside, it creeps like treacle. If you carry the whole world on your shoulders, you'll end up regretting that you hadn't been murdered at Satory or in the Luxembourg Gardens and your corpse covered with quicklime!"

Lislei did not unclench her teeth, for she would have screamed out her hatred for "the whole world": those Versailles troops who had slaughtered thousands, cutting off her brother's life and perhaps her niece's, those cocksure champions of the Commune who, with their harangues and empty dreams, had set Paris alight and plunged it into blood. No, she was not a "Commune filly"! Admittedly, during the final weeks she had sewn sandbags for the barricades. But she had been paid for that. It had been necessary enough to do something so that she wouldn't starve to death. And all those scraps of cloth stitched together in that workshop at the Hôtel de Ville did not even bring in enough to treat herself to one of those rats that butchers displayed shamelessly in garlands in their shop windows!

Lislei loved her brother, yes indeed, the one who had committed himself body and soul so that Paris might become, as he repeated endlessly to convince her – and probably to convince himself when he returned, depressed, from lengthy and verbose meetings of the neighbourhood committees – "a sovereign community of free citizens governing themselves by their own consent".

"My eye," she answered him, "what have you to gain from vilifying both the Emperor and those who succeeded him? You can see clearly enough that new bosses have replaced the old ones. But you and me, we're always hungry, we're on the bottom rung and there's no reason why that would change. At least we won't turn into scoundrels like the others, eh?"

And it ended up with recriminations in their Alsatian dialect in front of the contempt-filled eyes of Pierre's wife. One particularly exasperating day, Pierre shouted spitefully at his sister, who was only two years older:

"You're always a doubter, you shatter every hope, all enthusiasm, Lislei. Since Papa and Maman had their accident, you've carried on like my new mother, you're playing at being old, a kill-joy. We may be having ourselves on doing what we're doing, but you'd do well to let yourself go a bit, to loosen up. There's nothing better than a sweetheart for rediscovering a little madness. Yes, it is true that it's slightly crazy to believe weren't born into the world just to slave like a donkey!"

He regretted his flash of anger almost immediately, because Lislei stood up, her face drained of blood. She spoke not a word to him for several days. The wound was too fresh: a sweetheart, there had been one, and a real one at that; or so she had come to believe. Luckily, she told no-one about it. It happened at the beginning of the previous winter, while she

41

was standing patiently in a queue in front of a bakery, in despair, like the other customers, because of the unending Prussian siege and the all too familiar hunger which clung to the belly like an army of ticks. There she got to know a workman in a printing shop and, very rapidly, fell in love. The lively lad was handsome, spoke nicely and, one evening, she ended up by giving in to his advances in the printing shop he was supposed to be cleaning. She tried to forget the rather sordid circumstances of how she lost her virginity; he had laid ink-stained sheets of paper on the floor and did not concern himself overmuch with preliminaries. Pain shot through her when he penetrated her, and she left the workshop disgusted by the fluid trickling between her legs. She went home and, enraged, rubbed herself with ice-cold water. Then, choked with disappointment, she ended up accepting it: at heart, this was nothing more, perhaps, than "that", this union of bodies about which she had dreamt so much in the past; the important thing from now on was that she loved her printer. For the rest, oh well!, time would heal *the thing* in all probability, she hoped . . .

Their affair lasted less than a month: at the end of a harassing day, she rushed to the printing shop. Rejoicing in her heart, she pictured to herself her lover's astonished face as it took in her resourcefulness: at the cost of a thousand difficulties, she had managed to get hold of some beignets, and wanted to share them with him while strolling on the Buttes. She was already at the entrance to the workshop, her hand on the door-knob, when she heard him boasting to a colleague "about what he had done to the little brunette", calling her, between two bursts of laughter, *a pretty partridge, but so simple-minded . . .*! Opening the door no further, she dragged herself along the banks of the Seine until she was exhausted and, heart heavy with sorrow, she ended up sharing her fine beignets with an elderly tramp who was left speechless by this godsend.

She has grabbed hold of the bars to stay as close to fresh air as possible. A woman protests, crossly:

"Hey, funny-face, you're not the only one who wants to breathe in this fucking rat-cage!"

Even by hauling herself up onto the tips of her toes, she cannot make out the port, nor even the other cages of the upper batteries. The smell is putrid. Lislei thinks, overcome by shame, that she herself stinks, perhaps. Her last visit to the showers was some ten days earlier, the guards having decided to punish all the women in the right wing of the prison because two of them had been discovered naked in one another's arms. The bastards knew, moreover, that because there was typhus in some of the cells, this gratuitous harshness was in reality a deadly threat! The lice, my God, are pintsize hedgehogs.

Everything happened very quickly. Around five in the morning one of the screws arrived with a sheet of paper in his hand. From the man's shifty look, the prisoners understood that he was about to call out the names of those who must embark that day for the "New". Three groups had already been sent off some weeks earlier and, each time, the warders had to intervene with brutal force to quash the terror-stricken rebellion of the captives destined for deportation. One woman, more vehement than the others, had her jaw broken by a kick.

This time, the list contains no more than a dozen names. Most of those whose names were called allowed themselves to be led away without resisting. Two women, however, cried out that they did not want to go to Caledonia, that they hadn't deserved that. "Papa, get me out of here, darling Papa!" the elder of the two kept repeating in an astonishingly strident voice. The contrast between the woman's grey hair and the child-like violence of her terror threatened to stir up trouble. Voices were raised at the back:

"You don't have the right, you thugs! She's crazy, you know that well enough!"

Two screws flung themselves on the grey-haired woman to drag her away from the bench to which she was clinging. The one that seemed to be the leader thwacked her on the fingers with a truncheon. Lislei experienced the same cowardly sense of relief as her fellow captives when the shrieks of the unfortunate woman faded as she was dragged along the corridors of the prison. There had been at first a commotion in the hall because no-one understood why the list of those who were summoned was so short. At the end of the morning, an incredible rumour circulated among the captives: a prison laundress had learnt from one of the screws that the deportations were going to be suspended, and that the Assemblée Nationale had commuted sentences of transportation to New Caledonia to detention in metropolitan France! Women shouted with joy, some of them started dancing and singing. Lislei said nothing, did not even smile. Hiding her face in her hands, she tried to master the joy welling up in her heart and threatening to suffocate her. "Camille, Camille, I swear that I will find you again now!" she murmured.

When the same screws returned, Lislei did not react immediately when the one holding the sheet of paper called out her name. The guard came over to her and tapped her gently on the shoulder with the truncheon he had used on the elderly captive. She stared at the guard and realised that he would strike her without hesitation. As she rose to her feet, fear made her want to weep. The man laughed, then twirled his truncheon as he signalled "no-no" with his head . . .

The journey to the port was very short. All the way, Lislei tried to scream, but her voice would not obey her. Numerous passers-by, drawn by curiosity, looked on as the prisoner went on board. Some shouted insults at them. One man, one alone, raised his cap as they went by. When they, in their turn, reached the long wooden gangway leading to the ship, a dog ran over to sniff them. When it reached Lislei, it spun playfully around her. A sailor, growing annoyed, gave the dog a kick which made it scamper off like lightning. Another sailor, at the bottom of the gangway, laughed and put his foot out. The dog lost its balance and tumbled into the water. Lislei screamed: at first the bundle of fur plummeted into the filthy water of the port, then surfaced before starting to swim vigorously towards the wharf. The onlookers clapped.

A woman growled at Lislei's back:

"Keep going my little sweetie, you are blocking the way. You'd do better to think of yourself first! That mongrel, you see, is luckier than you or me . . ."

Lislei stops herself saying that the animal did not deserve to be kicked and that her little niece loved dogs very much.

"My God" is the only reply she makes, dumbfounded by the incongruity of what she was on the point of saying.

She continues making her way up the slippery plank, overcome by nausea at the thought of turning around, of seeing once more the soil she had been condemned to leave behind for ever: she would cry out with all her might, like that old woman – she is sure of it – arousing the whole town:

"Camille, save me, Camille . . ."

The frigate is swaying vigorously. The wind has risen and the sails are flapping with ever increasing force. Sailing out of the port is going to prove very difficult. For the last time, a sailor inspects the locks on the large cages occupying a good part of the deck of the *Calvados*. Every time he stops in front of a cage, he scowls suspiciously at the prisoners. The gun trained on the cages is fully charged, but you can never be careful enough. The one assisting him carries a rifle. He snorts, revealing his boredom:

"That's a lot of people, eh?"

"No more than on every voyage: 300, 320," the sailor grumbles. "This'll be my third trip, I'm beginning to find it very monotonous."

He adds with a lecherous wink:

"You've seen the women?"

"Some are pretty broken-down, but, my word, there are five or six I'd gladly have a taste of if there weren't these blasted nuns to keep an eye on them. Besides, I'm wondering if they are all going to be up to it. That one's vomiting her head off already and we're still in the port!"

The one checking the locks agrees, clicking his tongue:

"Those women in Paris, they are made to wiggle their rump, not to sail across the tropics!"

When they make their way past the cages on the port side, the sailor sighs with an amused sense of compassion:

"Hey, you mates of Mohammed, how are you going to find out which way's that Mecca of yours down there in the islands?"

The man with the rifle yawns. He seems impatient:

"Leave them in peace, these Ali Babas, they can't understand any of

45

your babble, and they're already terrified by the ocean, so it's no good making them even more cranky!"

The guard roars with laughter:

"It's normal, their God's scared stiff of rheumatism, he much prefers the good old dried-out deserts!"

Behind the bars, men in turbans, lying on their backs, watch the sailor and his guard make for the upper deck. No-one speaks. The business of casting off has started. Soon the prison ship shudders off. A young prisoner, not much more than an adolescent, jerks his hood over his head to hide his face. From the way his shoulders are moving, his companions realise that he is sobbing. At that moment, all would like to imitate him. But warriors like them do not weep, even when defeated, even when their hearts have never known so great a bitterness.

One of them takes a battered book out from his burnous and settles down to read. He is pale, with hollow cheeks. His neighbour, a great bean-pole, his face disfigured by a sabre scar, thinks that he is praying. He addresses him in Kabyle:

"Brother, you should not handle the Book before you have cleansed yourself!"

But his tone is too choleric and the voice grows comically shrill, betraying the true mood of the man with the gash on his face. The prisoner he reprimanded barely shrugs his shoulders. He screws up his eyes, amazed at the appalling banality of what is happening. For months, ever since the battle, ever since he was captured then sentenced to deportation, he has been anticipating this moment of departure. His throat is knotted tight. No, rather: there are stones in his throat and he no longer has enough compassion for the others. Above all, keep the eyes dry. Do not get carried away with a gnawing feeling of regret for the days before the defeat. Ordinary days, days of his mother, his father, living friends. Days of love and its warm fickleness. Without looking at them, he slowly turns the illuminated pages of the *Book of Songs*, which everyone, prisoners and screws in agreement for once, take for a Koran.

At the top of a page, he reads distractedly: ". . . Break open a man's heart and you will find the sun there . . ." He grumbles: "Me, if it pleased me to break my heart open, I'd find something there . . ." He sighs and does not finish the phrase. The boat has passed beyond the jetty. Rapidly, despite the clear sky, the buildings, even the clock tower of the town, vanish from the horizon. Soon, nothing is left but gulls streaking the sky with their cries. The wind, grown stronger, leaves salty moisture on his lips. "The wind weeps on our behalf" is the ironic thought the man with the book is tempted to utter. But he remains silent because he no longer trusts his own courage: the man next to him could mistake such a desire to cry out in protest for menace . . .

The man gazing out at the ocean seems to be at peace. Weighed down only by all the sorrow fixing him to the bench which will soon serve as his bed. Only his fingers twitch in desperation over the illuminated pages as the huge vessel, fully rigged, glides towards the end of the world.

PART TWO

PART TWO

4

Dense rainforest in the south of the island of Tasmania, spring 1875

To strive against the unbearable pricks of the needle-sharp thorns, the child bites his lips. His heart is about to burst: will the dogs end up sniffing out his presence, perhaps? He cannot endure any more sorrow and fear. How can this be possible? Could trees, rocks, the whole forest itself, see *this* and remain unmoved? Hidden in the spiky bush tormenting his back, he watches as the overexcited men disappear, one after the other, inside the hut. There are six of them, led by the one with the firearm who is barking out orders. The maniac with the carbine must be Irish; he has the same accent as one of the guards at the station in Oyster Cove, the one who was always trying to sleep with Aboriginal women by giving them rum and, when they refused, he called them ugly hags who feared neither God nor man. One day, he was found dead, his sex cut off, his body covered with excrement.

Tridarir's fingertips explore his forehead. He has not yet grown used to his hair being so short. His father, the day before, had not gone about his business with a gentle touch: using a flint, he cropped the hair right down to the skull. The child turned the wrong way and got hurt. He complained. Irritated, the father snarled that he was a whining possum. Then he started sulking. Hadn't his mother promised a few days earlier to pile his hair on top of his head, fastening it with a splendid snakeskin thong? It was he who had battered the snake to death with his club. His mother had been very proud of him because the brown snake is agile

51

and one of the most venomous in the bush. When he finished cutting the boy's hair, the father sniggered: "You have the head of a real gaol-bird, son!" The son scowled even more. It was this very sulking that saved his life.

Carefully, the father gathered up the woolly locks of hair and gave them to his wife to make into thread or string. Then they started travelling again, exhausted and in ill humour. All day, they had been tracking a wallaby. At the end of the afternoon, they succeeded in driving it against a rocky ledge, but the father's spear missed its target and the animal seized the opportunity to escape into the scrub. They had to make do with a handful of grubs and some roots the mother had scratched out of the ground with her scraping stick. Then there was the accursed hut and the flour inside, so appetising . . .

For months now, they had been suffering from starvation. His mother and father often quarrelled in these last weeks. The little Tridarir had even seen his father crying out in rage: "Thirty years a prisoner of the Whites, that's what I've become: I no longer know how to hunt, I am not even able to catch an ordinary wombat!" It made him ashamed of his father and the father sensed it.

Despite his age – he was already over fifty – Woorady remained a proudly impressive figure with his bulging muscles anointed with emu fat, the rest of his body covered only by a codpiece made from a simple shell. Walya, the mother, wore, for her part, a little apron below the waist. She had kept none of the two or three shifts she had been given at the station. A few days after their escape, she got undressed, bundled her clothes up and hurled them into a ditch. She asked her son, as naked as she was, to urinate on the pile. Tridarir pretended to treat all this as a joke. He urinated, laughing heartily, but he saw clearly enough that his mother was on the verge of tears. Several times, she spluttered violently: "Years of slavery, our people decimated, that's what they stand for, those vile clothes." The mother sobbed with anger and Tridarir felt a sudden urge to grasp in his arms this woman whose body had already become shrivelled, whose hair was tangled like weed, whom he loved so much;

but he did not dare. The call of a crane disturbed by a thylacine wolf, indistinguishable from a human cry, lodged itself for ever in his memory at that instant.

They had been hiding in the forest for a good three years. At first everything went wonderfully well. Certainly, returning to the old ways turned out to be trying because the two adults, after so many years of captivity, had lost most of the skills they had learnt in their earlier life as hunter-gatherers, not to mention little Tridarir, who was a constant victim to thorns, tumbles and scratches. Yet game was abundant, the climate relatively benign and the ageing parents were elated at finding themselves once again in the land of their childhood. Some days they even forgot this horrifying truth: they were among the very last representatives of the original inhabitants of Tasmania. Of the others who had escaped deportation and the massacres carried out by British colonists or convicts, there remained only a handful of old women at a station all but submerged in the marshes of the south. As for men, apart from the father and Tridarir, only a decrepit and half-mad dotard managed to survive!

The father and the mother sang all the time, explaining to the boy that they were bringing back to life the sacred paths of the Ancestors' Dreaming. There was no time to lose, they kept telling him, because, since there were practically no more of their people left on the island, nature would slowly die if it were not *sung*. For nature, song was like water, and there was never enough water! If nature died, if its breathing stopped, they themselves would not be slow to join the countless beings who had already gone before them towards death. But without leaving anyone behind!

"Who will inherit our Dreams, who will protect them from the agony of dying without any hope of survival? And if a Dreaming should not watch over our land any more, we will not have deserved to have existed, our disappearance will be more vile than death!"

And Tridarir saw both of them shudder with disgust at the idea of *this disappearance more vile than death*. Then, hunting for food all the while, they made their way across forests and plains, their anguished minds intent on finding again the old paths of their respective tribes, always on their guard to avoid deadly encounters with the militia or parties of head-hunters. And when they uncovered a track or a sacred site, that day was tinged with a strange air of celebration: the father stained his face with white pigment, while the mother traced curious networks of ochre all over her body, surrounding her breasts with concentric circles. The sacred place – to the boy's eyes in no way different in essence from the disorder of the forest around it – could be an ordinary rock or a stand of ghost gums where pink-crested cockatoos perched, a stagnant pool or an enormous ant-hill. Tridarir, amazed – and a little terrified – watched as his parents launched into long melancholy chants and then emerged from their trance, trembling and relieved at having saved a few of these invisible beings, at the same time so powerful and vulnerable, whom they called *Dreams*.

The child realised that his parents got confused sometimes in their hectic explanations: about the Beginning, about the mysterious era of the Dreamtime, when even time itself could not be reckoned, when the primordial beings had been created by the intense emotion of a Creature whom Tridarir's parents carefully avoided calling by name. "There is one of *His* dreams!" they said, tracing with a respectful finger the line of the rainbow lighting up the sky. "One of his feet rests on the hair of the mountain's head and the other is sunk in the sea's maidenhair and fills our brothers the sea-creatures with wonder." And the child looked in amazement at that rainbow which he was forbidden to call by name except in the silence of his heart. The Dreaming of the primordial beings had given birth, in turn, to the planets, to animals and to mankind. Wherever they passed, they scattered words and music in their wake, like so many tokens of their joy and their gratitude for having left behind on the earth a line of descendants. And it did not matter who it was or what it was that could remain capable, if their dreams continued to be sufficiently imprinted with desire, of imitating them, creating or at least perpetuating their life. Tridarir, for example, was born from the Dreaming of the Honey Ant, his mother from the Dreaming of the Emu, his father from the Monitor Lizard's. The boy marvelled in silence: how could he be the descendant of a Dream so different from his mother's and his father's since he never left their side? And above all, how to reconcile his parents' words with those of the Anglican pastors at the station, who poured scorn and contempt on what his parents and the other Aborigines believed? The pastors were the servants of the God of the British, and the British were so powerful that they enslaved all of them, the children of the Nation of the Ancient People – the *Abos* as they called them. Did that mean that the *masters* were right? So what did their Jesus, nailed to that peculiar tree, dream about? From the Dreaming of what awesome animal was he born, he who must be loved at all cost – and even eaten from time to time! – or else you went to hell, that scandalous bushfire in the sky? In any case, the child realised, his heart filling with rancour, what use was it loving him, that Ancestor whom the pastors claimed to be the sole Master of Life, since he had not deigned to protect them, him and his own people, from extermination?

". . . And you, Tridarir, you are at the same time the father and the son of your Dreaming," his father went on with the same heartbroken conviction filled with longing. "Since your birth, this Dream has belonged to you and you belong to it. You must protect it and nourish it, other-wise it will weaken and die. And your heart's flame along with it. But you must be worthy of your Dream, it must not be ashamed of you, otherwise it will flee from you. Ah! my son, it has been so long since our people were able to follow the paths of the Dreaming of our land, the beautiful land of *Droemerdeene*."

The Aborigine repeated that name *Droemerdeene, Droemerdeene . . .* as if he were caressing it with his tongue and his heart. His voice grew husky, it broke:

"These worms call it Tasmania, Van Diemen's Land or what other idiocy besides? But it's the land of *Droemerdeene*, ours, not theirs! Stinking arsehole colonists, gnarled dogshit!"

The father let fly other imprecations which rang out with a peculiar kind of obscenity because he was translating clumsily the oaths of British convicts and whalers. Tridarir realised that the words soiling their ears were replacing their tears. While spitting out his insults, Woorady seized his son's shoulder and shook him without restraint. The child was in pain, but for nothing in the world would he have admitted it to his father. He knew well enough what he was like, his father, at times like these: he was like one drunk with sorrow, drunk from a bitterness greater than the heart of a human being:

". . . Sooner or later you will take our place. Open your ears wide, split your skull open, do mischief to your head if you wish, but never forget: when we are singing, your mother and I, we are singing for the three of us, certainly, but also for the mad old women at Oyster Cove, for the dead of Bicheno, for those of the Great Tier and Kutikina, for the number-less people slaughtered in the bush who were left there to rot like the corpses of lizards, for the accursed dust which came to cover their bones. They have all left their Dreaming behind, and even if they are not our Dreams, we must sing them because we are the last. *The last of all the tribes that have ever existed here*! Can you understand that? And you, soon you must do the same: sing, so that a miracle might take place and the rain carry us away, as at the Beginning, the children of our people in the form of raindrops! Never forget that, even when you are nothing more than the last black man in this territory!"

On the verge of tears, the little boy tried to free himself from his father's brutal grasp. Then, brusquely, the father dropped him like a sack and disappeared for hours into the forest to let his despair brew. Until he came back, Tridarir felt he could not survive, he was terrified by the one idea: that the enraged father might abandon them or that he had been killed or captured by white hunters, whose smoking campfires they could sometimes glimpse in the distance. Worn out by astonishment, the boy ended up by falling asleep on his mother's knees. She stroked her son's fine skin to rid it of parasites and crusts of mud. The painstaking task allowed the mother to control her trembling chin and, above all, to empty her mind – because otherwise she too would have howled in terror. Calmed by his mother's protective hand, Tridarir's sleep was soon filled with showers of tiny black children pelting down on the towns and fields of those abominable invaders who had come from so far away and believed that everything belonged to them. One day it would fall to him,

Tridarir, he was persuaded by that dream, to create the rain which would people anew his beloved parents' *Droemerdeene* , . .

Then, at the beginning of winter, Woorady's health deteriorated again, and they had to leave the higher reaches of the wilderness, safe but inhospitable, for the lowlands. Three times, they managed to filch food from isolated farms and, on the third attempt, even a whole sheep, which made them almost ill from eating too much. No-one, it seemed to them, had caught sight of them. A month went by before hunger, once again, forced them into recklessness. That evening, the wretched wallaby did not want to let itself get caught. Tridarir fell behind his parents, out of sorts because of hunger and in a bad temper because his skull had been all but shaved. The mother was the first to notice the smell of food before catching sight of the hut. The father sniffed in turn, and whispered, anticipation making his voice break:

"Hurry, wife, there must be flour there, and meat perhaps!"

The father's greedy look stoked the fire of Tridarir's contempt. Luxuriating in hostility, the boy decided that his father and mother were intent only on filling their own stomachs and that their son, their so-called loved-one, no longer counted for anything in their eyes . . .

Until he was eight years old, Tridarir had lived only at the station at Oyster Cove; he had been born there and there he had learnt to speak the rudimentary and scornful kind of English that the British used in their rare contacts with the Aborigines. His mother, Walya, told him later on how his birth had stirred up great curiosity because he was the last Aboriginal baby born in Tasmania. Another woman, from the tribe of the Great River, had also given birth, two months earlier, to a little girl, but neither she nor her baby survived the confinement. Englishmen came from Sydney to inspect Walya's baby. The mother was afraid that the baby would be taken from her. One of the visitors insisted that the newborn must be sent to a scientific institution. At her bedside, they discussed the matter for a long time without paying her the least attention, prodding and poking her baby as if it were some prodigious creature. Maddened by fear, she tried to read their decision from the look on their faces. "They are devils" she decided when one of them picked up her son by the feet to examine carefully their tiny soles. Several times Walya let out an "Oh, oh, oh!" of horror, until the station nurse silenced her with a light slap on the lips. The men with monocles returned three or four times. Then, for some obscure reason of needing authorisation from London, they resigned themselves, with heavy heart, to going back to Sydney.

Everyone spoke of this birth as a miracle because the parents were not at all young and the father was coughing a great deal. Since the second deportation, from Flinders Island to Oyster Cove, Woorady had been spitting blood, and no-one gave him long to live. In any case, almost all the Aborigines of Tasmania had died. No more than a few elderly people remained, most of them ravaged by alcohol and the distress of looking on helplessly as their own kind, the beloved offspring of the Nation of the Ancient People, were dying out.

Tridarir's birth rejuvenated Woorady. Walya stopped drinking. She cleaned the shack which served as their home and arranged a little celebration for the dozen survivors still haunting the station that had been set up, a short time before, for British convicts.

Truganini, the oldest of the women Walya had invited, burst out in tears: "The Dreaming has lost its way! What is the use of a boy if there's no girl for him to put between his legs? None of us, on the whole island, can carry a child any more! When your son will be of an age to sire children, there will be no black woman left anywhere on the island . . . Nor any black man!"

And everyone, men and women, began sobbing, worn down by the unimaginable misfortune which had wiped out their people: the arrival of the English with their might and limitless greed, the occupation of ancient hunting grounds by sheep farmers, the bloodthirsty raids organised by the colonists against those tribes that showed any opposition, felling Aborigines as if they were mere kangaroos; equally that other death, slower but just as sure, from alcoholism; the diseases of the invaders or mass deportations . . .

There had been, as the deepest pit of this hell, the unimaginable campaign of the Black Line: soldiers, aided by innumerable volunteers raised among the farmers, had formed a gigantic line crossing the island from one coast to the other. When pulled in, like a murderous creel, it should have made an end, once and for all, of the remaining black people still at large . . .

Woorady was captured in the course of this apocalypse some thirty years before the birth of his son. He was lucky not to have been killed on the spot. Shifted from one place of banishment to another, he came to be stranded, together with the handful of survivors of the slaughter, on barren Flinders Island, where he remained a prisoner for many despairing years. It was there that he met Walya, who became his companion after the death of her first husband. At the time when the Governor of Tasmania ordered the final deportation to Oyster Cove, only forty-seven survivors of those who had made up, since the dawn of time, an entire population, came to be involved. Walya and Woorady were among them, just as sickly as those who shared their curse, all racked by an unquenchable longing for their contented life before the arrival of the Europeans, those cannibals with rifles who had succeeded in *eating up* an entire nation.

Several times, in the first years after his birth, Walya was tempted to kill her son and then to kill herself. The prospect of raising her child only to give him over to the unbearable loneliness of being the sole survivor of his people proved, little by little, intolerable for her. Each time, however, her courage failed her, and she started, like a madwoman, to hug the little boy with laughing eyes who followed her wherever she went. She sought refuge with Truganini, where she spent many hours, stunned by the absurdity of their existence: what use were the Dreams, what was the good of their Ancestors' great venture if it was only to end up there? Truganini grew annoyed and pleaded with her to go to look for her husband. The old woman was convinced that Walya could conceive again. "You will give birth to a girl, the Dreaming could not be wrong about that. It has given life to a boy, it must give life to a girl!"

"But that's impossible," the mother of child lamented, overcome by

59

shame. "We won't come to that . . . Life will come no more . . . We try every day . . . For nothing . . ."

Then she cried out again:

"And even if it were possible, it would be his sister! Think of it, Truganini, a man does not sleep with his sister! The Ancestors' wrath would be terrible. That, that is forbidden!"

Shaking with anger, Truganini swept her protests aside:

"What worse could come to us? To die out?"

Grasping Walya's hands, the old woman implored her:

"Oh, my sister in tears, all that is no longer of any importance. In the Dreamtime, all men and women were brothers and sisters. And here, perhaps this is the beginning of a new Dreamtime. We could not have existed for no reason at all! Do it before it's too late, Walya, I beg you, you still have moon-blood flowing through your belly. You are the only one . . ."

More than once, Tridarir came by surprise on his parents as they lay on top of each other, caught in an exhausting struggle, groaning and breathing heavily. Puzzled, he asked his mother what it was all about. She became embarrassed, avoided his gaze, and, inevitably, grew irritable and burst into tears. Wiping her nose with her fingers, she hurriedly launched into telling strange tales, about emus so much in love with one another that they transformed themselves into gigantic eucalypts precariously perched on the edge of a cliff, or about the kookaburra, the kingfisher who peals with laughter all day because, one by one, it plays tricks on all the animals in the bush . . .

Then came the time of the grave-robbers. At first it was only a rumour: they heard that men were digging up skeletons of the Aborigines of the island by their thousands to sell them to museums or collectors in Sydney and even in London! Worse, people claimed that some white doctors were ready to pay high prices for fresh, intact corpses, in order to study them. Panic seized the station when it was discovered that Umarrak and Pevay had disappeared, after they were seen getting drunk with white strangers. Truganini said bitterly:

"Since there are fewer than a dozen of us left, the price will go up every time one of us perishes. The last one's carcass will be worth its weight in gold!"

At the end of the year, an Irishman came to warn Walya that her child would be stolen from her. He had overheard a conversation in a gaming house between two English sailors. Because, as they were drinking, they had made insulting remarks about him and about Ireland, he made up his mind to have his revenge by warning the Aboriginal woman. Filled with contentment, he went away roaring with laughter about the coming disappointment of those sailor-kidnappers.

The same evening, Woorady, Walya and their son fled from the station. The former penitentiary was not guarded very closely because no-one imagined that such elderly people could have wished to return to their ancestors' hard life in the wilderness.

Three years later, their famished steps led them to the door of a wooden hut. The father went in first, finding straight away a sack of flour and another, smaller, of sugar. The mother, for her part, rummaged in the cupboard, triumphantly flourishing strips of dried meat, these, too, so poorly concealed . . .

Tridarir has been hiding all day in his prickly bush. He saw the hunters bring out the two corpses, hurling them to the ground. Someone cried out, disgust in his voice:

"God they're ugly! And to think that our pockets will be stuffed thanks to these fucking apes!"

The child has put his hand to his mouth, his teeth are chattering so much. When the father started gorging himself on sugar and flour, he called out to his son:

"Hey, don't make those eyes at us, little tadpole! Stop sulking, come and eat!"

The father patted his thigh in contentment.

"You surely are a funny one, my son, with that skull of yours smoother than a girl's backside!"

Her companion's jest made the mother laugh. She held out a piece of meat, which the child refused. Tridarir went out of the hut, furious

61

because of his father's good humour, equally furious at his mother's obvious complicity with his father. Stamping his feet in the undergrowth, he swore that nothing would pass his lips as long as his father did not apologise for the way in which he had hacked off his hair. At the risk of starving to death . . .

An instant later, the child felt his resolve weakening, the rumbling of his stomach reminded him forcefully that he had swallowed nothing for many long hours. He turned unwillingly towards the hut, grumbling against these parents who no longer bothered even to feed their child.

On the doorstep, he noticed first of all the smell of vomit. Then he heard moans. Because it was dark inside, he almost tripped over his father's body. His eyes closed, Woorady was squeaking like a mouse. From time to time, a spasm shook the upper part of his body. The mother was still conscious. A stream of greenish spittle oozed from her mouth.

". . . Don't eat . . . son . . . poison . . . it's the old trap . . . save yourself . . . they've used it against us . . . at the time of . . . save yourself . . ."

The father died first, rearing as though someone were battering his body from inside. The mother's death throes lasted until dawn. The child, paralysed by terror, could do nothing but cover with kisses those faces contorted with suffering. When, suddenly, a kookaburra burst into insane laughter, Tridarir knew that some men were on their way.

Crouching, the child tries to open his bowels. His belly is filled with pain, but nothing comes out. His legs twitch with the effort. He pushes once more. In vain. He understands that sorrow has bound his guts. He wants to rid his body of this sorrow as putrid as a heap of turd. He would shit out, if he could, his intestines, his heart, his eyes.

He stands up, wipes himself with a gumleaf. His lips are trembling. No, he must not . . .

It sounds like growling. He shouts with all his might, but his voice is hardly stronger than a whisper. The little boy is screaming, but his body, in the grip of terror because of what he has seen, stifles his cries of sorrow.

"Mum . . . Mum . . . Mum . . ."

Tears well up, clouding his eyes. Tridarir can no longer see any of the tangle of tree-ferns, myrtles, aerial roots twined around prostrate trunks. The little Aboriginal boy keeps up his whispered screaming. While he is wailing like this, he hopes, something in his head or stomach will perhaps burst and he in his turn will die. *Return to the land*, as his father used to say.

He has seen too much. The hunters argued for a long time, standing around his parents' bodies. "They're only worth something if their corpses haven't started to rot," one of them remarked. He suggested smoking the bodies. Their leader retorted that they did not have the time. At least a week was needed for the whole business, and he was afraid that they would miss his brother's delivery-boat.

"I've a better idea," he suddenly announced.

One of the dogs approached the bush concealing Tridarir. Attracted by the smell, it wagged its tail and poked its snout into the thorny thicket. The child's heart stopped when the dog's eyes crossed his. The animal started barking frantically.

"Quiet, you filthy mongrel. Here, gobble this instead!"

A sticky lump landed a few paces from the dog. The hunter watched with interest as the dog leapt forward and chomped on the blood-stained gobbet. The man had a knife in his hand. He spat with satisfaction:

"Doggy likes liver, doesn't he . . . In the long run it's no more diffi-cult than gutting a ewe, except that a ewe doesn't stink so much, and then . . ."

He laughed:

"And doesn't have such a big cunt!"

"Hurry up, idiot, the other ape needs bleeding! Clean them out care-fully and stuff them full of salt. That way they'll stay fresh at least until they're sold. Hey, Hughie, Lawson, get the bags ready!"

The child immediately closed his eyes. Too late. He had seen: his mother's stomach slit almost completely open, the man leaning over her pulling out her intestines by the handful . . .

The child vomited all over himself. The dog went back to the bush, but, having had its fill, quickly lost interest in the foul-smelling game protected by too many prickly thorns.

The men took the best part of the morning getting the corpses ready. As soon as they were gone, Tridarir took off, drunk with fear and disgust, without even casting a glance in the direction of the blood-soaked remains of what had been his parents.

And now, he is weeping softly, leaning against a eucalypt. He has never felt so lonely. He would like to tell the tree the secret of his great suffering. He knows, however, that the tree would not listen to him. The certainty of never seeing his parents again strikes him like clenched fist.

". . . And I have abandoned them, spilled on the ground like garbage!"

A guilty splutter sends a shiver through him. He has left his father's and mother's entrails scattered over the ground, at the mercy of the forest's insects and carnivores! Would the Ancestors receive dead people in such a poor state? Would they not condemn them to wander for ever through the stench of the earth?

Tridarir tries to get his breath back. He cannot just stand there with his arms dangling. He should bury what is left of them. He must. Perhaps that would allow his beloved parents to join the long-vanished tribes in their encampment in the sky, where numberless fires can be seen burning at night.

It takes him a good while to make his way to the hut. He stops now and then, overcome by giddiness. Cruelly, hunger makes him aware of his body again. For the moment, he almost manages to ignore it.

When the hut is in sight, the child recoils. It seems to him all of a sudden that he will not have the courage to gather up the entrails. The same tears return, the same words:

". . . Mum . . . Mum . . ."

It is not possible, it could not have happened. Who would tell him stories now, who would console him? And his elderly father, whom he believed to be stronger than anyone? What is the use now of the spear he once handled so well? Tridarir feels the stirrings of rebellion: he is too little, he cannot fend for himself without a father or a mother! A foolish idea surges in his head: he, who is still alive, has he not become older than both of his parents together?

He does not notice straight away the person who is approaching cautiously, a gun pointed at him.

"Well, well," the man sneers suddenly, "even the apes are here to blubber!"

And turning to the rest of the hunters hidden in the thicket:

"Hey, you bastards, don't say I didn't tell you that there was a third lot of footprints, and that they were made by a young 'un!"

5

At the same moment . . .
Prison Island of Nou, New Caledonia, 1,200 nautical miles from the coast of Tasmania . . .

"Hey, scumbag! It's for this afternoon."

The man gives a light tug to the chain linking his foot to the other convict. Annoyed, he whispers again:

"Have you gone deaf? I'm telling you it's for this afternoon!"

Kader shivers, but does not let it show. Rogg, misled by his lack of reaction, looks at him closely.

"Eh, Wog, don't you trust me?"

Rogg laughs sarcastically and adds, in that accent which he claims is Australian:

"Look, you are right! In the clink, mate, you can't trust anyone. If you're not careful you can even end up buggering yourself with your own hand on the sly."

Prisoner number 844 looks away, infuriated not to have enough time to think things over. This Rogg is as guileless as a famished snake. In reality, everyone knows that he is a French seaman who got mixed up in the business of abducting Kanaks to Australia, that he had done time for it in gaol, and that it was there that he learnt the scattering of English words he uses. Since yesterday, Rogg has been constantly chewing his ear about something that was about to happen.

The Arab continues digging as if nothing is going on. The two guards, who are supervising the small troop of ten prisoners "coupled" two by two, are not in a good mood. Where they are clearing the ground for the new track is too remote from the main part of the penitentiary. The guards are hot, and they have already struck one of the convicts because he had slackened the pace of his work. The captives are facing long hours of isolation in the scrub, where boredom makes even the best disposed of screws turn malicious.

Kader's heart is beating like mad: from fear and from excitement. For the moment, fear is the stronger because he is aware that a bungled escape means at best the lash followed by long months of solitary confinement, feet fettered and drinking soup straight out of your clogs. At worst, in case of complications, such as wounding or killing a guard, it is public execution by the guillotine in the prison yard, the *boulevard of crime* . . .

The man shackled to him is digging away at the ground, adroitly pretending to reasonable diligence, provoking neither the screws' suspicion nor their attention.

"We've been chained together for two days now, and it wasn't me who asked for it, cobber."

He growls:

"I wouldn't have asked to be chained to a Muslim, you can believe me! Though with your pale mug you don't look much like a Wog . . ."

He spits on the ground:

"It's really bad luck! The mate I was chained to carked it from the rotten shit they give us for grub. Everything was ready. And it's going to be today and not tomorrow. So, you fucking digger, are you coming with me or not?"

With the back of his sleeve, Kader wipes away the sweat clouding his eyes. He would so much like to believe in this chance of escaping, but three years in the chain-gangs of New Caledonia have taught him that most attempts to escape finish on the scaffold or between the teeth of the sharks that breed copiously around the archipelago. There had once been something even worse: someone had voluntarily let himself be immured between two walls, counting on an accomplice who was at large to get him out. The accomplice, after pocketing the money, vanished into the countryside. The fugitive was discovered in his brick tomb only a week later. Because of the smell! They said that he had worn down the nails on both of his hands scratching and eating the cement between the bricks . . .

Kader casts a sidelong glance at the man chained to him. How would he be able to trust his life to the hands of this "common criminal" who is so skilled in practically all the languages – and all the lies! – of every prison in the Pacific? Prison gossip insists that the would-be Australian did not hesitate to smash in the skull of an old woman in Noumea to relieve her of a few banknotes. He had not been sentenced for that murder, but for an affair involving the rape of the young daughter of an officer in the French navy. "Pokers" are not liked in the clink, but Rogg is feared because he is given to extreme violence: he almost strangled one of the captives because of a joke about his clothes . . .

The midday break has just interrupted Kader's gloomy thoughts. A Kanak, the sole captive in the group not to have been chained to another – no convict, not even the most repugnant would allow himself to be shackled to a blackfellow – has been put in charge of distributing food. Cursing Kanaks is the only thing which unites Algerian insurgents, deported communards and crooks of every kind. Wooden pail in hand, the Kanak makes the rounds of men laid low by exhaustion. He who could once boast that he was the nephew of the most illustrious emir of his country inspects his can with resignation: a thin soup with a few scraps of bacon floating in it. A good while ago, he gave up observing the prohibition against eating the meat of pigs: he would have been dead from starvation otherwise. But the feeling of revulsion is never far away. Kader chews slowly, his gaze lost in the vastness of the landscape. The sea is too blue, too beautiful with its little islands displayed like so many gems surrounded by their coral necklets. This accursed turquoise . . . Impossible for the convict not to think of Algeria . . .

He pretends not to notice the furious look that Rogg, eagerly waiting for his reply, gives him. Staggering Satan! he rages inwardly, why must the decisive choices of his life always be forced on him by others? Then with a faint grin: "Choice? As if this were one, to be slaughtered by your fellow worker or to be massacred by patrolling guards?!" In the penitentiary, everyone knows how disagreements between "mismatched couples" come to an end: the stronger – or the more crafty – ends up by skinning the weaker in a faked accident . . .

Kader is about to reply, but he wants to pretend to himself for a couple of minutes longer that he is still master of his own fate. This morning he has brought with him his *Book of Songs*, which everyone mistakes for a Koran. Just in case . . . He scrapes the bottom of his can. It is only a way of taking his mind off things, for the can is empty. Suddenly he thinks of Nour. Nour's image has stolen up on him like a swift dart. He growls angrily because he has been caught unawares. It is all this idiotic talk of escape that has allowed the chief enemy of anyone under a life-sentence to sneak out of its lair: hope. All day he will have to put up with these barbs! Months of relentless apprenticeship were needed to stop him thinking about the woman he loved, to bury once and for all the last impression of her he retains – the smell her sex left behind on his hands – deep in the tomb of memories. He will only allow his head, his body, his penis to plunge once again into the hell of regrets if he has a litre of tafia at his disposal. Otherwise, he would be howling in anguish in this universe where tomorrows were no longer of any account.

He coughs. In rage at himself and at the man staring at him with a mixture of anxiety and contempt. The cough is so violent that one of the guards casts a threatening look in his direction. Rogg, all alert, screws up his eyes, then, abruptly, smiles.

"How did you find out about it?" Kader whispers, fixing his eyes to the ground to stop himself from slipping. Rogg and he are among those captives who are considered dangerous. The three additional kilograms of iron attached to the clamps around their ankles beat painfully against their knees.

"What do you think, imbecile? I gave money to the other guard."

The afternoon is drawing to an end. From time to time, Kader's lip twitches with anxiety. He feels panic overwhelming him because he does not understand how his companion means to get rid of the screw. The three of them are making their way along the path leading to the clearing. Their task is to reinforce the sides of a well. The guard walks behind them, rifle in hand, constantly cursing the heat.

The journey lasts a good hour. When they arrive at the well, they are out of breath. The guard is soon in a rage at Rogg, who is ostentatiously sitting on the ground:

"Get up, you bastard, get working!"

The blow of the rifle butt is not particularly violent, but Rogg doubles up in pain. The astonished screw bends down over prisoner 3772.

"Don't start playing tricks on me, smartarse! What's . . ."

The knife plunged into the guard's throat so swiftly that Kader thought at first that he was imagining it. But the blood gushing from the guard's carotid artery almost immediately saturates the prisoner's shirt. Kader seizes Rogg by the shoulder. The Arab's face is ashen with anger. His jaws are so tightly clenched that he has trouble opening his mouth:

"But you are mad! This wasn't part of the plan, killing a guard . . . It's a . . . it's . . ."

The prostrate body of the guard twitches several times with weird convulsions before it grows still, hands clasping the neck in a last attempt to stop life draining away. Kader is torn between rage and terror. He no longer dares finish what he was saying: "It's the guillotine!" The seaman, knife still in hand, snarls at him contemptuously:

"Are you afraid, girlie? This way I could make sure that you wouldn't be able to back out. Don't get worked up about it; I've taken care of everything."

His foot prods the man lying on the ground:

"Him, he's no great loss. In any case, he was going to die of boredom on this blasted piece of rock!"

He is pleased with his joke.

"You're wondering how I got hold of the knife? You've seen nothing yet . . ."

From the inside of his yellow trousers, he pulls out a wad of soiled banknotes. "But yes, this'll open your eyes wide. It's money . . . Decent

amount of money, isn't it? But still," lifting it to his nose, "it stinks a bit
. . . There's a boat waiting for us. So, are you up to it?"

Kader would like to ask where that large pile came from. Overcome
by giddiness, he bites his lips. His companion laughs sarcastically:

"You don't really have any choice, mate! If you refuse, I'll insist that
it was you who killed him. Arabs, they love knives, everyone knows that."

Rogg bursts out laughing when he sees the convict's stupefied face. He
lifts the dead guard by the shoulders. The head falls back, revealing the
bloody gash. Kader thinks of the blood of a ram's head put out for drying.
Takes deep breaths to overcome his nausea.

"The other guard, he knew that you . . ."

"No, I only had to knock him senseless."

Clearing his throat, he continues mockingly:

"But you saw clearly enough that I had no choice. Go on, pick him
up by the feet. We'll tip him into the well. That will give us a few hours
to get ahead of the other guard."

Kader obeys, his senses dulled by the rapid succession of events. Their
task is laborious, because the chain linking the two labourers restricts
their movements. The corpse is dragged to the opening of the well, then
thrown in head first. They hear a dull thud – the corpse must have hit
the side of the shaft – followed by a *splash!*

"Hurry up, fat-arse. You aren't about to recite one of your heretic's
prayers over him, are you?"

Rogg grabbing hold of the rifle, hesitates for an instant about which
direction they should take.

"That way," he ends up announcing. "Wouldn't do to stumble on
Kanaks. They've declared war on white people, and even on off-whites
of your kind. If they catch us, it's off to the pot straight away!"

Kader shrugs, but Rogg is right: the danger is real. All the islands
of the archipelago are in turmoil. Kanaks have rebelled against the
colonists, recently massacring a police outpost in the scrub. The French
army unleashed violent reprisals against tribes accused of sympathising
with the rebels. The Kanaks harbour immense resentment against
convicts and deportees, because the majority of the latter, hoping for

a reduction of their sentences, have actively supported the army. Some transportees, communards or Algerian rebels who are not detained in fortified compounds, raised a squad of volunteers and are shamelessly tracking down rebellious Kanaks. Even El Mokrani's brother has joined them . . .

"Some Niggers would like to taste white meat . . . Perhaps they prefer white flesh to dark? What do you say about that, Wog? Your people are forbidden to eat pork, but what about the son of Adam, well roasted?"

Rogg, a little out of breath, roars with laughter. Kader cannot stop himself from feeling some admiration, mixed with repugnance, for the cool head of this emaciated man jogging at his side.

They have reached the head of a creek. The sheltering expanse of mangroves stretches out before them. The tart scent of vanilla wafts through the air. In the distance, further to the east, they can make out the line of a beach spiked with araucarias and coconut palms. Despite his apparent good humour, Rogg is worried. He hurtles down the dune, dragging Kader with him, towards an extensive grove of wild mimosas. The ground is slippery, and the two convicts stumble several times. Rogg makes his way around the bushes, cursing softly, goes around again, feverishly, rummaging in the undergrowth with the barrel of his rifle. He is starting to pant. Suddenly, he lets out a triumphant cry:

"It's there, it's there! Those stinking bastards haven't just made off with their money!"

He claps his hands together with enthusiasm. Kader is amazed by his companion's almost child-like glee. How can you laugh so freely when you'd just slit a man's throat?

"Get a move on, let's drag the boat out! Who knows whether they aren't already hot on our heels?"

The craft is quite small. A hessian bag and a pair of oars take up most of the bottom. Rogg has put the gun down at his feet, he rummages in the bag and pulls out a pair of pliers:

"Motherfuckers! these aren't thick enough to cut through the chains . . ."

Rogg, spitting contemptuously, hurls the pincers to the ground.

Resisting panic, Kader kneels down. The jaws of the pliers look ridiculously narrow compared to the thickness of the rings.

"Perhaps we could do something with them if we pulled them apart? How are we going to get into the boat if . . ."

Kader looks up, surprised at how stealthily Rogg is moving towards him. The other is staring at him, fixing him with a strange look of satisfaction. His tendons and his neck-muscles are bulging as if he were making himself ready for some violent exertion. His right hand is behind his back.

"But you . . . look at the mug you're pulling!"

The man, his jutting chin trembling, goes on smiling. In a blinding flash, the Algerian realises that the rapist is about to kill him . . .

Kader is seized by a foolish thought: to die, certainly, but not at the hands of a man sporting such a chin. A kagu is barking so close to them that the two men are startled. The flightless bird is concealed in the melaleuca grove. Its strident call, like the yelping of a puppy, almost drowns out the Arab's question:

"Afterwards?"

"What afterwards?"

"Where are we going afterwards?"

"To Noumea. There's an Australian boat . . ."

"This boat of yours, what is it called?"

"The . . . The *King of the Sea*, halfwit."

"And how are we going to get there, to Noumea?"

The conversation is faltering, now each of them knows that the other is on his guard. Kader's mouth is furry for lack of saliva. The convict has only one wish: to drop the pliers and to leap on the rifle. But the sarcastic look on his adversary's face reveals only too clearly that he has no intention of allowing that to happen.

The kagu barks again, as if begging for an answer. The kneeling man discovers that his opponent is on the way to winning the confrontation by virtue of the strength of his placidity alone. The seaman is holding a dagger in his hand, certainly, but his other dagger, equally efficacious, is his flagrant indifference in the face of death.

"He's going to cut my throat," Kader realises with alarm, "and me, I just stand here, right where I am, and stare at him like a terror-stricken goat!"

Rogg whispers, his eyes fixed to the top of the melaleucas:

"It's a nice enough day for us to escape, don't you think? All that's left is for us to suss out a nice little nook for . . ."

The knife is out before he finishes saying:

". . . Growing old in . . ."

Kader has just enough time to curl himself up. He lets out a short bellowing cry, which should have coincided with the pain of the blade entering his flesh. But the backwards drag on the chain attached to his foot has thrown Rogg off balance.

"Holy Mary of arseholes!" he swears, trying to stand up.

"Strike," Kader spews out, as if some other person were involved "strike, you blasted coward!"

The blow catches Rogg in the mouth. The convict roars with pain. The second and the third blow, better directed, strike him on the temple . . .

He has never felt so downcast. For a good quarter of an hour he has been sitting, legs stretched out, next to what is probably a corpse already. He has not had the courage to make sure. He knows that sooner or later the other guard will have to set out in search of his colleague. The Algerian sighs, almost wanting to wait for his pursuers to arrive. Only the obscene vision of a public execution – now certain – shakes him out of his torpor. He stands up at last, and takes a step towards the boat. His left leg, ulcerated from incessant rubbing against the shackle, brings him back to reality.

He looks at the pliers, hesitates. No, he could not. He is too cowardly for that. He shrugs his shoulders, drags the body with him, lays it crosswise in the boat in such a way that he is able to move his foot.

It takes him another exhausting half-hour to shift the boat to the water's edge. The chained foot was scarring him horribly. Again he tries to use the pliers to loosen the ring attached to the shackle. Though he manages to loosen it a little, he realises that an hour or two would be needed before he could hope to break the link. He has no time left for that. He frisks the gaolbird, removing the wad of notes and the dagger. He takes dried bread out of the bag. Then *only* one shirt and *only* one pair of trousers . . .

The corpse is slumped against the boat. "Scum!" he says to himself. From the outset, the rapist had intended to get rid of his companion in chains. The former candidate had escaped that fate, but only by dying of food-poisoning!

Kader slips on the shirt, realising – the chain! – that he can't put on the trousers.

"Be accursed until the end of time!" he spits at the corpse.

When the boat glides between the mangroves, Kader feels that a horrible panic is taking hold of him once more. Where will he go? He has not the faintest idea which direction he should take. Noumea, Rogg had said. And what if that good-for-nothing had lied? And even if that were not so, where is Noumea? To the right, probably. But how could he reach Noumea rigged out like this? To the left – but he is no longer very sure – lies the Ducos peninsula, where the majority of the communards are confined with relative freedom of movement. Those of the "Commode", in the envious jargon of the penitentiary. But would they have any cogent reason for helping him? As for the Algerians, those who were sentenced to banishment, they were deported to the Isle of Pines, too far for anyone as inexperienced as he is to reach on his own by sea. They too are allowed to move around their island without too much hindrance. At least that's what prison gossip claims.

He tries to work out whether he would be up to making his way to the Isle of Pines in several stages perhaps? "Isle after isle . . . yeah . . . enough time to die of hunger and thirst or to get caught by Kanaks and eaten . . . Unless, what's more likely, you get snatched up by the boats patrolling the harbour and along the coast of Grande Terre . . ."

Night fell abruptly, at first a fierce blaze on the horizon, then a moonless dark, with the twinkling of those stars of the southern hemisphere, for which Kader does not even have a name in Arabic, as the only source of light. He rows somewhat aimlessly, encumbered by the corpse. He has left behind the area of mangroves and is approaching open water. Pain shoots through his left foot imprisoned in its shackle. With the smallest movement, the overladen boat seems in danger of capsizing.

The sea is dark, menacing. This great Pacific swell lifting the vessel resembles a gigantic hand. Childhood fears rise again in Kader's heart: is not the ocean that famous perfumed lake where the souls of the dead find refuge? And if the ocean is so vast, isn't that because there are so many dead to be cradled in its depths?

Kader tries to pray, but cannot manage to do it. Grasping the pliers, he whispers:

"Darling *Yemma*, forgive your son for what he is about to do . . ."

It has been such a long time since he thought about his mother. She who taught him the difference between good and evil, who smothered him with kisses and reprimanded him with equal vigour, whom he would defend against the entire world . . . There is a lump in his throat. Like an abscess. Above all, act quickly, before he has to vomit . . .

The joint yields easily. A kernel of bone inside a nut of flesh. He then tugs on the foot with force. When the stump stays in his hands, Kader experiences a moment of horror. He has felt the sticky fluid trickle along his forearm . . .

6

The Ducos peninsula, New Caledonia

Lislei gets undressed quickly. Still a short hour before the screws start calling the roll. Even though the stilt-like roots of the mangroves shield her from being seen, she does not feel at ease. She is afraid that she might suddenly catch sight of a Kanak warrior with a sharp-honed axe, but the district is seething with militia and prison guards. Is she more worried, perhaps, that an onlooker might turn up and ogle her in her threadbare undergarments? Besides, shame upon shame, she is surprised to catch herself thinking that she would rather be discovered naked than decked out in those stained rags, frayed from having been washed and washed time and again. The administration of the penitentiary made no provision for the women confined to its care. At first, some of them were even obliged to wear men's clothing. Later, women's underclothes . . .

She is hungry. Under the new administrator, rations have been reduced even further. To make things worse, there have been fewer orders for garments from Noumea's high society. Her stomach reminds her that she should not tire herself out so much, but she does not intend going without the sole luxury freely available here, at this blasted end of the earth. She gets back into the water and swims a few strokes. She is one of the very few women confined to the peninsula to have learnt how to swim. Here the water is not at all salty, because this part of the mangrove swamp is where the river meets the sea. Lislei lets her thoughts wander. Her period has just come to an end and she feels that her skin needs to recuperate in open water.

She daydreams. She is aware that she should not allow herself to recall so often the caressing days of her childhood. The smell of jam, her brother's laughter, the way her parents used to grumble . . . There's a price to be paid for these sweet memories, because, later on, despair is never far away, and sorrow, her true state ever since the beginning of her deportation, returns to lash her soul once more. She has no-one with whom to share her memories, except perhaps Mathilde. But Mathilde is such a peculiar woman. She would give away her shoes and her ration of bread if there were any hope of helping anyone who asked. Some – like Lislei – love her, many detest her on account of that excessive kindness.

Lislei thinks about her mother again, a woman so filled with affection. And whose image is so distant, so much blurred after so many years. Lislei realises that her memory often plays tricks on her, for she replaces the intimate features of her mother's face, now lost from memory, with others which she makes up at the prompting of her reveries. "I am betraying you, my poor mother, but what can I do?" she sighs. The swimmer experiences such yearning for her to return to life, that calm and tender-hearted woman from Alsace, who used to call her her lass. If only her mother could clasp her in her arms again, as she had done when Lislei was terror-stricken because she noticed blood trickling between her legs. Her periods started very early, Lislei was not much more than ten years old at the time. When her mother found her in her room, she was sobbing her heart out. She was going to die, she spluttered, because blood wouldn't stop flowing from the wound inside her stomach which she must have given herself. Her mother, embarrassed, shook with laughter, then took her on her knees. She buried her face in Lislei's hair. Little by little, her uncontrollable laughter stopped, she sat still without saying a word, rubbing her nose against her daughter's head. Lislei felt her hair getting damp. She broke away vigorously, afraid that the inexplicable flow of blood might have also sprung up on her skull. The mother stood up just as abruptly. Looking away, to hide her moist eyes, she suggested, her voice husky:

"Come, Lislei, let's bake a cake to celebrate this."

After a brief silence, the mother asked, in a self-mocking tone from which there welled up, nevertheless, an inexplicable bitterness:

"Are you in so much of a rush as this to grow up, my lass?"

The water is warm and consoling. Lislei is on her back, eyelids closed. She loves this water, as comforting as a loving brother, she can weep her eyes out without restraint and pretend not to notice it. A curse on time; it courses more swiftly than blood from a wound, without ever flowing back!

The sun is high in the sky and gently warms her face, her thighs and the bush of hair between her legs which appears and vanishes as she moves her body to stay afloat. Lislei suddenly suspects that she has strayed too far from where she had set out. The more so because a flock of overexcited parakeets is fluttering above a guava tree . . .

Fear overwhelms her. Has she been carried away by the current? Or worse, has she swum past Kanak rebels lying in wait, who are busy preparing some evil fate for her?

Vigorously twisting her waist, she tries to change direction, but the current in the middle of the stream is too strong. Despite her anxiety she decides to make for the shore. When she catches sight of the boat and the hirsute man, a cry of terror rises from her throat, immediately stifled by the mouthfuls of water she has swallowed.

She is choking, she takes in another mouthful, goes under, comes up again. The man is still there. He is not a Kanak. And he's not a screw. She is so terrified that she does not immediately understand that he is imploring her:

". . . To eat . . . Help me . . . eaten nothing for three days . . . I'll pay you . . . I've got money . . . I beg you . . ."

Lislei has forgotten that she is naked. She swims like mad, her arms flailing frantically. To get as far as possible from the stranger. By the time she reaches the spot where she entered the water, she is exhausted, with a stabbing pain in her side that cuts short her breathing.

She slips on her dress and begins to run. She soon comes to a stop and, with painful little spasms, vomits up the water she had swallowed.

It is raining large, warm drops. The night has grown even darker because of the moisture. Beneath the up-ended boat resting against a tree, the man is shivering. For four days now he has been holed up in this muddy lair. He is hungry, hungry . . . He survived the first two days, marooned on the beach, on Rogg's sea biscuits. The third day he managed to kill a bird with a stick. The raw flesh of the notou was leathery and without any taste. He chewed on it for a long time until he grew discouraged. He tried eating roots, but they tasted so unpleasant that he was afraid of poisoning himself. This morning, he tried to bring down parakeets by throwing stones at them, all in vain. The parakeets seemed to make fun him, wheeling, screeching, then flying back to perch near him. His sole victory at the end of four days' furious effort with the pliers: splitting the leg-iron!

But would that be of any use? Perhaps the woman has already – and the man's heart shrivels with dread at the prospect of this – alerted the police or the screws. The fugitive worked out quickly enough that he was on the Ducos peninsula. In effect, the inlet looks like a crab, with Noumea where its head should be. He had escaped from one of the crab's claws, Nou island, to be recaptured on the other claw, the Ducos peninsula. From hell to purgatory, in a way! He lacked the courage to put to sea again because the bay is thick with patrol boats searching for fugitives. But he can stay here no longer. The forest is not far away. Without too much bad luck, he will be able to hide there and get hold of something to eat, fruit perhaps. While waiting to see things more clearly. Unless the insurgents making war on the colonists capture him on the way and stick his head on a spear as a trophy . . .

Once again he is overcome by the weariness of hunger. He moves as little as possible to prevent his stomach from contracting. That woman . . . her naked body . . . It has been an eternity since he saw a naked woman. And yet, what did he catch sight of this morning? A tuft of black between her legs, her backside when she turned around with furious and terrified eyes. And all that in a flash!

So is there still a life where naked women exist, with a vagina, thighs, a mouth? Sex . . . In the penitentiary no-one talks about it yet everyone is obsessed with it. Being deprived of freedom is intolerable, but Kader has discovered that there are degrees of the intolerable: to know that you would never again hold a woman in your arms and that your penis stiffens for nothing is the red-hot blade of what cannot be tolerated. "The vagina of the intolerable," are the words the fugitive utters without a smile on his face.

Kader shuts his eyes. Little by little a feeling of shame – but a kind of joy too – seeps into him. Saïd was chained to him for a whole year. They understood each other well enough, but hardly ever spoke. For fear of getting pointlessly irritated, but also because Saïd came from Kabylia. Neither had mastered the other's language well enough to allow them converse freely. In the name of the same country, they had fought against a common enemy. In the rout, they lost for ever their country and those dearest to them. That was enough to make them take care not to spoil their good relationship, so precious in the pitiless world of the penal outpost. The administration of the prison always took care to couple prisoners who had nothing in common. That was a part of their punishment and diminished the risk of escape, because hostility between two prisoners in a "bad marriage" implacably transformed them, in the course of what became hell for them, into gaolers without pity for one another.

It began when the bunk shook, so imperceptibly that at first Kader doubted whether he had felt anything. A faint beam of moonlight through the bars lit up the cell. The sound of snoring filled the large space with its usual racket. Discreetly, he turned away from the companion who was always tied to him, even in sleep, by the accursed chain. Saïd's hand, moving rhythmically, was inside his trousers. Saïd kept his eyes half closed, breathing a little too rapidly. Yet, but for the action of his arm, he seemed to be asleep . . .

Kader had, until then, adopted the strategy of denial: women were a land where he would no longer venture, he had decided that his member was dead. Or, more accurately: that the question must no longer concern him, for there were, in prison, only ignoble ways of answering its call.

He, the son of a chief, nephew of an emir, could not reconcile himself to take or to become a catamite! When his sex grew erect, Kader felt that his intestines were betraying him. The prisoner grew tense, the tendons and muscles of his neck bulged. A good hour of cold fury was necessary before he could take control again of his belly swelling with desire. He came to feel, within the folds of that belly, a frightful emptiness, while struggling with an overpowering sense of culpability: hadn't he become, with the passing of time, his own gaoler, a gaoler incapable of exacting retribution, but a gaoler without compassion for his own penis. He had watched with a revulsion mingled with bewilderment – and perhaps admiration – two gaolbirds in his own cell who, in return for money, had managed to get themselves chained together; one evening they filled a bowl with their blood and sperm, which they drank "for the sake of becoming one"! After someone denounced them, they were tortured with thumbscrews: fastened between wooden clamps, their thumbs were crushed until the phalanges were shattered. They were not chained together again, needless to say, and the elder drowned himself from sorrow, dragging his new companion into suicide with him.

When, that night, Saïd lifted his eyes to him, asking forgiveness by raising his eyebrows, Kader did not react. Throat raw with anger, he turned away, so as not to be looking at his companion any longer. He tried to go back to sleep. Profound sorrow took hold of him. Then, as if a dyke had burst within him, he also put his hand to his member . . .

This habit of masturbating simultaneously, the one granting, in a way, permission for the other to begin, lasted until Saïd's transfer to the Isle of Pines. They never spoke about it. Perhaps, at certain moments, they grinned at each other in unintended complicity, but they reined themselves in immediately. The two had been warriors: how could they have sustained such laxity without shame? When the blacksmith undid the chain linking the two convicts, Kader shook the hand of the simple mountain lad from Djurdjura without saying a word. He had almost let slip a "thank you", but stayed silent, suddenly aware that that was the one thing which should not be said . . .

*   *   *

The man hears a noise. He does not know any longer whether he is dreaming or if this is reality. He is not really hungry any more. That disturbs him slightly because he should be feeling famished. The only things left are the spasms, their sharp pain rising slowly to his brain. He tries to stand up, bumping his head against the boat. In any case, his legs are shaking so much that he abandons the idea of getting out and running away. Astonishment gradually strikes root in his exhausted mind: how could his penis grow so stiff while the belly underneath it is yelping like a rabid dog? Bile rises to his lips.

"Hey, you, look over here!"

Two women are inspecting him with intense curiosity. Despite the darkness enveloping the scrub, the fugitive recognises the woman he saw in the afternoon. The other woman is older. Her face is ugly, and she is whispering, fear seeping from the suspicious look on her face:

"Is it you, the one who escaped?"

She is holding a stick in front of her like a shield. Her voice is shaking with disgust:

"Is it true that you've killed two people? They've found your chum on a beach, his body hacked into small pieces . . ."

The woman's face is hard, tense with contempt:

"Go on then, what are you going to say? You know, don't you, we wouldn't come off too badly if we turned you in, perhaps we'd even get a remission of our sentences?"

7

South coast of the island of Tasmania

There is raging dispute. First Lawson's voice is heard, urged on by Hughie and Flynn with cries of "Yeah, yeah!" The child listens intently, his heart battering away.

"We're not going to rot away on this bitch of a farm for a fortnight. Your brother Bruce should have got here with his boat by now. Remember: three days . . ."

The voice seems to be seeking the support of the others.

"Hey, you blokes. Three days was what he said!"

A commotion follows. Tridarir realises that he will not be able to hear what O'Hara, the leader, is going to say in reply. He is the only one of the four who, paradoxically, keeps his voice down when the discussion becomes heated. Equally, he is the only one, up to now, to have filled the child with terror. Tridarir swallows hard. In the darkness, he wipes his lips on the top of his shirt. On the third day of his captivity, Hughie gave him an adult's shirt and trousers because, he grumbled, "a naked lad's indecent, it's not Christian, even if he's a Nigger."

O'Hara replied with an icy smile:

"Since when have you had religious scruples? That," he pointed to the child, "that's an animal, and an animal's always naked. Does it shock you to see a kangaroo's backside? No! Or has the little savage's arsehole got you all excited then?"

He went away, laughing uproariously. The others imitated him, embarrassed all the same. Hughie, in a rage, muttered in reply:

"A Nigger's a Nigger, and a kangaroo's a kangaroo! I'm not saying he's human like us, but I'm not saying he's an animal. And a lad's a lad; there are some things you shouldn't say!"

The discussion, in the large room next to the barn of sorts where Tridarir is tied up, is obviously drawing to an end. O'Hara has certainly managed to get them to agree: they will wait on this isolated farm for as long as necessary . . . They are all a little scared of O'Hara, even Hughie with his mountain of flesh. They realise that, without any hesitation, he would treat them with just as much cruelty as he used against the Aborigines. O'Hara is all smiles when he is in a good mood, but he can start bellowing, without the least warning, in such a terrifying way that the first time he heard it Tridarir pissed all over himself. That happened in the main room of the farmhouse. O'Hara stared at the little puddle around the captive's feet without saying a word. Then he fetched a bucket of water, tipped it over Tridarir and, miming the action of pissing, rewarded him with a fierce kick in the backside.

"You piss and you shit in the tub, snot-face, and nowhere else!"

The boss of the head-hunters was looking with satisfied air at the child lying on the ground, whimpering softly from pain but not daring to cry.

"O'Hara, it's only a kid . . ."

The Irishman replied contemptuously:

"So, you can manage to gut the father and the mother, but you feel sorry for a brat stinking of shit a mile away. He won't be pissing on the floor the next time, I promise you. Do you appreciate cleanliness, yes or no?"

Flynn smiled, but only for O'Hara. He is much too afraid of Hughie: the latter could take out on him his sense of frustration at not being able to stand up against O'Hara. The giant contents himself with muttering between his teeth that it's no use mixing things up, that chopping up the parents was work, while striking a lad with such force, that's not the same . . . Lawson, however, betrays no reaction. He picks up his pipe, fills it and puffs on it, observing the whole scene with that look of disdainful indifference which he adopts for every occasion.

*   *   *

Several times Tridarir tried to convince himself that nothing of what had happened was real: the poisoning, how his mother and father were gutted, his capture, this confined dark space filled with the putrid smell of rotting meat, *his parents' meat*. How could that be possible? At first he persuaded himself that if he begged his abductors for a whole day, a whole night, and then throughout the following days, they would make up their mind to get him out of this impossible world and put him back in the "real" world.

Impossible world . . . because it is impossible! For how, otherwise, could the corpses of his father and mother, stuffed with coarse salt, be lying next to each other in a large crate? Hessian bags inscribed with letters and numbers are scattered all around him. Lawson, who never comes into the barn without lighting his pipe – because of the smell – was the first to open one of the bags right in front of the child's eyes. Tridarir realised, from the way the man was looking at him, that he had tipped out the pile of bones in front of the little Aborigine purely for the pleasure of observing his reaction. None of the grave-robbers knows that Tridarir can understand English. Nevertheless, Lawson has fixed the child directly in the eye:

"This here is one of your kind, a fine broth of a lad from Bicheno. Set your mind at rest, he was well and truly dead by the time we pulled him out of the bush. You apes are good at hiding them, these stiffs of yours!"

He strokes the bleached bones.

"The skeleton is in good condition. Like the others, from elsewhere, from the Great River, the ones from the Lake Country . . . Ah, we've done good work! We'll get a good price for these, but, the devil take me if I am mistaken, less than we'll get for the meat of your old man and his missus though . . ."

Trying to catch the look on the Aborigine's face:

". . . and much less than for you, little rat. You're out of luck, you are the jewel in our collection: the last little Nigger still alive in Tasmania. There's nothing left for us any more except a few shrivelled old Abos, and then you, you pop up, you're there, like a spring lamb! You can count on us, we'll get the bidding up and up, you can believe what old Lawson, his darling mother's bastard son, is telling you!"

The child kept his eyes lowered, gritting his teeth so that they would not chatter. Lawson ruffled his hair, marvelling at its thickness. Tridarir was sure that Lawson – and the others – would not have taken it well if they found out that their prisoner could speak their language. A beast – and in their eyes he was hardly more than a beast – does not speak English! Lawson gathered up the bones, stuffed them into the bag in an offhand way, making them clatter against each other. Whistling a merry tune, he slammed the door behind him. The child heard him asking Flynn if he wanted to play cards.

Tridarir waited a good while for his teeth to stop chattering. He tried to weep, but in vain. Only in the first two days had his tears flowed. And then, like a fist in the face, the certainty struck him that you weep only when you expect to be consoled. But who would there be to console him if his mother and father were dead? Once only, in the barn, did he see their faces again. The crate had been opened for more salt to be added. The features of Walya and Woorady, just like the rest of their bodies, had crumpled, shrivelled by the action of the salt. They seemed to be in a terrible rage because they were lying there, handled by their murderers like dried fish, when they should have been concentrating the little energy they still commanded on finding and tending the Ancestors' sacred paths. Tridarir was tied to a post, Flynn and Hughie were sprinkling salt over the naked corpses. The child learnt, for the first time in his life, both compassion and the absolute pointlessness of compassion: it was not even within his means to pay a little respect to the flayed bodies of those elderly people who had brought him into the world and managed to protect him, more or less, against the white man's devilry. Also for the first time since his capture, he was overwhelmed by a feeling other than sorrow and fear: it was up to him now – but how? – to save what was left of them.

Tridadir was staring wide-eyed in order to fix in his mind the faces of his tortured parents. He searched his memory for the words of the songs of the Emu and the Monitor Lizard, the Dreams of his mother and father.

87

"Oh Honey Ant, help me not to stray and to sing properly the paths of the Dreams of the mother and the father of my life, help me to recover the sounds of their journey to the land of our elders. Help me, Ant, to help them . . ."

It was at that moment in his prayers that he realised that he was weeping profoundly, but without tears. Because he was no more than a child and because a child cannot remain alone in the world. And if a child is alone in the world, then the world is out of joint, twisted, diseased. And this whole world was about to die, like those great red gumtrees gnawed by termites which suddenly topple over. Spasms of retching, filled with sorrow, choked his larynx, clouding his face, almost reaching the point where his eyes meet, then sink to his belly. How he would have welcomed a flow of bitter tears burning his eyes! Tridarir knew that the healing liquid – the water of the lake of sorrow slumbering deep in the earth, for which each living creature is a source – would never come to assuage his suffering and his fear in that fashion!

Then he started humming once more, ever so softly, fragments of the sacred songs, replacing, so as not to fall silent, forgotten verses with those he improvised or borrowed from other Dreams. From one instant to the next, he was inventing a single song, born out of the three songs he retained almost intact in his memory, those of his parents and his own song. He had the vague inkling that this was probably sacrilege, because each song indicated a precise itinerary, and mingling the three would result in a tangle of paths along which his parents could easily lose their way, without hope of ever reaching the meeting place in the Dreamtime.

But what else could he have done?

Lislei casts a last glance at the bay and its line of low hills tinged with blue. Behind the port, a chaplet of houses flanked by trees climbs towards the sky. The *King of the Sea* is there, at the end of the wharf, between two fishing boats. The vessel is small, ugly, with inadequate rigging. How would it manage to make its way to Australia?

As she sets foot on the ship's gangplank, her heart is ready to burst. She would have been happier if it had taken her longer to find the boat.

Long enough to screw up her courage and to get the explanations she will give the owner clear in her mind. Access to a vessel is usually strictly forbidden to her. Because she was sentenced only to deportation, she has relative freedom of movement around Ducos. Like all those sentenced to banishment, she has a hut at her disposal, which she built with the help of others. But she should not be in Noumea, even though it is hardly far from the peninsula. She grips her shawl tightly, her hands are shaking, she would like to give up. Her time is limited, she must be back before the evening roll-call. The Arab's money has already been useful because the road worker will be coming, in the early afternoon, to take her in his cart back to the outskirts of the town. He believes that she has come to see a lover. In any case, that is what she led him to understand.

The paintwork on the rail is peeling. The ship is not really in good shape. Two sailors eye her with irony. She asks to see the captain. The younger of the sailors inspects from head to toe this ill-dressed woman who is blushing. The two have obviously decided that the visitor is too poor to warrant polite treatment. She repeats her question. One of them calls out to her in English:

"Here, girl, we . . . don't speak French here . . . we speak English!"

With his finger, he points towards the open sea:

"We're from over there . . . You understand . . . Australia!"

Lislei takes a deep breath, remembering with gratitude her former employers from London, and decides to put her English to the test.

"I . . . I would like to see the captain."

Hearing her strange accent, the seaman bursts out laughing. He nudges his companion:

"Hey, the lady speaks English! And why do you want to see the captain?"

"It's . . . it's private!"

"Private, really?"

"Yes, private."

The seamen laugh uproariously.

"Just look at that: a beggar woman who wants to talk privately with the Cap'n. There are inns for that, Mam'selle!"

"Poor, but not ugly, the slut! He has good taste, the Cap'n has!"

Her cheeks on fire, Lislei is about to slap the sailor who has just insulted her when a guttural voice booms out behind her:

"Hey girl, what are you doing on my boat?"

He spoke in a heavily accented French. Lislei's anger crumbles straight away. The man looking at her, apparently well into his sixties, is tall with his stomach spilling over his belt. He has a windblown face, skin blotchy from drinking. His cloth jacket is relatively clean, but his shirt is filthy.

"I want . . . I . . . I'd like to see you, Monsieur."

The man grows a little less hostile, without abandoning his contemptuous frown. He is face to face with Lislei. Her features seem to please him.

"You two, get working! And you, come with me."

The cabin is at the front of the boat. Lislei walks, almost limps past the two hands. She clenches her teeth when one of the sailors makes a soft kissing sound with his lips.

The cabin is tiny, but polished from bottom to top. There is a striking contrast between the neglected appearance of the deck and of its commander and the shininess of the cabin's planks and brass fittings. Lislei hardly dares to breathe as she tries to control her shaking legs. It is fortunate that her dress hides them. The man inspires revulsion in her. He is taking his time, sucking on a pipe. He does not say a word, content to "palpate" her with his eyes. He looks as if he is weighing up even the smallest recesses of her body. A vague nausea overwhelms the woman. She is sure that he is going about things so ostentatiously only because he knows that, if he wants to, he could rape her there, on the spot. *She is on his ship!* In any case, as a consequence of what she is trying accomplish, she has cut herself off from any chance of complaining or calling for help, because the penal administration's reprisals would be terrible. For her and for Mathilde . . .

The woman exiled to the end of the earth runs over in her mind what she is intending to say: to speak about money first, then about the voyage to Australia. Never has she been overcome by such a feeling of boundless desire: if all goes well, she will be free again! That word – free, free – has made her mind's mouth water, has caressed her ears. By dint of saying it over and over again, she has gathered up enough courage to undertake this attempt to confront the menacing captain. Mathilde does not yet know that she, Lislei, has also decided to make use of the Arab's money to escape to Australia, the dream of everyone who has been banished to these islands. Her friend, for her part, drank in the fugitive's story and decided to help him. She said that a communard must sympathise with anyone who had fought for the freedom of his country, "even if he is a fanatical Muslim," she added without concealing her disapproval. In reality, Mathilde harbours such hatred for the authorities on the island that she would have given shelter, with the same eagerness, to a parricide who had slit his own father's throat, had the father been one of the screws!

"We must lend him a hand. Otherwise those Versailles bastards are going to capture him and . . ." – she made a horizontal slash with her hand – "cut off his head!"

Lislei has no liking for the fugitive and feels no obligation towards him. Most of the time, he seems to be in a daze. Mathilde, scorning the danger, hid him in her hut. She'd risk her life for a cat, that one! As it is, she is one of the few communards to go as far as supporting the Kanaks' uprising! "We've taken their land from them and their hunting grounds; in exchange we've given them stony fields, endless bondage; we've violated their women and their burial sites! Now, in order to be able to kill them with a clear conscience, people say that they have run riot, that they are eating their victims. It's hardly surprising that the Kanaks are about to turn the invaders' skins into bagpipes! Even the gaols have been built over the lands of tribes who'd been expelled at gunpoint!" As far as these stories about the fate of the Kanaks are concerned, Lislei would more or less agree with Mathilde, but we all have our share of suffering, and she does not feel courageous enough to add others' misfortunes to her own.

The risk they took was enormous. Because the man had killed and because he could turn on them. Because the peninsula is seething with guards and soldiers. Because, in similar cases, the prospect of a pardon has already prompted some of the most hardened communards to snitch on others.

The man eats little, hardly speaks, even though he expresses himself in nearly correct French and not in *Bechelamar*, the local dialect – but where did he learn to speak French? From time to time he leafs through a tiny book, becoming so abstracted that he sometimes seems to be on the point of falling asleep. Mathilde whispers to her friend that the book must have something to do with his religion and its peculiar prophet.

For Lislei, the Arab's story has made no sense from the start. How could a common criminal, who, rumour insists, is a hardened malefactor, have allowed himself to be caught out so easily? In reality the Arab must have been pretending when he agreed to the plan for a double escape. They killed the guard, then the Arab, probably helped by his compatriots, turned on the man chained to him. These stories of betrayal, by knife and mutilation, aren't they said to be common in Africa?

Mathilde told Lislei that the fugitive had been shipped to New Caledonia in the middle of 1872 on board the *Calvados*. Lislei's heart missed a beat. That means that they travelled on the same ship! In itself, this is not at all astonishing since deportations to the archipelago were carried out in large batches with only a few crossings. But Lislei quickly came to the conclusion that this coincidence gave her certain rights over the man she had discovered. "My God," she began turning over in her mind with growing bitterness, "why should this person gain his freedom while in my case I continue dying a slow death on this accursed island?" And the more the possibility of escape took hold in her mind, the more her despair-filled resentment magnified the importance of the "coincidence". Thoughts of escape raced through her mind as soon as the man showed her the money and swore that he would leave them a large part of it if they helped him to get in touch with someone in Noumea. The very idea of escaping from the hell of this slow death at the end of the world made Lislei's mouth dry and silenced the promptings of her moral senses. My God, to be free, to be able to go wherever your fancy takes you, to eat your fill, no longer to endure insults, humiliations, or the expedient tricks for finding a little tenderness, the adulterated liquor she and Mathilde drink to forget what they have become, and that damned sun which rots you right there, on the spot, before finally pitching you into the grave! She never imagined that she would be ready for any kind of treachery as long as she could get back to her France, with its rain, its snow, its cold and perhaps . . . and perhaps her sweet, her darling Camille!

Lislei would like to forget that her decision to join in the escape, whatever the cost, makes that more difficult to accomplish. And even impossible. In that case the Arab will end up on the scaffold and she – with Mathilde! – confined to a dark cell, if not worse . . .

There, face to face with this arrogant, filthy captain, she is overcome by sickening fear: the worst is no longer a mere possibility . . .

"You've come for what, Madame?"

He stressed "Madame" with emphatic irony. He studies her reaction, weighing with interest the first signs of revulsion in her frowning features, then vexation and finally consent when her eyes signal resignation.

"I've come . . . that's to say . . ."

"Yes?"

"I've come . . . to arrange an escape . . ."

The man knits his eyebrows. All he does is mutter: "Ah!" The irony is gone. He draws on his pipe, takes it out of his mouth:

"Is that all? As if, just passing by, you happened to notice a sign: Escapes To All Countries Arranged Here. Competitive Rates."

He said "excapes" and "rats". Lislei is almost smiling. She is, at the same time, so terrified that she launches into a muddled explanation: there are two of them, a Frenchman and herself (she supposed that the captain would not be happy to have an Arab on board), that someone had suggested the *King of the Sea* to them, money, yes, they have it, plenty of money, only passage to Australia, it won't be a problem for him, they wouldn't take up much space . . .

The seaman continues drawing on his pipe. He looks at the porthole, apparently preoccupied with a spot of dirt on the glass. Lislei stays silent, worried by the excessive indifference of the man's attitude.

Abruptly, he turns and seizes the collar of her dress:

"Who are you, whore? Are you a stool pigeon, or what? You want to lay a trap for me with your pretty kisser, is that it? Who told you to come to my boat? The police? You're going to tell me or I'll smash your teeth in one by one!"

He shakes her violently:

"You rotten bitch! One after the other, your front teeth first, then your back teeth and then your pretty little face will look like an old baboon's backside! Do you understand?"

Lislei can hardly breathe. She tries to break free but a blow full in the face stops her. Struck down with pain, she puts her hand to her face. Her jaw seems to be shattered. The seaman is still holding her by force. Lislei realises from the look in his eyes that he is ready to start again. Indeed, he is already lifting his arm. Her terror is too great. Then, her voice blurred by tears, she confesses everything all at once.

The man is visibly relieved. He murmurs sarcastically:

"So, it really is Rogg, the fellow they found with his foot where his hand should be. Bastard! He was done in by one of Allah's apes . . . Well, bully for him! He's made me three days late already."

Letting Lislei go, he picks up his pipe again. He sucks on the stem while reflecting:

"So the Arab's got hold of the money, is that it? How much?"

Lislei mentions the sum, unable to disguise her fear of being struck again. The captain puffs two or three times, scratches his neck, hesitates, before a look of curious greed breaks out over his face:

"It'll be all right . . ."

Lislei feels herself overwhelmed by gratitude towards this person who has just treated her with such brutality. A faint smile begins to play around her lips. The seaman interrupts her:

"The deal with Rogg concerned one person only, so that will be for the Wog. It'll have to be this very night and no other! If you're hoping to join the company, well . . ."

Lislei's smile freezes.

"You'll look after me during the crossing . . . I mean to say . . . You understand?

94

I get lonely at times. It shouldn't be as hard as all that for a Parisienne, but, it goes without saying, it's up to you to decide, darling . . ."

The woman, stroking her chin, has not yet fully untangled the meaning behind the man's words. Her nose is running. She is livid, with a large red spot on her jaw.

The other bursts out laughing at the woman's stunned look:

"Your ticket of leave, my little chick, is your cunt!"

His flash of wit increases his amusement. He dries his eyes with the back of his sleeve:

"Your rump, and all that goes with it, that's your ship to Australia, darling!"

8

South coast of the island of Tasmania

. . . Above all, not to wake up on this accursed farm where the hunters have been driven mad by irritation. Something is about to happen. For him and for the others. And that could only be something even more horrible. Well then, he must dream. Get his fill of dreams. Dream the living mother. Dream the living father. Dream the sheltering forest and the crazy cackle of the kookaburra. Dream about feasting on kangaroos and emus, savouring the eggs of fairy penguins and mutton-birds' too.

The child curls himself into a ball, filled with a voluptuous drowsiness. How fine is the gift of sleep, to be cradled, enveloped by the sheath of dreams, new-born next to his mother's skin. He, Tridarir, would like to die, to become nothing other than this desire: to kiss the earth and the undergrowth, to give thanks for the friendship of animals and plants.

A purple heron takes wing. The little Aborigine taps on his father's swelling belly – tap tap tap – and that helps the elderly father breathe more easily. They have lit a fire near a rock resembling a recumbent thylacine wolf surrounded by her cubs. This has been a beautiful day, and the meat smells so good. His mother places the yams, which have been soaking all morning, over the embers. His mother, his poor mother with her faded, flaccid breasts, smiles. She rubs his back, and her tenderness, an unfailing shield, is stronger than all dangers. Even those that are unimaginable!

The child, in his sleep, stretches his arm out too fast, jerked by the rope fastening him. His lips are twisted by a grimace of pain which he cannot manage to erase from his dream. Because he clings to this wisp of a life with all the power of his sleep. The child's smile is filled with indulgence. Imagining that their little boy has fallen asleep, they seized the opportunity to hide behind a bush. They are doing something incomprehensible, and a little comical too, as is the way of grown-ups. His father, usually so violent, is lying on top of his mother. His actions are filled with kindness, and his mother moans, but with gentle suffering.

He is running, the sleeper, with weightless legs, in the dream-forest, filled with a sense of irony and also a little unhappy, but why? He hurries between the trees, seeking his dear Woorady and Walya who taught him how to hunt the Giant Kangaroo, which is able to kill outright all those clumsy enough not to pay it respect. Ah, how joyful he is, the child snoring in the foetid room, his father and mother are suddenly so young, and there are still so many things left for the three of them to do . . .

King of the Sea, *somewhere on the Pacific Ocean*

. . . With huge waves, the wind churns up the sea's indifference. Without cease, the slow undulations roll from one shore of the world to the other, carrying news of horrors men do not heed. Lislei shivers, despite the heat and the foul air in the hold. She sleeps. She tries to sleep. Despite the rolling of the ship, seasickness, the creaking timbers. But galley-masters crowd around her sleep.

The waves beat against the hull. It is a lass who is sleeping. Adult in appearance, she is only six years old. Her mother has just caught her by the arm. Lislei has been playing in the sun too long. The mother gives her a glass of apple juice. She has always been terrified of the risk of running mad from sunstroke. The father jokes: sunstroke in Alsace? But he shouldn't be talking to her either, they were drowned in the Rhine so long ago. Yet the father's voice is nevertheless scathing: this is not Africa here! Lislei wants to smile because of her parents' fondness for disputes like this. Her brother Pierre pulls a face because he hadn't been given anything. You have done wrong, my girl, her father grumbles without

97

warning. He frowns. He would like to look angry, but he is only very sad. He has the look of someone worn down by reality but no longer able to do anything about it. You have done wrong in the eyes of your mother, your brother and in mine. We loved you so much. Freedom at such a price?

Lislei speaks in her own defence. She breathes in the smell of bread and quince jam. Oh my childhood! It is a dagger of joy that cuts into her. And tortures her. It's to be with you again, my dear family, that I have done this. I am too far away from you, Maman, Papa, Pierre, it could not go on any longer. Maman, protect my sleep, Maman! Remember, you used to lie down beside me every night, I did not go to sleep before hugging you dozens of times. Understand me, I would die if I had to stay in a country where the bats are so enormous!

You still have sperm between your legs, that pervert of a commander's spunk. And you don't even wash yourself, you slut. What have you done to our love for you, our beloved daughter? You have betrayed everyone. You've let Camille, our granddaughter, die. Even your Mathilde, you've deceived her. You didn't let on to her that you'd be leaving, she must still be waiting for you, that dyke of yours!

Their tone is so gross – this is the language women prisoners use among themselves! – that Lislei starts, yanked from the pit of her sleep by a whipcord. And by a scream rising from her belly which, fortunately, fails to break out. She just has time to ask herself: is this father, is this mother, and why doesn't Pierre defend her?

The woman is wide awake. Her teeth are chattering; she feels the moisture of what the commander has deposited in her vagina. Four days of sailing and this comes around once each day. Sometimes twice. As if the man urinated on her. Or covered her in snot. And the Arab, wrapped in his silence, who gorges himself on her humiliation.

She is at the rear of the hold. She hears her fellow fugitive's breathing. He is at least a metre from her. Is he asleep? The first night, she had been terribly afraid of him.

If she had been able, she would have sobbed out loud . . .

* * *

. . . Squeezed between two casks of rum, he closes his eyes. It would be possible to keep them open, so dark is it in this hold where the stale smell of alcohol and waterlogged timber wafts around. He would like so much to persuade himself that freedom is waiting for him at the end of the voyage. But he has no money left, no documents, and he knows that fugitives guilty of crimes of blood are shipped to France by the Australian authorities. He committed one, two if the murder of the guard is imputed to him. Two crimes, the guillotine twice. First the head, then what? The testicles? Not the other way round? That would make it worse. A bitter snigger. Where could he go? Algeria, in any case, is out of the question for him, it has become a part of France now. With her soldiers. With her justice. With her injustice.

He tries to doze. Even though he has hardly left his hiding place since they came on board, he has the sense that it is evening. And late enough. The ship dances a jig. Sometimes, it is necessary to cling to something to avoid being tossed from one side of the hold to the other. Some time has passed since the captain – or commander? – returned to the deck. It's practical, that copulation as regular as clockwork: the old man comes down, making the steps creak, the Frenchwoman gets up and joins him at the other side of the hold. The captain doesn't give a damn that the Arab should witness his loose conduct, at least by ear. Perhaps it arouses him? On the first days, he cursed the woman at the top of his voice as he was penetrating her. At no instant could Kader discern the least sound coming from the woman. Except once, on the first day, a cry of pain after, probably, the dull thud of a slap or a blow of the fist.

Kader feels no pity for her. Each of them must pay the price of their escape. Which of the two has paid more? He, with his murder or she in yielding her body? He has not spoken a word to her. Even when she announced: "I am escaping with you, otherwise I'll turn you in!" He agreed with a nod of his head and she took care of the rest. She was trembling with joy and fear when the ship left the port. Too easy. He is astonished to realise that he does not know the features of her face very well. Nor even her name, besides. Sometimes, he thinks he can hear her weeping. He cranes his neck. But perhaps she can "hear" in the dark that he is eavesdropping on her, because the snivelling stops.

The fugitive's head nods gently. Thinking about that woman humiliates him profoundly. To be there, a filthy voyeur, while a man toils away at her, almost within hand's reach. He cannot, however, stop himself from growing stiff. He grows so stiff that he feel stabs of pain in his belly. The lust of a jackal, he curses himself. If this goes on, he is going to masturbate, and she will be aware of what is going on.

Sleep overcomes him. He would like to smoke. "Every prisoner found in possession of tobacco will receive six lashes; if he has matches as well, twelve." At the beginning of his internment, he got eight of them, through a bizarre method of calculation on the part of the prison authorities. His pipe lying on the ground was alight at the moment when it was discovered, but the screws could not manage to find his matches. Ah, how he screamed that day, flogged in front of all the convicts in the prison yard! Others had conducted themselves better under the lash, and treated him with fierce contempt on account of his weakness.

The boat is pitching violently. A matter of sou'westerlies or sou'easterlies. The movement resembles more and more the swaying of the fronds at the top of those palm trees where he and his cousin Hassan used to hide. Something within Kader's body relaxes, lowers its guard: the man is dreaming. Rather, he is swimming, immobile and swift, between the folds of his slumber. There is no longer any danger in this dream. The proof: the dreamer is clutching his little book to his chest; a curious verse soars out of it like a butterfly: "Love me no more, one day oblivion will come."

Drink from the cup of happiness and good health, Hassan, perched as ever in his palm tree, wishes him, for no good reason at all. The cousin on his perch adds, his expression filled with wonder: Do you know that there is a market in Paradise where they sell oranges? Oh, how I would love some oranges, sighs the dreamer, because my mouth is parched by the salt of the ocean! The woman – he realises little by little that it is Nour – presents him with a pitcher. She whispers, with an expression of unbearable melancholy: Here is lemon juice tasting of bergamot. And a smile arises in the eyes of the one he loved. The sleeping man makes a sign of despair. Ah, he has been well and truly caught. Sleep has led him into the snare of the past. Nour, Nour, the past is a land where I will never again dwell. Why do you insist? Never, never will I come home again. And in Kader's heart, which is also the centre of the dream, there blooms a sudden starburst of sorrow . . .

9

Tonight, Captain Bruce has not come down. At the time when he should have appeared, there was a loud clang, as if the ship had strained against something and could advance no further. There were shouts and muffled bumps against the hull.

At first she imagined that there had been an accident. A shipwreck. She thought, dumbfounded: "My God, the same fate as Papa and Maman! Drowning, is that to be it, my punishment?" She shivered, probably groaned, because the "Other" asked in his strange throaty accent:

"What's happening, what's happening?"

In his voice, the same panic.

The noise continued. They realised soon enough that some men were coming on board, and that the first clang had been the vessel dragging on the anchor, followed by the sound of rowing boats scraping against the hull.

"Have we arrived?" whispered the man next to her. She felt his breath. She said nothing, her body growing tense.

An hour later, the uproar increased tenfold. Commands and curses, shouts and the deck creaking.

"I think there are more hands than when we left. They're bringing something on board and . . ."

His voice is filled with anxiety. A shudder ran through Lislei, she has just reached the same unspoken conclusion as her companion in flight: if they are loading goods, it must be because they have not yet reached their final destination: Australia. But where are they then?

The hatch is torn open. Two men climb down, one of them brandishing a hurricane lamp. Lislei and Kader are huddled up against two casks. The woman has recognised the captain. His companion is talking rapidly in English. It is a matter of money, a great deal of money. The lamp illuminates his face and Lislei is taken aback by the resemblance between the two men. Brothers, certainly – the same head, the same vitality, even the same arrogance – and the newcomer is the younger of the two, she has guessed. Two wolves, one plump, the other sinewy. The captain has put his arm around his brother's shoulder. Lislei is consumed by bitter rage: the eyes of the master of the vessel are overflowing with affection for the man next to him, who is waving his arms around as he pours out a torrent of words. She detects an obvious brotherly pride in the way the elder is nodding his head. My God, so that scum Bruce is capable of human feelings; as for her, he treated her is if she were less than a bag of rubbish, but that does not stop him from adoring his young brother. And if he is a family man, this wretch probably behaves towards them in the same way: good father, good brother, good neighbour!

She clenches her fists, chokes back her anger because the pair is drawing nearer. But the taste of bile lingers in the mouth of the deported woman, filling her with disgust.

The man gave a start when he noticed the dark shapes between the casks. He tilts the lamp towards the fugitives.

"Who are they?"

"Don't worry, brother, they are . . . they are my guests!"

The man threw a questioning glance at his brother, then at the two "guests". The captain, who seems to find the situation amusing, taps his brother on the shoulder.

"I'll explain everything to you, O'Hara."

Kader came forward as soon as the two had turned their backs to him. Cowed by the powerful presence of the two brothers, he cleared his throat.

"Why have we stopped . . .Where are we?"

Captain Bruce scowled at him, not sure what attitude to strike. He has a pipe in his hand. He inhaled greedily.

"You, Mohammed, may have paid your way, but you're too nosy all the same. It's up to me to decide when this tub sails . . ."

Then, changing abruptly from menace to friendliness:

"We are less than a mile from the coast of Tasmania. The mainland's for tomorrow, after Bass Strait. That's if my god and yours will allow it . . ."

He burst out laughing, as if he had just cracked a joke:

"If it's Heaven's will, you'll soon be flying with your own wings. Like gulls. Be patient, little birds!"

His companion has not altered his sombre expression. He probably doesn't speak French, and is puzzled by his brother's good humour.

A few minutes after they left, other men climbed down and began removing the casks of rum. Three of them, one built like a giant, did not belong to the crew. Their task took them the best part of the night. Kader whispered to the woman:

"That must be contraband. Otherwise they would have unloaded it by daylight."

As was her way, Lislei did not reply. Around four in the morning, the sailors went away. Nothing was left in the hold except a few sticks of wood, rope and fishing tackle.

Lislei spent a long time leaning against a crate. She had not dared to go back to her makeshift mattress. She tried to struggle against drowsiness, but she was fast asleep when Kader got up to urinate. He smiled: she was snoring gently. The girl had threatened to turn him over to the screws, she had risked her neck to escape, and now she was sleeping like a lamb, exposed to goodness knows what danger. Kader sniggered: "Silly goose, for you I'm nothing but a hyena, or some such beast, eh?" He was sorry he had not put the lamp where he could make out her face. Because of the scarf she always wears, he has not yet been able to decide whether or not he likes her looks. He is overcome by sharp resentment against this sleeping woman who never deigns to speak even a word to him.

The latrine is at the other end of the hold. "Just like my luck," Kader grumbled while relieving himself, "to escape with a bad-tempered slut. She opens her thighs for the captain, but claps her mouth shut for me. Go and get stuffed by misfortune and all its long-pricked mates, you bloody whore."

He shook his sex, disturbed by his thoughts. Those are not his own thoughts, but prisoners' thoughts. Filthy, scabby, like prison. Has his mind become so infected?

Annoyance, tinged with despair, eats into him. What had been the use of Damascus, poetry, love for his own people, all the rest?

Lislei caught her breath. Gently, silently, happiness blossoms in her. Dawn rose without haste, in a succession of soft colours, like a young girl, you would have thought, who is preening herself while getting dressed in a room as vast as the horizon. The breeze is lively. Occasionally two or three clouds float by, frills on a billowing robe.

Lislei's heart is ready to burst. This is the first time when the cause is neither anxiety nor fear. Despite the captain's express orders, she has climbed the steps leading from the hold to the open air. The hatch had not been bolted.

How tiny the ship seems to her! How could they have travelled so far in such a dilapidated craft? Her eyes are heavy from lack of sleep, but her spirits are as clear as the water around the boat. Hidden behind a coil of ropes, she takes in the landscape with hungry eyes:

"My God, how beautiful . . ."

From afar, the island traces a line against the horizon, with patches of jagged reefs in front. Trees, many trees, a long rocky outcrop, a little stream with a sandy beach complete the picture. Lislei makes out beached boats and ants – men – busying themselves around a dark pile. Barrels, in all likelihood, and something that looks like one or two carts.

A bird embellished with marvellous pigments flutters above the boat, soon joined by others of its kind. Lislei smiles with joy: the presence of the island has made the terrifying ocean, which tossed them around for so many days, seem more kindly. *Terra firma*. Despite the stink of the ropes, Lislei is sure that she would be able, if she wished, to smell the lush vegetation.

"This ship is deserted? Where have the sailors gone?"

The voice of the "Other" broke the spell, its tone bringing back her sense of anxiety.

"You . . . Did you see anything?"

Both of their heads are above the hatch. Lislei blushes, embarrassed by her hostility: he has spoken politely to her, she realises, addressing her as *vous*. No-one has done that since . . . how many years has it been? . . . since that accursed day when a policeman dragged her off by her hair. She looks away, not wanting to betray any sign of gratitude. Kader feels a pang of pity for the young woman. Her dress is spotted with tar, the red scarf around her hair is filthy. He himself is hardly more resplendent. She is elated, he realises, despite her sulky look. Madam thinks that she has already reached Australia.

"No," she mutters awkwardly, recovering a little of her liveliness. "They're all on the beach, busy with the rum."

Kader has noticed her changed attitude. He laughs dryly. "It's time to get away from this cesspit. Much longer here, and we'll both turn green with rot. We probably don't smell very nice, you and me . . ."

Taken aback, Lislei glares at him. Outraged, she is casting about for something to say. Without finding anything: he is right, during the voyage they were able to care for themselves only in the most cursory fashion. Even the most private things . . . Besides, he was the one to tip out the stinking bucket each night. The creature drives the point home with sarcasm:

"A hunter would be able to follow our trail without any trouble. Just smell yourself, and me too, if you're not convinced."

Lislei's jaw drops, offended by the mocking familiarity of someone who hardly spoke a word to her during the crossing.

"Oh you, you . . . you . . ."

The man makes a pretence of shielding his face.

"See for yourself how you smell: I stink like a wild boar. And since we are in the same . . . er . . . woods . . ."

A smile plays around Lislei's lips: the wretch is trying to make her laugh! She sneaks a look at his not very handsome face, much more pale, to her mind, than an African Arab's should be.

"You're right, neither of us is very decent."

The phrase, as soon as it is uttered, takes on a different meaning. Kader, his lips taut with bitterness, agrees.

"Yes, filthy indecent."

He makes an effort to laugh once more. He was not able to control his voice, and his laugh breaks off abruptly. The atmosphere has changed. Lislei, all her good humour gone, returns to her gazing. But the island no longer seems so filled with mystery.

"Filthy indecent." The woman's gorge rises. Now even a murderer is able to throw that in her face, and she can do nothing to counter him. *He's seen everything . . .*

A light tap on the shoulder from her accomplice brings her out of her sullenness. She shrugs, ready to make a cutting reply to anything he might say. A finger on his lips, he orders her to be silent. He points with his chin towards the rear of the boat. A soiled canvas sheet has been thrown over what seem to be crates and sacks. Lislei looks at him questioningly, again in the grip of anxiety. Pointing to his ear, he urges her to listen closely.

Waves splashing against the hull prevent her at first from making anything out. Then her face grows dark.

"It sounds like . . . groaning? And even . . ."

An expression of horror spreads over her face.

"It's a . . . no, it can't be!"

10

Lislei threw back the cover.

"It can't be!"

Kneeling down, she is clawing at the sheet. "What have you found, filthy frog?" Kader mutters between his teeth. Leaning against the coil of ropes, Kader is unable to see what she has seen. He is anxious because the seamen are likely to return from one moment to the next. He is afraid. Truly afraid of that captain and his brother. Admitting it to himself gives him a vague feeling that he needs to vomit. He realises that he is ready for any kind of cowardice. So close to freedom and this hussy threatening to spoil it all!

Lislei raises her voice, it is drained of all expression:

"Come, help me! Quickly!"

"Just as yellow-bellied as I am", he laughs to himself before crawling out of his shelter. When he joins the woman, he sees that she is shaking, but not from anger.

"What is it?"

"Look! Are you blind?"

He is exasperated by the woman's fiery tone:

"What should I be looking at? There are crates, bags, tools . . ."

Lislei is livid:

"I'm not talking about picks and shovels. Between the crates, there, at the back . . ."

The cover has not been fully thrown back. He follows the direction of her finger. Between two crates, three-quarters obscured by the sheet, they can make out a black bundle. A ball in the middle of which shine . . . two terror-stricken eyes.

"*Ya Ouled el kahba*! It's a child!"

The Arab's oath made Lislei shiver. Her neighbour is lost for words. He stammers:

"Is he alive or . . . dead?"

"Alive, idiot, he wouldn't be complaining otherwise. Come, let's throw the cover right back!"

Kader is conscious of the insult, but the surprise of the discovery is so enormous that he remains speechless. He pulls at the cloth. The black child is lying on the deck, wedged sideways between two crates.

"What is this, this bastardy?"

The captive's hands and feet are secured by thin cords which are eating into his flesh. The little boy is muzzled, but, thanks to the saliva, the gag has ended up slipping inside his mouth. The child moans softly, his huge eyes fixed in terror on the two adults.

"A Kanak child, you'd think. But what would a Kanak lad be doing on this ship? I'm sure he wasn't with us in Noumea."

Appalled, Kader turns to Lislei:

"Why do they treat a young fellow like this?"

Enraged, Lislei cuts him off:

"Stop asking all these questions! He can't be left like this! Look, he is dying of fear!"

The child has curled himself into a ball, as if he were protecting himself from the blows that are bound to be on their way. Kader tries to shift one of the crates with his foot. It is so heavy that he has to buttress himself against the mast.

"What's this terrible smell?"

"He smells no worse than we do", Lislei comments dryly. "You were the one to say it."

"I'm not talking about the boy, but about the crates."

The captive wriggles, trying to stop the woman from touching him. He is whimpering frantically. Kader frowns:

He is going to alert everyone with his cries. Tell him to keep quiet!"

A twinkle of contempt at the corner of her eye, Lislei scoffs:

"Because, as far as you are concerned, I can understand his lingo?"

Twisting his body to push the woman's hands away with his feet, the child crashes violently against the head of a pick. Pain immobilises him; opening and closing his mouth, he is like someone choking and trying to recover his breath.

"He is bleeding, he is bleeding!"

Lislei casts Kader a beseeching look:

"But help me untie him. The child's terrified. What's got hold of you, are you going to drop dead from fear?"

She whispers, her eyes misting over:

"Are you such a coward?"

A muscle makes Kader's lower lip twitch violently. He is on the point of exploding with the words: "But afterwards, what the fuck are we going to do, you little nitwit?" which form in his head – but only in Arabic, because of his anger – when a creaking noise startles them. A hoarse voice is calling to them from the storeroom:

"Better to be a coward than dead, my young lady! One lives longer like that."

Captain Bruce is beaming. He holds his cap in one hand and a pistol in the other.

"Go on with your conversation, my lambs. Me, it doesn't bother me at all, but my brother and his friends will be a little less pleased that you stole the reward of several weeks of hunting. Isn't that so, Hughie?"

Kader shivers. The man called Hughie is like a giant, but that is not what makes the greatest impression on him. The captain, with his pistol pointed at them, could fire at any moment, merely to amuse himself. Besides, he is about to fire. His contentment is too evident. The realisation hits Kader in a blinding flash; assuredly, he is going to wipe them out. From the outset, Kader should have known it: helping a gaolbird accused of two killings to escape must amount, even in the eyes of the police in Australia, to being an accessory to murder. With an accusation like that, he would inevitably have a heap of trouble in front of him. Money, yes, but only if the fugitives are made to vanish.

And if he hasn't killed them earlier, it's only because of the lust of his penis. The captain wants so much to sleep and to keep on sleeping with the Frenchwoman that he preferred the risk of putting off their execution. "Thanks to your cunt, little sister. If it had been less tasty . . ." A mocking smile stealing to his lips, Kader wonders what kind of a face she would pull if he paid her his compliments aloud.

Kader gulps, wipes his face with his arm, realises that his hand is shaking: surviving through all these days for nothing, only to die in sight of this island with its obscene beauty.

The sea rises. The wind is blowing with much greater force. From time to time, a gust fills the air with a sudden slap of salty droplets. The landscape remains magnificently indifferent, however, despite the savage beast with his pistol and his prey limp with fear. Already, the scene around him is making itself indolently ready for what is to follow straight away: the annihilation of some of the actors on the damp timbers of the deck, and the satisfied laughter of the others.

Beads of sweat trickle down his back. From the innermost depth of his being, Kader is huffing with resentment: "God, Thou makest a plaything of us. So is that it, Thy secret since Adam: to crush us as though we were tiny creeping creatures, while surrounding us with the glory of Thy creation?" The fugitive is paralysed by horror. He must, nevertheless, react in some way. A bizarre thought comes into his mind: the island, the ocean would lose all their meaning if he died, but do they know that?

Because he is going to die. The others too. The woman certainly, perhaps the child. Without appearing to be doing it, the captain's finger has lowered the catch on his pistol. How to die? Two or three seconds to decide: with courage or cowardice? Something within Kader wishes to act with greater honour, even at the cost of his life. And something else, with far more determination, would make him decline shamelessly into baseness to preserve this life.

It is the woman who interrupts the final twitch of the finger on the trigger. Lislei does not imagine for an instant that the captain is about to fire. She calls out to him with violence in her voice:

"Captain, it is shameful to treat a lad like this! You must set him free, you . . . you . . ."

Her anger makes her babble. The seaman bursts out laughing:

"Hey, the slut's not short on pluck!"

His finger is still stroking the trigger. He has the look of a cat who has decided to give a few moments' reprieve to a deserving mouse:

"Set your mind at ease, Parisienne! The Nigger is in no danger. He stinks, he is as ugly and as vicious as a rat, but he is worth his weight in gold for us. Money, big money for us!"

"Then why mistreat him?"

Curiosity is mingled with indignation. Lislei blinks. She still fails to realise that the man intends to close the "discussion" by butchering them. The captain appears to be highly amused by the confusion:

"Do you know what an Aborigine is? No? It doesn't matter all that much. Here, in Tasmania, for a hundred years now, they've been crawling around like lice on a scabby head. Tens of thousands, hundreds of thousands of them, go and find out for yourself about this race of black rabbits. They're very different from the ones on the mainland, much more backward. They haven't even learnt how to light a fire! When the white people arrived, they decided to clean out the island. You couldn't leave fucking Niggers in charge of God's paradise on earth, could you? So, we cleaned them out . . . Me, I took part too. My brother and I were among the best black-catchers. And believe me, our service as hunters, it didn't come cheaply!"

There is nostalgia in the seaman's voice.

"Ah, that was some business, it brought in five pounds for an adult, two for a child! And easy work. And no-one asked any questions. The farmers paid well, they weren't misers. In summer you went fishing, in winter you hunted Niggers. Those were the good times . . . Nowadays, we are reduced to smuggling rum in this decrepit tub . . . Luckily, there are still collectors and museums! You see this little Nigger, he comes from the island . . ."

Lislei stares at the captain, fascinated by her own disgust. The man wants to confide in her. The idea slowly grows in the woman's mind that this sudden loquaciousness is a portent of even greater misfortune. Kader feels a stitch in his side, he summons up all his energy to still the irregular heaving of his chest.

". . . The little blackfellow hasn't the least idea of his price. There are, all in all, no more than four or five specimens of his kind left. A few old Nigger women, always at each other's throats; it won't be long before they kick the bucket. This one's unique, because he is very young and more or less in good condition. So he is very, very precious for us, darling, especially since we had a lot of trouble catching him."

"You speak of him as if he were a rare animal. All the same, he's only a lad! It's not his fault that he was born an Abo . . . Aborigine as you call it."

The seaman's eyes are almost closed. He mutters between his teeth:

"He only had to be born, the monkey. They're beasts, these fellows. They would've polluted our race if we'd done nothing to protect ourselves."

He grimaces contemptuously:

"Tell me, little Frenchy, do you think you are of the same kind as this . . . this rotten filth . . . these black pigs? What do you say, are you for or against your race, you slag?"

Stunned by the sudden outburst of anger, Lislei steps back.

"Stop," the captain roars.

Hughie contemplates the scene attentively, looking like a huge hound snapping at its leash and ready to disembowel the prey its master has pointed out to it. Kader experiences a kind of inner desiccation which quells the trembling of his legs. He is now unconscious of his own fear. He leaps backwards. Lislei lifts her arm to protect herself.

The shot is fired at the instant when the Arab seizes the child and, throwing himself against the rail, holds him high above the water. The child screams in terror, but stops almost as soon as he notices how close he is to the water.

Kader shouts with all his strength:

"If you fire once more, I'll let go of your treasure. He will drown straight away. You will not have the time to fish him out. As for us, we'll be dead, but you, you'll kiss your treasure goodbye. Drop your gun!"

His face grey with fury, the captain starts to make a show of begging for mercy:

"Hey, man, calm down, don't be an idiot!"

"First throw down your gun."

"All right boy, I'm dropping it, but don't let go of the Nigger."

Bruce puts the pistol down on the deck, but Hughie is already hurling himself at Kader. The captain bursts out: "No, Hughie, no!", trying, by grabbing hold of the giant's shirt, to restrain him. Hughie, with a heave of the shoulder, throws off the seaman's restraint. The captain, losing his balance, pitches forward. "My ankle," he has just enough time to groan, before watching, lying flat on the ground, a strange bout of fisticuffs: the Wog hurling the little Aborigine at Hughie like a cannon ball, the other pushing the child away with the back of his arm, his adversary seizing a pick and planting it, with a dull thud, in the giant's chest . . .

"Devil, I'll make you pay for this, both of you!"

Forgetting his ankle, Bruce is quickly on his feet and looking for his pistol. His eyes meet the woman's. Straight away, each understands the other's intention. She leaps at the same time as he does. Her foot is on the middle tread of the steps when the seaman doubles up, grasping his left ankle with a cry of pain.

Lislei holds the pistol in her hand. She points it at the man holding his ankle. The latter drops his head, hunches his shoulders while waiting for the shot. The woman's eyes are popping out of their sockets with hatred and fear.

Everything happened so quickly: the captain at her mercy, the stranger with a giant's muscles stretched out in a pool of blood, the half-dead child, one of his legs all but flayed. And this pale Arab who is holding her by the arm, imploring her:

"Don't shoot, or we are dead. Give me the gun, the others are about to come back, they must have heard the shot!"

11

Kader is struggling against the drowsiness overcoming him little by little. What they have just accomplished is enormous; it is nothing in the face of what remains to be accomplished. And there is so little chance for that to come about . . . He wants so much to ignore all this, not to have to think about it all the time. Behind the captain, he can make out the island. At first he thought he was mistaken. But a boat has already put to water. Soon followed by another. The sea is rising, it will slow the progress of the boats past the reefs. Count on half an hour, three-quarters at best, before the boats are alongside the ship.

The captain gets up cautiously. He examines the man menacing him with his own weapon. Senses his hesitation. Turns to follow his passenger's gaze.

"You're not short on audacity. All the same, it's not clear that it'll get you anywhere."

Kader did not hear him. He starts:

"Eh?"

"I am saying that you are smart and you are going to use your head. Do you follow me, boy?"

Kader finds it difficult to throw off his dejection.

"You played that one well," the seaman adds with unfeigned admiration. "I like a scoundrel with a quick eye. And what are you going to do now?"

Bruce is amused by the other's stunned expression:

"You're in a real fix, my good man. My fellows will soon be on board and that means things aren't going to go too well for you. In fact, I am ready to make a deal: you give me back my gun and you'll be admitted into our company of collectors. We take the child and . . . and all that and you'll get your share just like the others. You'll not only be free but rich!"

Beaming at Kader, Bruce holds out his hand. But his cunning, narrow eyes cannot entirely disguise the tension running through his body:

"Come on, give me back my gun. We're going to talk business now. I hope that you haven't damaged it too much, *our* merchandise . . .

The child! Where is the child? How could he have remained, until this instant, so indifferent to the lad's fate? He remembers the little black-fellow's terror when he was holding him above the waves. And it is he himself who is the cause. The warrior exploited a child . . . Lislei is leaning over the Aborigine. His head is on the woman's knees. He is no longer gagged. Lislei is struggling to undo the knots. She takes to them with her teeth, spitting out bits of rope. The child moans, but he is no longer fully conscious.

"Get me a knife and a clean piece of cloth. Water . . . or better still, rum."

There is acrimony in the woman's voice, but, above anything else, there is sorrow too. Seething with fury, she examines the knots and starts biting on the rope again.

"She feels greatly for the little fellow," Kader observes with a sudden flow of emotion. His voice hoarse, he interrupts the captain:

"Give me your knife. Did you hear me: your knife! One false move and I'll flatten you."

The man scowls:

"You're not going to set him free are you, this bit of crap those other savages left behind? He is quite capable of leaping into the water. Don't listen to that slut, you're not going to let yourself be impressed by her arse. This Nigger's money. Money, do you understand? I've invested a good part of my wealth in this affair. I'm telling you it's going to bring in a great deal. Arab or not, in the final count, you're white all the same, shit! I've travelled a lot, you people keep slaves too, don't tell me any different!"

With an oath, Bruce pulls a long knife out his pocket.

"Throw it behind you. With your left hand. Good. Now, some rum. And you are going to show me where you've hidden the other weapons!"

Screeching breaks out just as the two men reach the captain's cabin.

"*Ya Rab*, what is that?"

"That" changes into a whine of horror. The pair retraces its steps, one prodding the other without any consideration. The scene they are witnessing makes Kader freeze: the little black boy, now free, is still on his back; with his hands above his head, he is screaming and struggling like a mad thing; Lislei, one of her hands still clutching the knife Kader gave her, tries to soothe him with the other . . .

"Don't touch him, he thinks you're going to harm him! It's the knife . . . the knife . . ."

On his knees, the child continues screaming while Lislei backs away from him. The woman is appalled. Panic-stricken, she murmurs:

"Have I hurt you, little one? Forgive me . . . I didn't want . . . Forgive me . . ."

Little by little the screaming loses its force; it changes into yelps, just like a puppy's. Suddenly, as if he had become aware of where he is, the child makes for one of the crates, and sniffs it. Then he strokes it with his cheek, stretches out on top of it and bursts out sobbing. This is even more horrifying because they can no longer hear him, they are only able to see how his shoulders are heaving.

"What have you done to this kid? What is it, that crate?"

The captain shrugs, muttering a curse in English. Beside himself, Kader strikes him in the face with the barrel of the gun.

"I am speaking to you! Answer me: what is in that crate?"

The man begins to grimace with pain, but stops himself because the barrel of the gun is a finger's breadth from his temple. But Kader's mood does not seem to make too great an impression on him.

"Take a look yourself, if that's your fancy!"

The child lying on top of the crate – his arms embracing its two sides – has not noticed Kader's presence. Face turned to the timber, he makes rapid clicking noises with his tongue, interspersed with weeping. For

Kader, at first it sounds just like purring. Then like words, their sense drowned in tears.

Kader has seen more than his share of people crushed by grief. During the insurrection against the invaders of his country, and also the unprecedented yet futile courage of the vanquished. On board the convict transport, when every wave put a greater distance between the prisoners and the people they loved. In the cells where those who had just been flogged watched themselves drinking soup from their clogs . . .

But here, Kader thinks, he has met "Sultan Sorrow" in person, the "King of Despair" of the dirges chanted by the peasants of his country. His lower lip throbs like a pulse in time with the lugubrious song: "Sultan Sorrow has come, and not even God himself is higher than he." The fugitive feels a sickening sense of compassion. Only one thing could make a child cry like this . . .

Because of the shadow cast over him, the lad starts. He has the same terrified reaction as he did with Lislei, slipping to the ground and squatting on his haunches.

"Give me the knife."

The crate gives off a stink of rotting flesh, which becomes unbearable once the blade forces the lid to spring open.

He would like to go to sleep right there, no longer to see the little black boy's boundless sorrow and the two salt-shrivelled bodies. He puts the lid back in place, without daring to lift his eyes to the lad. His mother would have said: "He has met the black camel of misfortune, it is a tireless camel ceaselessly roaming the earth, seeking human beings, without ever feeling hunger or thirst." And that camel is truly mocking the child to death, mocking him until its lips crack from laughing.

Lislei, she has also seen it. Tears are running down her face. She is at the end of her strength, her sides are heaving with convulsions. She cannot get her breath back. All she can say, with difficulty, is:

"Camille . . . He is like . . ."

Kader frowns, turns away. He looks at the sea, at the island. The swell is strong. The boats are still far away. His eyelids are leaden. He has a few moments of absentmindedness, with the sensation that a mill-wheel is churning away inside his skull. No, he is not brave. No, life has absolutely no meaning. Apart from making ready for death. At the time of the final battle against the French, he stuffed a handful of hot peppers into his mouth; he fought like the very devil, because the pain in his mouth masked the abominable fear of being killed. And his companions called that courage!

"Ass-arse, where are you going to dig up peppers on this ship?" he mutters to himself in Arabic.

Bruce has not stopped smirking out of the corner of his mouth. On his face, the verdict is clearly written: the two halfwits are trapped, and their capture, if not death, is no more than a question of time.

"Come here, you."

The gaolbird's voice is flat, without aggression. The seaman limps over to Kader, mockingly exaggerating his handicap. A smile breaks out over his mouth.

"So, we're going to see reason?"

Kader chokes back the blasphemy rising to his lips. He swallows slowly, commands in an expressionless voice:

"You're going to help me throw your mate overboard."

"Are you out of your mind?"

"You see this pistol? You loaded it yourself . . ."

Bruce stares at the Arab in disbelief. His finger is twitching dangerously on the trigger. The seaman's features contract. He shrugs and hisses, with apparent nonchalance:

"Stupid idiot, stop fooling about! You are going to run into serious bother, little man . . ."

"Shut it! Hey . . . you!"

He hesitates, not knowing his accomplice's name. He holds out the weapon to her.

"Aim at his head at the least suspicion. Have no pity. It's him or us, don't forget!"

The giant's corpse is huge. The head of the pick dug a large hole in his chest. Blood, already congealing, is still seeping out of the wound. As a measure of safety, Kader takes charge of the feet. He has not put the knife down. When he makes a sign with his head, they tip the corpse over the rail. A large wave immediately swallows it. Further out, the corpse bobs to the surface like a cork, face to the sky.

"The sharks in the water will soon be swarming around him. Blood attracts them, you know that better than I. And your mate's a proper barrel of blood."

Kader wipes the sweat from his brow:

"Good, now, you are going to weigh anchor, set the sails and get the ship going."

"What?"

The seaman's face, red blotches all over it, expresses complete amazement:

"Have you gone mad! Set sail? Even if this was only a fishing boat, you'd need at least three people to sail it. At worst two. And skilled people . . . You're stark raving mad! Why do you reckon I'd do that? All I have to do is to wait until my brother and his men are on board and that will be . . ."

"I'll kill you before that!"

Bruce spits on the deck with contempt:

"Your word's worth no more than this gob! You're only an Arab, that's to say a half-Nigger. You're hoping to make me afraid, but if you kill me you're dead!"

"If your friends get here I am dead in any case. I've nothing to lose. So, you are going to obey me. You are going to raise the anchor and we, the woman and I, we'll help you. If necessary, you can tell us what to do."

The captain's face is covered in a web of wrinkles:

"You are not going to make me obey you, you filthy shit-eater!"

"Ah, you think so?"

The slash is so sudden that the seaman has no time to protect himself. Save for exhaling a "Ha!" of pain. Lislei recoils. The captain, hand pressed against his head, is staring incredulously at the arm of the man brandishing a morsel of blood-stained flesh in front of his nose: *his ear*.

"Your blood is going to flow pretty freely. Your clothes will get soaked. If you won't obey me, I'll grab you by the balls and . . ."

Kader pauses. Time to steady his legs and to stop them from trembling. Bruce, for the first time, is staggering under the blow. His hand is red, he looks at it furtively to convince himself that the mutilation is real. The skin on his face crumples with fear.

"If, by mischance, your mates come in sight of the boat, I'll throw you into the sea. Stinking of blood all over, you'll attract the sharks in a couple of seconds. Your friend has taken care of raising their appetite. You understand now why I was determined to throw his body overboard?"

Kader hurled the tip of the ear into the water. Without taking his eyes off the distraught seaman:

"They say that they don't finish off their prey straight away. First they gnaw the flesh, mouthful by little mouthful. They'll taste you first, you understand . . ."

12

The storm did not arrive. They were dreading it for a good part of the afternoon. The wind had grown much stronger. At first, after the anchor was hauled on board, that made things much easier for them: the wind was strong enough to fill the two large sails, giving the impression, all of a sudden, that the ship was tearing itself out of the water. The pursuers in their rowing boats were already within view and brandishing their rifles. Kader stayed close to the captain's heels, threatening him with a more horrible death each time it seemed to him that the latter was slackening his efforts.

When the rowing boats disappeared below the horizon, Kader carefully lifted his finger off the trigger. He had not abandoned his sense of admiration for the seaman. Despite his severed ear and the pain which must have been tormenting him, despite his sprained ankle, the man had managed to steer the ship remarkably well. He had to do almost everything himself, without any help, for Kader and Lislei understood hardly any of the technical terms he used. He was quite successful at showing them how to carry out certain simple operations by miming them, but soon decided to do without their clumsy services.

Kader almost said "thank you" and stopped himself just in time. "As ever, how the spineless fall into temptation!" he thought. Bruce glanced at him with a furious look, which made the fugitive freeze: he would kill them without hesitation if ever they gave him the opportunity. Kader then called out to the woman. She protested dryly that she was not called "Hey, you" but Lislei!

"Me, I'm called Kader," he replied in the same aggressive tone.

He whispered in Lislei's ear that she should carefully search every nook and cranny on the boat, starting with the cabin.

"I'm certain there are still weapons on board. He is too sure of himself . . . How's the child doing?"

"Not well. He's hiding behind the crate. He is terribly afraid of us. All of us. And then, he is so . . . He is suffering greatly because of his papa and maman."

"How do you know they are his mother and father?"

Disdain glinted in Lislei's eyes.

"She camel," he muttered bitterly as he was looking at her retreating back. "She takes me for a butcher and a murderer. And she's not too far from being right."

The wind abates to a less terrifying intensity. The sailing ship, despite looking so unseaworthy, is making good progress. At length Bruce informed them that they would be touching the coast of Australia tomorrow, towards ten, eleven in the morning, and even perhaps at dawn if the wind kept blowing with the same force.

"We've got between 150 and 200 miles to put away," he let drop casually, with a sneer forming at the corner of his mouth.

The task of watching over the seaman proves exhausting because they must always stay close to his heels. The captain limps from one part of the vessel to another, checking this part of the tackle and that, pulling on this sail or that. Kader cannot tell the difference between actions that are necessary and those intended to distract him from his vigilance, or to seize a hidden weapon. When Bruce wanted to defecate, Kader did not avert his eyes; the seaman pointed out cantankerously that he was not going to turn shit into an offensive weapon.

Lislei spent a good part of the day rummaging through the ship in vain, then she devoted herself to the child. At first, he refused to touch the gruel she had made for him. She put the bowl down on the deck and pretended to lose interest in him. It was not until the end of the evening that he picked up the bowl. Lislei came into the cabin, all excited:

"He has eaten!"

"What, who has eaten?" Kader muttered, lost in his thoughts.

"The little . . ."

"Monkey, she means, by Jove," Bruce cut in. "Your new friend's hooked on a little baboon. She must be getting broody! You should take advantage of it, she's nice all over, the sweetie, you know . . ."

"Shut it!" Kader screeched.

"Hey, you're not going to stop me, are you, from saying a monkey's a monkey? A human brat, I know what that is: I have three fine children and a wife who are waiting for me nice and proper at home. These Abos, on the other hand, they have no idea of a family. People who go around naked, fornicate with their fathers and daughters and feed snakes to their children, are they human, are they, for you?"

The seaman laughed, ogling Lislei.

"Women are strange; she sleeps around left and right, and wants all the same to have a little snot-face to cuddle."

Lislei went away, her shoulders taut. Kader had time to notice that a hint of a sob was rising in her throat. He stayed impassive, but a fit of shame overcame him for having stood by while the woman was insulted.

The air grew cold again. Darkness fell all of a sudden, as if someone had decided, without warning, to change the scenery: day for night. Bruce has lit an oil lamp. A bandage around his head, pipe in his mouth, he sips from a glass of rum, ignoring his keeper. From time to time, he makes sure that he is on course, checking the instruments and tracing lines on a chart. Beyond the sheet of glass covering the large window of the cabin, nothing can be made out, not even stars. Heavy rain is falling, increasing the sadness overwhelming Kader.

What a filthy world. Filth, filth, filth! Kader has the feeling that the convulsions of his brain are turning into so much spittle inside his skull. He cannot even manage to sort their misfortunes into the right order: this woman's misfortune, his own, or that, incommensurably greater, of the lad! They had salted his parents as if they were ordinary mutton. And all that talk about how he would be the last representative of his people? That pipe-sucking Australian calmly insists that the other inhabitants of the island had been massacred one by one. And this head-hunter is a good family man who boasts, at one and the same time, about his three kids and his skill as killer! But is it even imaginable that a whole people could disappear from the face of the earth just because someone else had wanted it to happen? This cannot be possible, could God be so treacherous?

Lislei has rushed into the cabin. She is soaked with water:

"He can't be left out in the rain. I threw a cape to him, he refused to put it on. The lad's in a fever, but he is thrashing around like a devil and . . . he bites!"

She shows him, almost with pride, the scratches on her arm.

The captain roars:

"Bringing the Abo into my cabin is out of the question. In the hold, in the storeroom, wherever you like, but not in here with me! He'll soil everything!"

"I am going to bring him here," Kader cuts him off, "whether you like it or not. We are all going to stay together from now on. I don't trust you at all, if you'd like to know. Lislei, hold on to the pistol!"

The capture is easier than anticipated. Noticing the woman and the captain, and convinced that he had only to deal with them, the Aborigine hurls himself in the opposite direction. He crashes against Kader, who is lying in wait behind the lifeboat. The man grabs hold of him by the waist. The lad flings himself at Kader with all his might, trying to claw him, but his teeth are chattering. Soon, his strength abandons him. He is shaking all over.

"Little fennec, you're expecting me to gobble you up, aren't you?" Kader murmurs in Arabic. "I am not the devil you take me for. That's Iblis, the old fellow, and his cronies, not me! I've never harmed a child, and I'm not going to start now. Me too, I've been a child. And if I could go back to being a child again, I wouldn't say no, believe me."

Kader's chin rubs against the child's skull.

"Well, well little brother, you've had a pretty close shave. You'd think your skull's a spiky desert bush. What's more, you stink like a goat who doesn't know how to wipe its backside. Who's rigged you out in these rags, eh, my little mate in misery?"

Speaking in Arabic – the language of the time before exile – to a child infinitely more of an exile than him, makes the fugitive's throat contract. The child is soaked to the skin and shivering like a trapped pigeon. Kader clears his throat:

"You have endured things which an adult could not tolerate. You are an old man in your misfortune, that's what you are, little brother. We, compared to you, are just your children."

Kader relaxes his grip. Almost straight away, the child jabs him with his elbow.

"Ouch, that won't do! Stop jibbing like a mule . . . Ouch, stop . . . Lislei, I've got hold of the kid. He is ill. He needs something warm. Some broth with bread, and dry clothes. And a little rum perhaps."

When he steps into the halo of light, he notices the woman's disconcerted features. That does not displease him. Like the onrush of a soothing sensation in the midst of terror.

The night turns into a Calvary. It is vital for Lislei and Kader not to give in to sleep. Ignoring the captain's fury, they laid the feverish child on a makeshift bed. His little black eyes remain profoundly suspicious. His face is grimy, and the bruise from this morning's fall has stayed on one of his cheeks. Despite Kader's efforts, the child refused to get undressed. Lislei managed to make him keep down a little of a peculiar brew of porridge and dried fish.

"Luckily your friends managed to put in more provisions!" she grimaces for the captain's benefit.

The effect of food and alcohol is immediate. Very quickly, the child can be heard snoring. Lislei strokes the head covered in scars:

"You can't leave a kid in such a state. Tomorrow, we must wash him."

"Making plans for the future already?" is the captain's sarcastic comment.

His words lash them like threats. Lislei with the knife and Kader with the pistol have placed themselves at either side of the cabin, in order to surround the captain. The latter sniggered when Kader suggested that he should get some sleep.

"I'll lower the sails at sunrise and then I'll get a few hours' sleep. Me,

I'm as tough as hide. It's you, my lambs, who are going to have trouble keeping your end up."

He filled a fresh pipe. For more than an hour, there was nothing but the rumbling of the captain's stomach and the child's snoring. The first alarm came at around three in the morning: exhausted, Kader had nodded off, leaning upright against the door. Lislei, with a little cry of panic, makes her fellow fugitive wake with a start.

"Moisten your face with this."

The pupils of Lislei's eyes reveal her anguish, because she herself has almost dropped off to sleep. While Kader wipes his face with the damp cloth, Bruce stays slumped in his seat without letting any of the conversation slip past him.

It is at dawn that an object brushes against Kader's head. He is in Biskra, and even though the weather is unusually cool, he is taking his afternoon rest under the date palm in his family's garden. He is exhausted and would like his rest to last for hours. Ah, he would sleep away the days . . . But who is that nuisance worrying his temple with a twig?

"Hey man, above all, don't budge, or I'll blow your head off. I'll shoot you if you move, you dirty little boy!"

The command is whispered, but Kader feels as is if he had heard a thunderclap: Bruce has placed the tiny barrel of a revolver just above his ear.

"You, whore, don't get all excited with that knife! I've plenty of time to kill him and then to kill you. So, don't make a move! The party's over. Put down your pistol and you, your knife . . . There, thank you . . . In fact, we have arrived. Look over there. I'll have to cast anchor soon because of the reefs. If the latrines here didn't stink so much, we could already smell the gumtrees!"

He smiles perkily:

"And what's more, there's sunshine! I told you, this old fellow is as tough as hide, and you – you're just sheep. But what a shame about all that heavy snoring! You stopped me from sleeping, you filthy swine!"

The man wants to get everything off his chest:

"My weapon? It's easy, but you couldn't know. Its common enough on these tubs. It's normal, you run across heaps of them in port, sailors are not choirboys. For emergencies, you arrange a little hiding place . . ."

He presses an innocuous-looking knob on the panelling:

"It's a nice little drawer, isn't it? I've got something even more precious inside: my life (he shows them the weapon) and the wherewithal (he flourishes banknotes) for . . . hum . . . sustaining it. You see, I'm not a spendthrift, there's also the money for your passage . . ."

He plays with the banknotes, feigning dismay:

"By Jove, if you'd thrown me to the sharks, no one would have had any benefit from this . . . this happiness. That would have been a real shame!"

His face takes on an abstracted look:

"You've put me through quite a lot, you two. Perhaps it's my turn now. What do you think? Get down on the floor, swine . . ."

With his foot, he kicked away the revolver and the knife. Without letting the prisoners out of his sight, he slowly bends down to pick up the weapons. The seaman plays with the knife. He smiles when his eyes meet the eyes of the Aboriginal child curled up on the bedding:

"You, my little savage, you've found some funny idiots to take care of you. The good life, I don't think it's going to last for you . . ."

His voice is unctuous:

"My ear, you should have given it to this little cannibal to nibble. He would have appreciated real Australian meat. You, are you a wastrel, eh? Are you sorry?"

Kader makes a vague gesture with his hands. The woman looks at him. She looks at the child. She is livid. Kader has never seen anyone so white with fear. He too is afraid, he can hardly feel his body any longer. Above all, the knife fills him with dread.

"Answer me!"

His voice remains entirely flat, but the captain has kicked Kader violently in the ribs, followed by a second blow to his chest.

"Yes . . . I'm sorry . . ."

"Ah, you're sorry, son of a bitch!"

The heel is pressing on the centre of the thorax. Kader gasps out a large puff of air. He has doubled up because a thousand needles are cutting into his lungs. The pain is intolerable. He tries to shield his face against Bruce's fury. The other's lips are dribbling. Rage makes him stammer:

"My ear, eh, was it your mother's hole that brought it into the world?"

He circles around Kader, looking for an angle for another kick. He steps over to the child's bedding, nonchalantly prodding him in the back with the hand holding the knife. That is the moment the child chooses to bite the seaman's calf. The attack is so unexpected that the captain, thrown off balance, stumbles. Bruce cries out, shaking his leg to break free of the lad.

"Son of a bitch, I'll kill you!"

Impeded by his weapons, he cannot manage to stand up. He drops the knife in order to push himself up with his left hand. But Kader has already seized the other hand. The struggle is short because Lislei has grabbed hold of the knife and is furiously jabbing it into the nape of the captain's neck:

"Let go of the revolver, or I'll kill you, you thug!"

She pushes the blade until a drop of blood appears. She hisses into the seaman's ear:

"Don't give me an excuse to wound you, nothing would be dearer to me, cur!"

They are all on the ground: the child at the seaman's feet, Kader on his back, Lislei opposite him, holding the captain's head between her legs while her free hand is tearing his hair with all its might.

The Alsatian woman's face is red with sweat. Her scarf has fallen off. Her dishevelled hair hangs over her eyes as she utters "Ohs" and "Ahs" interspersed with obscenities. The captain's terror-stricken moans as the blade pricks him increase Lislei's frenzy. Kader is amazed by the Frenchwoman's animal vigour. For his part, the child's eyes follow with approval the treatment Lislei is inflicting on him who looks so much like the leader of his tormentors. The contortions of his entire body seem to support what the woman with long hair is doing. He ends up starting to bite Bruce's calf again.

"Stop," Kader says softly, placing a hand on the arm flourishing the knife. "I've got the revolver, it's not worth the trouble, Lislei."

"No, I'm going . . . going to . . . yes, cut his throat . . ."

Lislei claps her hand over her mouth, appalled by the word that has just escaped from it. Noticing Kader's worried expression, she tries to recover her bearing, then, as if each muscle in her face had been given its head, her mouth smiles while her eyes are melting in tears.

"Oh, Kader, I was so frightened . . . I was so frightened . . . It's not right to be so afraid . . ."

Her tears are contagious. The little Aborigine lets go of the calf, rubs his nose in puzzlement, sniffles two or three times before bursting into loud sobbing. And Kader, astride a murderous old seaman, finds himself between two people he hardly knows, who are weeping their hearts out.

He has no idea what he should do to console the child and the adult who are forming a ring of sorrow around him. Besides, he himself is hardly in a better shape. If he gave in to his desires, he would place his two hands in front of his face and would, in his turn, begin to choke with suffering.

Little by little, however – and what a reward – an unexpected sense of gratitude flowers in him. Mixed with a comic realisation: the captain, overpowered by three people, ought to find the time passing very slowly . . .

Tridarir would like to fall asleep. His father taught him that, when something is hidden from understanding, it is necessary to lie down, and, for a long time, set about dreaming with determination: the explanation would at length present itself to him. "Everything has already come about, and if something seems strange or new to you, it is only because it has been forgotten by you, by me or by your mother. But there will always be someone amongst us, the shards of the Nation of the Ancient People, to dream the answer. Seek out someone who dreams better than you, and he will give you the explanation."

Tridarir loves his father and mother; his heart, at this moment, is overwhelmed by the grief of knowing that they have been packed into boxes like the spoils of a hunt. He is terrified by the thought that his father was perhaps wrong. He, Tridarir, understands nothing at all of what has happened to him, and he feels certain that, even if he should sleep through the remainder of Time, things would stay just as shadowy for him. No-one will help him, because there remains nothing of the Ancient People apart from two or three senile old women.

The man and the woman who have rescued him – and this is already a puzzle for him: in what way do they differ from the hunters? – are busying themselves around the crates. After they overcame the fat seaman, Tridarir has been caught up in a series of events the purpose of which he cannot begin to grasp.

At first, the woman washed him, despite his protests. She almost manhandled him to get him into a tub. She is much stronger than he would have expected. She pulled his ears when he wanted to bite her to free himself, rubbed him vigorously while letting fly little horrified cries at the sight of the scars covering his back. She then dressed him in the clothes of the huge man, which she took out of a trunk. While all that was going on, the prisoner, with his slipping headband and the raw stump of his ear, spewed out an interminable series of oaths and howls, like a horrible kangaroo which is being dismembered alive. But, and this is the one thing which really made Tridarir rejoice, it is now the turn of the white man to be tied up. The ropes securing him to the mast are impressive. Tridarir floats inside his new clothes, even though the woman cut off the bottoms of the trousers and rolled up the sleeves on the shirt. He is a little disgusted at having been swathed in the clothes of the man who is the brother of the chief of the killers.

The woman, she too, washed herself, but first of all she took care to put the tub somewhere in the storeroom. The man simply stood naked on the deck and sprayed himself from a bucket which he plunged into the sea. He was so happy that he sang at the top of his voice in a peculiar language which did not resemble that of the white people of the island. He made use of the same trunk, amused at how ridiculous he looked in his new clothes, because the trousers were too short. He rummaged in his own sack of clothes, pulling out a tiny object, a book perhaps. He smiled at Tridarir.

Tridarir cannot share the man's happiness for he can only think about his parents stiff in their wooden prison. Through caution, he pulled an imitation of a smile, without forgetting that the man had almost thrown him into the sea. He has already realised that, for the invaders, black people's capacity to suffer remains incomprehensible. So much so that, most often, a man of his people does well to mask his suffering under an animal-like impassiveness when dealing with the invaders: among some of them, a black man's tears provoke at times exasperation, at others feverish hilarity, both capable of making them decline into greater cruelty.

It is Tridarir who whispers the words. And it is Tridarir who listens as if he had not been the one to utter them. "My mother called me: my little wombat." The little wombat wants to howl, he would like to raise his voice, but he cannot find the appropriate cry for the unhappiness tying his tongue: to be nothing other than the only one of his people, to have parents, uncles, aunts, neighbours no more, soon to be no more than *the last* to know how to speak *his* language!

Then, oppressed by what he has just realised, he stares vacantly into the air: no-one can imagine the immensity of his sorrow. But even that immensity – which crushes him – is not enough to allow him to mourn properly the disappearance of each representative of his people, beginning with his father and mother. For, if each of the dead does not perceive a due measure of affliction among living beings, then it is as if that dead person had never been a living creature among the living creatures of the earth. More terrible, his mother had assured him that the departed could go on living in the camping grounds in the sky only by virtue of the dreams of those who outlived them. If there were no-one left to dream of them and to present them with the gift of sorrow which was their due, the numberless campfires, around which the Ancestors who have followed each other since the Dreamtime seek to warm themselves, would disappear at the same instant.

To dream of the dead is to give them warmth. The departed need that heat because up there the nights are very cold, despite the multitude of fiery stars.

. . . *Powamena*, my mother, it is impossible for me here, all alone, you know that well enough? Nothing but you, how could I give you warmth with your fat belly and soft breasts, you know that well enough? And *Nimermena*, my father, all legs, with his huge trunk? . . .

The child does not see the man and the woman coming near him.

"*Powamena . . . Nimermena . . . Powamena . . . Nimermena . . .*"

This is not a true song. It is simply "Mother . . . Father . . . Mother . . . Father . . ." He can find nothing to add because he no longer believes in the power of his own words. Otherwise, he would not be here, he is too young, he has none of the Knowledge, neither of men nor of women. What is to be done since his parents did not have the time to initiate him? He has not even been circumcised. Tridarir is afraid of blaspheming but, nevertheless, he cannot rest idle. When the woman touches his shoulder, he starts. It is his sole reaction, for the song – a trace, a skeleton of song – occupies all of his head. She insists, her face is so concerned the he recognises on it the soiling of long sorrow.

The woman takes him by the hand and leads him to the back of the ship. The man in trousers that are too short follows them.

In front of the crates, she says something, accompanying it with a series of gestures. She made as if to lift the crate containing his parents, dragging it to the side, then hurling it into the sea.

Tridarir is appalled. So, all these white snakes are just like each other. She wants to throw the remains of his father and mother into the all-devouring Ocean! Does this bitch of a *ria-lowana* want to prevent them from returning to the warmth around the fires in the sky, to the company of those who had gone before them? She is seeking to make their death complete, so that they would be more dead than dead! Then it would be necessary . . . necessary to make them . . . But what should be done, in truth, with bodies from which life has departed? Tridarir, staring wide-eyed, cannot utter the least sound, he is choking, he has just realised that he does not know how to help the dead return to the Land. He has seen how white people deal with their dead: purely and simply by shoving them into a hole. But a hole is black, sticky mud turns the bodies of those who have gone over putrid. Stinking so much of the ordure of the earth, the dead could no longer reach the final camping grounds!

Tridarir has leapt on top of the crate, grasping it on each side. A nail wounds his palm, but the child feels nothing. He has become a wild animal. He cries like one possessed, threatening the man and the woman with his teeth:

"My Pa . . . my Ma . . . Don't touch them . . . don't drown them . . . still alive . . ."

The child's face is as ravaged as a frayed rag. He is no longer crying. He feels a pain in his chest, so fiercely is his heart beating in its too-narrow cage. It wants to leap out, that little ball of despair, and howl in their ears: look, those in the crate, they are not nobodies, they are Walya and Woorady, my mother and my father, two great hunters, they were put to death like noxious beasts, you do not understand that it is the greatest misfortune in the world, the earth should weep, the water should weep, and you too, and even this flesh-eater who sells people and their bones, you wash yourselves and you laugh, and I am the only one to suffer sorrow, it is not possible, my Dreams are false, there are holes where my eyes should be, no-one can understand me, there is no more Walya, no more Woorady . . .

The little black boy is shaking all over. The woman steps towards him. The woman is trembling just as much. She listens attentively to the sharp yelps, interspersed with "Pa" and "Ma". Little by little, the child loses his voice. It has become so hoarse that it is no more than a growl in a martyred throat.

The woman turns to the man. His face has gone completely white. She says something to him.

13

"He is speaking in English!"

"What's he saying?"

Lislei is at a loss for words. She has put on her old clothes again, but not her scarf. Her damp hair falls over her face.

"He is saying: father, mother, don't drown them . . . they are still alive . . . not completely dead . . ."

Kader feels a lump blocking his gullet.

"What should we do?"

Until now, things seemed simple enough for Kader: to get away from the ship as quickly as possible, all three of them obviously, using the lifeboat. Ashore, they would regain their freedom and, each on his own, take off like the devil, only asking only for a little luck to help them save their skins. As for the captain, his ship is so close to the coast that he will easily find someone to rescue him by the time fugitives are at large.

"Look, we can't leave the lad here," Lislei whispers.

"You're the one who wanted to throw the crates in the sea. We could have got away without touching anything. The child, we could have taken him by surprise . . ."

"Don't they respect the dead where you come from? These are his parents, his father and mother, not meat you buy and sell. Even Arabs should be able to understand that!"

Her sarcasm makes Kader shudder. He reins in an insult because the child is staring at him with a hatred too great for one of his age.

Lislei turns to the trussed captain:

"We can't leave these skinned corpses, these poor wretches in the hands of these . . . these . . ."

She cannot find the right word. Kader tries to step towards the Aborigine. The child grabs hold of the pick, but Kader is too quick for him. Catching hold of the boy by the waist, he forces him with a twist of the elbow to let go of the pick. The little black boy struggles frantically, but in silence. Kader feels that he is holding on to a terrified animal compulsively thrashing around with his paws to free itself of the hunter's grip.

He looks questioningly at Lislei. Tridarir, realising that the man has relaxed his grasp, seizes the opportunity to bite him on the wrist. The surprise and the pain are so acute that Kader slaps the child violently. The blow strikes Tridarir's ear; he totters, falls to his knees. He blinks his eyelids, struggling to keep them open. Lislei cries out:

"How dare you?"

Appalled, Kader stares at the child who is losing consciousness in front of his eyes. The ugly mark his hand left behind spreads over the whole cheek. Nausea overcomes the fugitive. Never has he felt so miserable. To strike a child in the way that he would strike an adult! Has prison degraded him to such an extent?

He kneels down next to the almost unconscious child. The other makes a last show of protecting himself before letting his hand drop. Kader, ashamed, takes him in his arms. He sighs in Arabic:

"You weigh so little, forgive me, little brother. First yesterday, then today: I drop you on your skull every time I come near you! I am not as wicked as you would imagine. I would have preferred to seem as awe-inspiring as this when I was a warrior on the battlefield. The slap came all by itself, I did not want . . ."

He glances at his blood-stained fist:

"As for biting, you know how to bite! But you are protecting your parents, aren't you? As for me, if ever I have a son, I would be very happy if he came to my defence with the same ardour as you. What do you want me to do? I am not God. Your father and mother are well and truly dead, it is necessary for you to leave them. Peace be with them . . . And with us, we have great need of it . . ."

Lislei is behind the man. She would like to know what he was murmuring so softly into the lad's ear. His voice is hoarse, caressing, drained of that accent which, in French, sometimes makes him sound ridiculous. She was about to berate her companion in flight as a brute, a hooligan, a murderer. She stays silent, intimidated. The Arab's face is bleached of colour:

"Find me some pieces of cloth. I'm going to tie him up, you stay with him while . . . burying his parents . . . at least, I mean to say . . ."

He pitched all the crates overboard, as well as the sacks of bones. He prayed for a few moments, looking out to sea. He owed the kid that much at least. The old sacred words of his childhood came back to him: "*Though the sea became ink for the Words of my Lord, verily the sea would be used up before the Words of my Lord were exhausted . . .*"

He gazed at the nearby land, with that lump lingering in his throat. He came to an end with "*Enter in peace: this is the Day of Eternity.*" He could not stop himself from thinking about those verses of the Koran with a sense of irony: "After what your people have endured, that is something you'd have to struggle to make yourself believe. The only one in Paradise today is the shark who's going to gobble up your parents."

While this is going on, the child wakes up. He seems not to react, indifferent to having been tied up again. When the first "splash" explodes, he straightens up. Lislei leans down to his face and plants a kiss on it.

From his mast, the captain has started cursing again, calling Kader and Lislei thieves, Mohammedan vermin and sewer slut. His jaw set tight, Kader went back into the cabin. He emptied the drawer of its contents: money and documents. When he steps past Bruce again, the latter calls out that he will kill all three of them, and that if he can't manage it, his brother and his band of hunters will cut them into pieces so small that even the rats will refuse to eat them.

Kader replies in Arabic: "Son and brother of a rat, yourself!" and lets fly a vigorous kick to the seaman's testicles. The man spits out an "Argh" of pain from the shock.

"I know, Bruce old man, that it's not very valiant of me to treat a prisoner so brutally, but you, you are not a human being, you're simply a fucking vulture, a child-killing piece of shit!"

Kader has avoided Lislei's eyes. Tense all over, he makes for the pulley on the lifeboat. Lislei, tying up a bundle of clothes, fights back a smile. She looks the other way, afraid of being unable to suppress a glint of admiration for that kick. Certainly, the act was not very honourable, but she herself would have gladly let one of them fly, that kick in the private parts. And twice rather than once, reinforcing it with a number of pointed home truths!

Despite the sunshine, the sea is rising. A wind has come up, increasing the swell. It is necessary to row strenuously against the current, to avoid the sharp outcrops of the reefs, taking care not to capsize the lifeboat by changing direction with clumsy strokes.

When Kader first treads on solid ground, he feels a pang, almost of pain: the sand is white, the rocks surrounding the creek are huge and, less than a hundred feet away, a baby sea lion is comically waddling towards the shore. Kader feels like laughing, he *wants* to live, but he has been unaware until now how much he clings to this devil of a life! The realisation rushes to his head. Like an excess of liquor, of dubious joy. But is it really joy? He sinks his feet in the sand of this new land. The sand is firm. That commonplace awareness soothes Kader's anguish. Perhaps fate had decided to offer him another chance. To give them another chance. Lislei's face – she is still in the boat – is beaming, hers too. Two brief glances exchanged between them, distrustful at first, then ironic, make it clear: they have had the same thought.

And that thought is revealed straight away to be what it is: stupid. Nothing, it seems, promises an end to their troubles. On the contrary, indeed: because of the death of the seaman – an Australian! – on the ship, the district police are probably going to be hot on their tail very soon. If they are captured, they will be sentenced in Australia. Among the prisoners in New Caledonia, the story goes that judges in Australia have a pronounced weakness for hanging murderers. As for the child . . .

In an anxious mood, Kader offers his hand to Lislei to help her jump. She refuses, suddenly in an ill humour:

"Look after the child, I'll manage by myself."

"It doesn't hurt to be polite."

He mocks her in Arabic:

"Sing to the ass, it'll thank you with farts."

"What are you jabbering about?" Lislei protests as she jumps into the water.

Kader shrugs. He drags the lifeboat to dry ground. This is not a light task because of the ceaseless rolling of the waves. The little Aborigine stares at him with hostility, but allows himself to be carried without resisting. Lislei is at his side when Kader unties his bonds. Straight away she massages the child's wrists and ankles.

Tridarir gives a start when the woman's fingers brush against the badly healed scar on his foot. The Aborigine gazes at them gloomily. His slightly bulging forehead gives him the incongruous look of an adult.

"Ask him his name," Kader ventures, lowering his eyes. With stupefaction, he becomes aware that he is intimidated by the little boy, almost scared of him.

Lislei makes a gesture of refusal, changes her mind, whispers:

"What is your name, kid?" she asks in English, without getting a reply. She repeats her question more slowly, without success. The child's features remain expressionless, almost stupid.

"He can't understand me. Nevertheless, I am sure he was speaking in English."

Kader is worried. They must leave this beach as soon as possible. To the left, the shape of Bruce's ship is clearly etched against the water. From the beach, the distance between the ship and the shore appears less impressive than it seemed when they were rowing in the lifeboat. A seaman as experienced as the captain could free himself more quickly than anticipated. Once again, the familiar presence of fear.

"Lislei, it's time to make ourselves scarce. If someone sees us on this beach . . ."

His companion does not listen. The lad's mutism seems to have had a great effect on her. A little fan of wrinkles raise the flesh above her nose. Her hair is almost dry, she brushes it aside with an impatient hand. Her eyes, despite their exhaustion, are magnificent. "You are beautiful, *gaouria*," the fugitive acknowledges in his heart of hearts. "Almost as beautiful as . . ." He stops himself in amazement, he was about to think "Nour".

For this slut to remind me of . . . He blushes, overwhelmed by the sense of his own treachery.

"What are you . . . ?"

Lislei has noticed the man's distress. Kader cuts her off dryly.

"If the old man struggles free or if someone catches sight of the tub, then we'll be . . ."

The child is on his feet. His voice is insistent, jerky. Standing in front of the adults, he nods his head, persistently repeating words incomprehensible to Kader.

Ashen-faced, Lislei holds out her hand to the child.

"What is he saying?" Kader asks.

"He is asking where the forest is. His forest. He wants to go home."

"We must explain to him . . ."

"Explain what? That he'll never see his island again, after his mother and father have been thrown overboard? He's only a little child, and you, you're acting as if . . ."

Lislei splutters, she interrupts herself; it would turn into sobbing if she went on with her diatribe.

"It had better be done. And if it's not to be you it'll have to be me. How . . . how do you say 'sea' . . . 'your island' . . . and 'forest' in your wretched English?"

The Frenchwoman mumbles her reply.

Kader traces two circles in the sand, one small, one large. The fugitive is furious: are they going spend every single moment preoccupied with this snotty savage? And how long will this idiocy last?

He beckons to the Aborigine. The lad, his brow obstinate, is constantly giving voice to his litany. Kader points to the small circle: "Island, your island . . . Tasmania . . ." then to the second circle: "Australia, not your island . . . Australia . . ." He makes grooves in the sand between the two circles: "Sea, big sea!" With a sweeping gesture he points to the beach "Here Australia, not your forest and over there . . ."

His hand is pointing towards the horizon:

"Over there: Tasmania!"

The child seems to be paralysed for a few seconds, as if he were turning over in his mind the adult's impossible explanations. Then, all of a sudden, he bursts out screaming. As if he had been touched by a red-hot iron. He rushes to the edge of the water, pushing Kader out of the way. Pointing to the horizon, his eyes bulging, he whines. He is almost chest deep in water. He is overturned by a wave. He gets up, coughing, spitting, his finger constantly pointing into the distance. Lislei and Kader have hurled themselves after the child. He is about to drown for, once more, a frothy breaker submerges him.

When Kader drags him out of the water, Tridarir is shaking with convulsions. Water spews out of his mouth. Between two fits of retching, he moans "My forest . . . my forest." He is crying, his pupils are hard, filled with hate.

"We must change his clothes," Kader manages to say, looking away, "he'll end up catching a cold. He can't be left like this, eh Lislei?"

Lislei unties the bundle of clothes. She has her back to Kader, but her whole body expresses her contempt for the man who dared to mistreat an orphan.

"Lislei?"

She makes no reply, because she would insult him.

"Lislei, look! The ship!"

There is so much alarm in his voice that she lifts her head.

"What about the ship? Do you think I've nothing else to do?"

Her hands still inside the bundle, she gazes at the landscape. Everything is absolutely normal. She is on the point of bursting out with sarcastic remarks when, suddenly, she is struck by an anomaly: the sailing ship should not be so close!

"You'd think that . . ."

"Yes, it's moving . . . and that shouldn't be possible, the captain shouldn't have been able to set himself free so quickly. And then, the ship's making straight for the reefs . . . That bastard isn't such a fool as all that!"

Kader wipes his brow in anxiety.

"That must be the anchor . . . I let it down myself . . . yet I turned the windlass almost to the end. I'm sure that . . ."

The ship has picked up speed. Kader wants to shut his eyes because collision with the reefs at the entrance to the channel is inevitable.

Lislei is fascinated. She pictures the old seaman howling in rage and panic. When the ship noses up to an outcrop, she stops herself from calling out. For several interminable seconds, there hovers the strange image of a ship lying only a little way above the water. The craft seems to hesitate over which direction to take. Then, very slowly, it keels over.

"The mast . . ." Kader whispers.

Lislei has understood: as soon as the foremast reaches the horizontal, the captain will drown. She looks, dumbly, at her hands encumbered with clothing. *Clothing*!

"The little one. Where is the little one?"

"The little one? What little one?"

"But you have calluses on your heart, you!"

Lislei has run off in pursuit of the Aborigine. He is already at the top of the dune. By the time Lislei reaches the bottom, the child has disappeared from view. Kader, he too, is running. They reach the top at the same time. Lislei is sweating, panting. She cups her hands to her mouth:

"Come back, kid, come back, kid!"

In front of them extends a tangle of dry grasses and eucalypts.

"My God, which way has he gone?"

The man is surprised by his accomplice's dejection.

"We are going to find him, your Tasmanian, he can't have got far," he whispers, placing his hand on the woman's shoulder.

"Don't touch me, murderer!"

The word "murderer" rings out like a gunshot. Horrified by what she has just uttered, Lislei stares apprehensively at the Arab. The latter, his eyes like slits, is thunderstruck. He goes limp, trying to control his fury:

"And you, you're nothing but a whore! Me, perhaps I am a murderer; you, you are certainly a whore, a filthy little whore! You can't ask for a better witness than me for that, eh?"

Lislei raises her hand to strike the man. Kader lifts his arm to protect himself, then lets it drop:

"The mast . . ."

From the top of the dune, the spectacle of the sea is magnificent. It evokes an impressive purity, all savagery, flecked only with the foul spot where the ship has capsized.

A temporary blemish, for the tops of the two masts are tickling the surface of the sea. A somewhat more powerful wave suddenly submerges them with a single blow. Only the stern of the craft remains visible.

Kader swallows hard: how easy it is to live through the death of others! Nothing in the landscape reveals how a seaman, with his last gurgle, must have come to detest all of creation because of what fate had dealt him.

At the other end of the beach, the baby sea lion has returned with others of its kind. Soon, their joyous yelps are ringing out. It seemed as if they were celebrating the recovery of their territory, invaded for a moment by three unknown rivals who had no business to be there.

14

He is running, he is running, Tridarir. His lungs are going to burst, his legs will crumble like rotten timber. A little while ago he felt cold, now he is sweating. Sometimes, he thinks that he can recognise the group of rocks heralding the Great Tier with its characteristic clumps of red eucalypts, and so hope floods over him: this surely is the trail leading to the forest, his forest, where he will soon find shelter, where he will be able to evade from now on the most cunning ruses of the "Black-Eaters". Keep running to the top, turn towards the sun . . .

And then, each time, the disposition of the rocks, the shape of the mounds of earth, the thicket of thorny bushes reveal themselves to be terrifyingly unfamiliar.

Tridarir refuses, even for an instant, to lend his spirit's ear to the tales of the unpredictable individual on the beach. It cannot be so, it is inconceivable! If he had left his island, he would have become aware of it: the colour of the soil, the trees, the texture of the grass, the taste of the air, something would have warned him. Tridarir placed his tongue against a pebble, gently at first, then with greater pressure, then he licked the acrid bark of a tree: no, even the taste is similar! The man, with his tracings in the sand, is either deceitful or insane . . .

The son of Walya and Woorady wipes his brow with the sleeve of his shirt, picks his nose distractedly, more from perplexity than through necessity: the man and the woman, that couple are certainly strange! The man had treated him with brutality twice in a row, but afterwards spoke to him with such kindness. The woman, she looked after him, fed him.

She did not hesitate, on the other hand, to announce that they were going to throw his parents away as if they were ordinary rubbish. All the same, the two have probably snatched him from a horrible fate. Perhaps they only wanted to get rid of the old *Ludawini* to keep the money from the sale for themselves. Why, then, did they throw the bodies and skeletons overboard?

When Tridarir sees once again the image of the crates in the water, all that lives and moves beneath his skin, his muscles, his stomach, his heart, sputters and shrivels. He would like to weep, to injure himself, to die: he was unable to protect *his* dead. The dead do not know how to swim, so how would they find their kindred in the Timeless Land, where life continues without life? He would like to beg his father's and mother's forgiveness; he knows well enough that from now on no-one will grant him forgiveness. Can there be any doubt that he should have jumped in after them? Not from the ship, seeing that he had been tied up. But from the beach? The child grimaces to stop himself from weeping; he lacked courage. The water was icy and they say that there are such monsters in its maw . . .

He should not stay there, at that place too open to discovery. Other corpse-hunters could appear. Once again, he has lost his way. He tries to steady his breathing. He would like to piss, to calm himself down. He pulls out his little penis, presses on his testicles. His feet are shaking. No urine comes out. He makes an effort to concentrate. The clear stream manages to emerge. He waters a small clump of ferns. A tiny rodent bolts, probably infuriated by that peculiar shower. Tridarir smiles, bites his lips.

Forcing himself to reflect, like a grown-up warrior: which direction, then, would his parents have taken after collecting, always a risky business, sea-birds' eggs on the shore? To get back to the forest, they used first of all to hide among tree-ferns in an open space. A huge boulder served as a landmark for them. When Tridarir examined it carefully, the boulder reminded him of a human face, with its a mouth set in a haughty frown. "This is one of your Ancestors, he is irascible," his father whispered in awe, bowing before the rock. He would strike Tridarir's face if the latter proved slow to emulate the gesture of respect. In that way

Tridarir came to dread the apparition of the sentinel rock. What wouldn't he give at present to come upon that grumpy forbear again and pay it respect, head to the ground if that's what he wanted!

Tridarir is hungry. To hunt. But not in these weird clothes which disgust him. He takes them off, throws the trousers and the shirt far away, retraces his steps, tramples on the clothes, shreds them with the sharp edge of a stone. This is nothing, only a bout of vengeance against the old *Ludawini* on the ship and his accomplices. For a brief instant, he has the delicious dream that he is doing harm to his parents' murderers, that the hunters are beseeching him in vain to spare them . . .

The sun is high in the sky. Tridarir has made up his mind, at last, to turn around. To allay his anguish, he decides to make a spear. He has seen his father doing it. Find a sharp tool and a straight branch . . .

The child is almost elated when, after several attempts, he has in his hand an object which looks like a weapon. The wood is thin and the tip not very well sharpened, but it is better than nothing. So he is not so clumsy, he considers with self-satisfaction. How do you hunt kangaroos then? He should ask . . . And it is, each time, the same shock: *there is no longer anyone to ask*!

He swallows hard to choke back the spasm rising in his throat. Good, he'll make do with a rodent, with a lizard or a handful of grubs. Besides, there is a snake over there warming itself on a large rock. The hand grasps the makeshift spear. Tridarir has already killed snakes; steamed, they don't taste too bad. Obviously, he has no means of lighting a fire. That doesn't matter, he'll eat it raw. When he lived with his parents in the forest, what they ate was, most often, uncooked. His mother considered raw food to be in the order of things. Until the arrival of the accursed *Ludawini* in their huge vessels, the women of the island managed very well to prepare food without fire. "Since the Dreamtime, we have been eating quivering meat. Why change?" Her son did not dare to contradict her – she would have accused him of having sold out to the Whites – but he far preferred cooked meat to raw.

Tridarir is proud of himself because he is less than three paces from the reptile and it has not betrayed the least anxiety. Perhaps it had gobbled up a mouse, and is digesting it, lulled by the intoxication of having had its fill?

The hardest thing, now that he has reached the top of the boulder, is to hold his breath, to stand up slowly and aim the spear without haste. The head . . .

Drops of sweat cloud his vision, trickling down to where his lips meet. With a precautionary tongue, he licks the salty liquid . . .

"Whoa!"

The cry flew from him: his snake-dinner slithered into a crack in the rock! Tridarir straightens up, stiff all over and disappointed. In front of the child's morose gaze, there extends a cultivated field. A structure, probably a farmhouse, rises in the middle.

The heart of the little black boy is thumping violently. The farmhouse looks so much like the one from which they stole a sheep! An intense nostalgia overwhelms him. He laughs, despite everything, because he remembers how his father had thrown, with irritation, a piece of mutton at his head. Woorady had not appreciated his son's impatience: "Stuff yourself up to the eyeballs, but don't stay near us when you want to shit; everything you've eaten is going to turn into heaps of stinking crap, there'll be so much of it that it'll submerge your backside and everything around it!" Walya pealed with laughter, making her son and the irascible father break into interminable cackling.

Tridarir tenses the muscles of his chest to throw off the almost voluptuous sorrow of these memories. He begins to recognise easily enough these little moths from the past: that gentle fluttering in the skull, warm all over, that exhilaration of joy. And all of a sudden, it bites, it slashes.

The little Aborigine sniffles. He weighs his flimsy spear in his hand. Attentively examining the surroundings of the farmhouse, he begins to make his way down the path.

They have been wandering around for a good part of the morning, each walled up behind anger and desire. Kader hates the woman who has called him a murderer and he dreams of finding swift passage to Mecca, and from there to Damascus. Damascus . . . ! His eyes grow misty at the memory of his elderly father with his wounded pride, of his affectionate and impressionable mother and even of his "aunt" Armande, the pastry cook from the Auvergne who taught him his first words of French.

What became of them, are they still of this world? He saw his father for the last time at the trial in Constantine. He almost failed to recognise him. Hajj Omar, he too had spent several months in prison before being released on account of his family ties with the Emir Abd El Kader. His mother had stayed at Biskra. The son understood, from the unhappy look on his father's face, that his mother was gravely ill. Hajj Omar did not seem in better shape. Captivity had transformed him into a hoary old man, coughing without cease, with nothing to recall the impetuous and generous warrior who had protected the Maronites on the orders of the Emir. They were only able to touch with the tips of their fingers, the gendarmes forbade them to get any closer. In his father's face he read the same despair as he was experiencing, that sense of the sordid and underserved end of the world, giving rise to the wish to spit on all of creation.

The father whispered: "May God protect us, my son!" Kader had enough malice to answer him: "God, Papa? What God, He who has cast us into such misery as this?" Hajj Omar stammered with horror as he was already being pushed aside by a gendarme: "Do not add to your misfortune, son."

"Aunt Armande" had come to the trial. Kader avoided her eyes during the interminable days of the hearing. With spiteful anger, he decided to suppress his feelings when he discovered, in the back row, that fat woman whom he held responsible, in part at least, for the misfortune which had come crashing down around his family. Now, while he readjusts the rope of the sack weighing down his shoulder, he experiences once more that fury mingled with gratitude which shattered him when he saw her breaking into tears at the announcement of the verdict.

Lislei continues walking, her body taut under the weight of the bundle and of humiliation. With difficulty, she manages to step around the thorns beating against her legs. Since their violent exchange, she has been turning over in her mind the insulting word "whore!" Her rancour against her companion in flight has transformed itself, little by little, into contempt for herself.

If he, Pierre, saw what his sister has become, a common slut, with her coarse features and bloated face, who sold herself for a freedom which reveals itself to be a dead-end! When an abject gaolbird can call her, whom her brother loved so much, a slut without her being able to accuse him of lying. During their childhood, Pierre and she had sworn never to be unworthy of one another. She had betrayed their oath, he would be ashamed of her if he came back to life! And her parents? And Camille? And Mathilde? That had really been her sole achievement, to betray everyone! Capping it off, no later than this morning, with that little black child wholly paralysed by sorrow . . .

"We must find him again! It is not possible . . . He's a child . . . They are going to . . ."

Kader, amazed, sees her putting down her bundle and seizing him by the arms:

"I beg you, we must look for him . . ."

"But . . . but, that's what we've been doing all along."

Lislei's eyelashes are sticky with sweat:

"No, we are looking for him, but without really looking. We must . . . we must find him. If not, they are going to kill him or treat him like cattle in a saleyard!"

"You are speaking to a murderer . . ."

"You are a murderer and me, a whore. On that, we are in agreement. You and me, we're nothing special. But that's no reason to abandon the kid to his fate. When it comes down to it, he saved our lives. It would be . . . it would be . . ."

Her voice is close to breaking. Kader, disconcerted, is anxious to avoid the eyes of the woman clinging to his arm.

". . . Shameful . . . it would be shameful for you and for me . . . We have nothing left, and we are nothing. Perhaps we are even going to get caught by the police! If, on top of that, we don't even try to help the lad . . . That's the only thing left now. We find him and then, afterwards, each of us will go our way . . . I beg you . . ."

The woman blushed. Abruptly, she lets go of the arm she has been grasping so fiercely. Kader, as embarrassed as she is, retorts harshly:

"You are holding us up, Lislei. You keep on speaking, you keep on speaking and the brat, all this while, he is the one that's on the run."

For a brief instant, Lislei remains speechless. Concealing her joy, she picks up her bundle. Kader has gone ahead of her. On the horizon, the shape of a building appears, the first in this seemingly deserted place. Perhaps the little black lad has made his way there. The Arab adjusts his sack once more, checks on the contents of his pockets: the *Book of Songs* is there, likewise the pistols. He is not unaware that all this fussing is a way to prevent himself from being overcome by an enervating sense of gratitude. This is the first time, in years, that someone has appealed to . . . yes, to his honour. For the fugitive convict, that word from the past conjures up an incongruous perfume, mingling the smell of orange peel and clumps of dates. His cousin Hassan and he, children then, were on their way to hide on top of date palms. Stuffing themselves to the full, they talked passionately about the great deeds which the future held in store for them . . .

A bird of prey makes its solemn way across the sky, followed by egrets with snow-white plumage. The man has taken off his wide-brimmed hat. He scratches his crotch. From time to time he brushes away the flies sticking to his face. Several gaping gashes, or rather scars left behind by claws, disfigure one side of his face. Lislei and Kader are surrounded by three huge dogs, mastiffs, one of them a bitch, baring their teeth and setting up deafening growls.

"Leave it," Lislei murmurs, for Kader has put his hand to his pocket, "I am going to talk to him."

Without being able to understand any of it, Kader listens to the conversation. This is his first meeting with an Australian and he feels thoroughly foolish. The farmer, on the contrary, does not give the impression of being very surprised to see them turning up from nowhere. There seems to be no-one apart from himself on the farm. The buildings are in a pitiful state, implements rusting away in a disordered heap. A cockatoo perched on a water tank is drinking with little pecks of a febrile beak. Lislei, sporting a broad smile, embarks on a long explanation. The farmer, inside the pen, nods mechanically in agreement, but his raised eyebrows reveal his mistrust clearly enough. He holds a long-bladed knife in his hand. Constantly keeping his eyes on the newcomers, he picks up a lamb and turns it on its back on a crude cross-shaped device. Despite his age, the man is uncommonly strong. He binds the animal's legs, cuts off the animal's testicles with a single swipe of the blade, throws them into a bucket. He then plunges a pair of pincers into a pot, passes it over the wound, frees the lamb – which bolts away, bleating in pain – and addresses himself to the next.

Lislei, fascinated by the briskness of his actions, stammers out that they are travellers who have lost their way and that they would like a little food and hospitality for the night. The farmer's eyes betray derision at the word "travellers", but he calls out to the dogs with a short, sharp cry. They, almost immediately, abandon their aggressive postures and return to their master's side, expecting to be patted and fed.

"We'll have the same fare as they will today," the Australian frowns while distributing kidneys to the dogs. "They're delicious with onions . . . but for . . . hmm . . . travellers who've lost their way, whom the stage-coach has left behind. Would that suit . . . the lady?"

Lislei nods and turns as red as a beetroot. She has not been taken in by his over-polite tone. The fellow believes none of the story she told him. He goes on with his work, without paying any more attention to the couple whom he must consider vagabonds or somewhat shady beggars. It is true, Lislei realises with shame, that it is difficult for them to make a good impression, she with her filthy dress, Kader in clothes too short for him.

"What did you tell him?" Kader murmurs in exasperation. "We're not going to bake in the sun like morons, are we, waiting while he goes on with his butchering?"

Lislei shrugs her shoulders, wipes the sweat from her face, explains that he has "invited" them to eat with him, but that he hasn't swallowed a single word of the tall tale she had spun for him.

"Would you swallow any of it?" Kader mutters with lassitude. He lifts his sack and makes for a stand of trees near what looks like the entrance of a barn. Immediately, the three dogs rush at him.

"Look out," Lislei screams before another clamour makes the hell-hounds stop dead in their tracks. The farmer, furious, shouts at Kader. The dogs do not take their eyes off him. Their muscles are twitching with impatience, only waiting for an order from their master.

"He is saying that he has not given you permission to go over to that side. You are at his place, on his land. His dogs will disembowel you if . . ."

Rage, following on fear, seizes the fugitive. The muscles of his neck are tormenting him. He pulls the pistol out of his pocket.

"Warn him that if his dogs move, I'll kill them!"

"Stop, don't fire, I'll reason with him!"

The farmer, seeing the pistol, has changed his attitude. He makes a prolonged whispering sound, accompanied by clicks of the tongue. He seems to be talking to his dogs. The bitch whines, as if she had been punished. The two other mastiffs lower their heads, let out plaintive barks, then all three go over to the Australian, tails between their legs. Kader is astonished by the transformation: the three killers are begging to be patted, rubbing themselves against the farmer's legs, just like affectionate puppies at the side of their suckling mother.

The farmer harangues Lislei, who has trouble understanding his vehement English, in no uncertain terms. Kader observes the scene, pistol still in his hand. When the farmer's tone becomes less aggressive, he puts away his weapon. The old man, all the while talking with Lislei, examines the other visitor with a mixture of irritation and curiosity. This son of a bastard is afraid, Kader realises, for his dogs, not for himself; he must keep on tickling the trigger just in case. Kader makes a questioning sign with his head.

"He asked me why you don't speak English."

"And you . . ."

"I replied that you are a Hungarian immigrant, that we have just arrived in the country . . ."

"Hungarian, what kind of a story is that?"

"You are from Hungary, that's all. A subject of the Austro-Hungarian Empire, to be more exact!"

"But I don't speak . . ."

". . . Hungarian . . ."

"And you?"

"We are both in the same pickle. Me too, I'm Hungarian and I can't speak a word of Hungarian!"

An unexpected spark of good humour flashes in Lislei's pupils. Which vanishes, like a snuffed-out flame, when the farmer barks a few words, among them an enraged and prolonged "Out!" His arm pointing in the direction from which they had come permits no ambiguity. Lislei translates nevertheless:

"He accuses us of lying, he is ordering us to clear off his farm immediately. What's to be done?"

"What do you want us to do? We are going to obey him, no doubt about that. Suggest to him, first, that he sell us clothes, some food and . . . and horses."

"Are you making fun of me? And the money, where will you get that from? An Arab genie?"

The woman's anguish has given way to sarcasm. Tickled by a puff of vanity, Kader is on the point of answering her quite uncompromisingly when a pain-filled exclamation rings out, immediately drowned by frantic barking.

"What's that, that din?" Lislei manages to ask. She has questioned the Australian in French. She is livid because the squealing can be heard again.

"It's . . ."

Curiously, the dogs followed them without any show of aggression. At first, a cart is blocking the way. In front of the open door of the barn, another dog, a bulldog, is barking, its snout pointed at the interior. Its muzzle is bloody, froth is seeping from its jaw. The animal resembles an enraged wild beast.

The farmer mutters a curse, rushes inside the barn, elbowing the couple aside. He comes out, his features set in anger, one hand holding by the neck a struggling, completely naked black child.

"Let him go, but let him go," Lislei shouts at the top of her voice, "you are strangling him!"

The jerking of the little Aborigine's body resembles the way a drowning man flails around. Lislei clings to the farmer's arm; he pushes her out of the way without ceremony. She trips and ends up face to the ground between the dogs' paws. The beasts growl, encouraged by their master's attitude. The hound with the blood-stained snout shoves its fangs into the woman's face. Feeling its warm breath, Lislei shuts her eyes and screams out in terror. When the pistol shot rings out, she opens her eyes and finds herself staring at the wall-eyed bulldog. Surprised by the explosion, the animal lifts its muzzle, expecting some explanation or a word of encouragement from its master.

Kader, his finger tight on the trigger, makes a sign with his head to the woman and the child. Seething with rage because he cannot heap insults on the farmer in English, he bursts out in Arabic:

"Son of a sow, I'll make you eat your balls steeped in the juice of your own shit if anything happens to them!"

The farmer stares contemptuously at the man menacing him. The muscles of his face are twitching, making it break out in a curious network of wrinkles. Kader has no difficulty discerning the considerable effort the old man is making to control his fury. The Australian decides to whistle to his dogs. With the same alacrity, they abandon their attacking posture and disperse. Then, as if he had been holding until then a bundle of linen, the man throws the naked child to the ground.

"What are you meddling in? It's only a Nigger, a filthy bit of Nigger crap!"

The voice is overpowering in its scorn, but it is governed, above all, by astonishment. Lislei is on her feet, she is choking with indignation:

"It's a child. You don't have the right to treat a child like that!"

"For God's sake, he's a Nigger, an Aborigine, a cannibal kid. They are not like us, they don't feel pain like we do, these creatures. You understand what I'm telling you, I hope?"

The man frowned, inviting them to be reasonable. Lislei is aghast at the farmer's candour. She is searching for something to say in reply, remains unable to speak. The farmer notices her perturbation and means to exploit it to his advantage.

"He hit my dog with a piece of wood. Have you looked at the damage, such a fine beast?"

The child is still on the ground. He rubs his neck, trying hard not to moan. He is in dread of a fresh volley of blows. Kader experiences a rush of admiration for the lad: "Little grub, may the earth be gentle to you! You've dared to defy a dragon capable of tearing you to pieces with one snap of its teeth. At your age, I would not have had the courage. The only advantage I had over you was to have more clothes on!"

The Arab follows the exchange between Lislei and the old man. The Australian walks in front of him, ostentatiously ignoring his weapon.

"Can you guess what he did to one of my sheep? This morning, I came by surprise on this fucking Nigger just as he was trying to kill a ram. He was stabbing it with some kind of stick, it hadn't been very well sharpened. This vermin clawed me when I was trying to control him."

The man aims a gob of spittle at the child. The latter stares at him with a sombre look. He is on his knees, lips tight, so frail compared to this muscular farmer.

"He messed up one of my best breeders, just think of it! I can assure you that this snotty brat hasn't escaped the hiding he deserved. And with his own miserable spear, what's more! Afterwards, I locked him up, left the dog to watch over him."

Lislei and Kader have seen the marks the blows left on the buttocks and the back. The Arab has the taste of ashes in his mouth. He hisses:

"Ask him what he reckons he'll be doing."

As if he had understood the question, the white-haired man looks defiantly at him, blows his nose for a good while on his fingers, wiping them on the barn door.

"Tomorrow, I'll take him into town. There, the troopers will make him talk. As a rule, there shouldn't be any Abos left in the neighbourhood.

They've all been chased away to the north. But they're worse than dingos, that riff-raff. They hang on! You think you've got rid of them, they crop up again as soon as you put your arm down! If there's a brat, it means his bitch of a family can't be far away, and the tribe too."

Lislei translated the reply. Kader experiences an instant of disarray. The child (and the fugitive recalls that he understands English) is staring at him in silence, but the look in his eyes is only one of intense supplication.

"Tell the old man that we'll take the lad with us."

The man bursts out with recriminations and curses. He splutters, drops of saliva accumulate between his lips. The dogs, aroused by his shouts, have gathered around him again, menacing once more.

"A pistol would do you no good against my pack. Kill one and the others will tear your guts out. This vermin of a Nigger, he's damaged one of my finest beasts. That ram, someone must pay for that!"

Kader sniggers, after Lislei's terror-stricken translation:

"Tell him we'll pay for the damaged sheep."

The old man protests, and adds sarcastically: "As if scabby beggars had money!" but his face takes on a cunningly attentive look. Lislei is scarlet with exasperation:

"He insists that he does not have the right to set the lad free. He finds our interest in the Aborigine more than fishy. He swears by all that's holy that if the constable finds out that he has let a cattle thief go, it would cause him a great deal of trouble."

The gaolbird is sniggering even more sourly:

"Tell him that we'll pay for his damned sheep only on condition that he sells us the boy, the cart with a horse and two or three other bits and pieces . . ."

"Buy the child? But he isn't a . . ."

Kader, his tone still mocking, cuts her short:

"It's much easier to look after something you've bought, isn't that so?"

"Do you think this is a time for jokes? And with what money?"

"The old man on the ship . . . the secret drawer? Does that say anything to you?"

A smile, the first real smile she has given him, lights up Lislei's features, disfigured by dirt and fatigue.

"Have we enough? I mean to say: money?"

The goalbird, still under the influence of that smile, nods his chin in agreement. She is so filthy and so poorly rigged out, and he is so trapped in terror at the prospect of being recaptured, that he has managed, quite simply, to overlook how beautiful she is. The beauty of a poem, of a *qasida* of the desert, he realises, almost shocked by the outrageousness of his comparison. Because she does not in the least resemble a daughter of the Sahara. And, in any case, not Nour.

"Calm down, idiot!" He is annoyed at having been so moved. But this feeling, which has assailed him without warning, clings to him like a tick. The woman nods her head gently, her voice husky with embarrassment:

"Among those bits and pieces, could it be possible to include some women's clothes? He is a widower. Perhaps he kept some dresses and other . . . under . . . I mean . . . garments in a cupboard?"

She raises her eyebrows because the man standing in front of her has burst out laughing.

"Why are you braying like an ass? Is what I'm asking for so hilarious?"

Kader tries to defend himself, but his uncontrollable good humour spills over his face:

"God protect you, cousin, but . . ."

Lislei senses a sudden desire to laugh and to insult him. When she turns towards the child, he betrays a sign of recoiling. He seems to be rooted to the spot, hesitating between his usual panic and this delicious-tasting relief, too unexpected to be real.

"Come on, little wolf, we've some strange things to talk about."

The child hazards a step, a second. Lislei pulls him to her. She passes her hand over his bumpy skull and jests:

"That's not a great piece of work, is it? Who gave you such a bad shave? Next time, I'll be in charge and you'll see the difference . . ."

She has spoken to the little Aborigine in English. Tridarir looks at her. He pauses for an instant. His eyelids are half closed. His shoulders shake:

"What, are you crying?"

The woman's face has taken on a desolate expression:

"But look, my little boy, what have I said that's so terrible? I only mentioned your hair . . ."

15

"None of them at my place," the innkeeper warned them. "You two, you can sleep upstairs, but your Nigger will have to hit the sack in the stable. And that's much too good for him. Maybe he'll steal one of my horses . . . Are you really husband and wife?" he adds with suspicious eyebrows.

Lislei replies, her cheeks on fire:

"What do you take us for? Of course we are husband and wife, Mr and Mrs Harry and Elizabeth Sutherland!"

"And what country do you come from?"

"From . . . from Hungary."

"Where's that?"

"Where . . . Over there!"

The innkeeper muttered something between his teeth about arrogant foreigners who believe they're allowed to do anything they like as soon as they land in Australia. Lips tight, Lislei restrains herself from yelling in his face that he too is a stranger in this land, that he'd probably been nothing other than a transported convict, and that only the "Nigger" can claim to be at home. An inner voice reminds her with irony that the lad is not at home either, that the fundamental difficulty behind their flight lies precisely there.

Weary of battling, she shrugs her shoulders.

"So, you'll take it, the room?"

The landlord examines, with a mixture of curiosity and hostility, this young woman, who is pretty enough but dressed in those frayed garments which must date from half a century ago. The man waiting for her outside is just as nervous as she is. As if they were on the alert.

Lislei is exhausted by this endless journey under the sun and by those clouds of flies which do not leave them for an instant. The cart was not fitted with a tarpaulin and, because of a problem with the axles, it had, on two occasions, almost pitched them to the ground. Sleeping again in the open tonight, in fear of snakes and shivering until morning under a flimsy blanket, is at the present moment a prospect beyond her strength to contemplate.

"Yes," she sighs, ashamed at her sense of relief.

"It's payable in advance . . . You understand my English? As for food . . ."

They have been wandering around in this accursed country for only ten days or so. Everywhere the reception is the same: full of good will, friendly until Lislei mentions the little boy. Then the tone of voice turns harsh. Everyone is quite happy to welcome them, her and her "husband", as long as they have the wherewithal, but not the blackfellow. That kind belongs out of doors, people told them aggressively; and besides, how could that bother the little savage since the likes of him spend their lives out of doors and sleep naked under the stars. "But the nights are freezing," she protested. "That makes it clear, Missus, that you are not from these parts," a stockman said to her sharply. Cursing all the while because his beer was warm, the cowherd reproached her for wasting her pity on those good-for-nothings:

"When these Nigger devils are cold, do you know what they do? They always take with them five or six dingos, the local mutts, even more hairless than they are. When the temperature gets too low, they lie between two dingos and warm themselves by rubbing up against them . . . Supposing that they only rub against them!" he guffawed, slapping his thighs.

Three days later, as they entered a dusty, sun-parched township, a man on horseback pulled up beside their wagon. He was not in uniform, but a certain incisiveness in his attitude allowed the policeman accustomed to obedience to show through. He put some questions to them about their presence in the district and about the Aborigine who was accompanying them. Thanks to its intricacy, the version of their story they had cobbled together during the first days of their flight seemed credible enough to them. But face to face with this individual with an inquisitorial mien, Lislei almost let herself get muddled: they've always been Hungarians, certainly, but one of her husband's great-grandparents was English, "you see!" That John Sutherland chose to remain in Hungary after one of the many European wars against Napoleon. Her husband, Harry, and she, Elizabeth, had emigrated to Australia because they hoped, like numerous emigrants before them, to find gold and to make a new life for themselves. The kid, they'd picked him up on the road yesterday, dying of hunger; they intended giving him back to his relatives or to the first group of blacks they would meet on the way.

The policeman inspected the cart, laughing gently:

"Is it with this broken-down contraption that you intend going in search of gold or Abo tribes? It's more likely that you are rushing headlong into trouble . . ."

The man hesitated. He was in a hurry, and obviously regretted it. Lislei suspected that he wanted to go on with his interrogation. Something had aroused his suspicion: this woman who spoke too much, this man who said nothing at all and did not seem particularly European, this tale of a Nigger plucked from the side of the road like a mushroom . . . He finished by dropping:

"Get rid of the Abo as quickly as you can. In this country it's easier to end up with a Nigger's spear through your chest than to find nuggets of gold. Follow my advice: get rid of him in open country and make off as quickly as possible. You were wrong to take him with you, and above all to put clothes on him. You are giving him bad habits. He is going to think he's like us. Already, quite a few of them in the north and the west have been persuaded that the land belongs to them and they haven't hesitated driving their spears into settlers and prospectors. It's an insult to the decent people of Victoria to treat a Nigger kid like a white child. You are bringing disorder with you, lady. A blackfellow is an ape and should not look like white people. Otherwise, nothing is in its proper place any longer!"

He spurred his horse, trotted off a hundred paces or so. Without giving them a backward glance, he called out:

"I don't like your story very much. There's something murky about it, I'm not sure what, but I don't have the time to delve into it. It would be better for you if you didn't tarry too long in these parts. What's more, tell your mute of a husband that he'd do well to learn our language as quickly as possible. We don't like having people here who have no love for England!"

Kader has put the away the cart and led the horse to the stable. He has been gnawing away at the nails of his anxiety. Things had not turned out at all how he had envisaged during the crossing. He should already be in Sydney or in another large coastal town, melting into the crowd, calmly keeping an eye out for whatever vessel would get him near Damascus. Or would, at least, have put enough distance between him and the French and the English. Money is not lacking for that: money for subsisting at ease for several months and, moreover, to pay for a passage to the other end of the world! Instead, here he is, on the road, shilly-shallying in this cart across this lousy country in the most inadvisable way possible: a couple accompanied by what seems to make the Europeans around here bristle the most, an Aborigine, and a young kid at that. The two of them are all right, for Lislei is, after all, very useful. Without her knowledge of English – hold on, he should ask her where she learned it . . . – the first steps they took in Australia would have been fatal for them. But the child, he represents a complication which has turned out to be more or less insurmountable.

They have found out his name: Tridari or Tridarir. Lislei has decided to call him Trid. Nevertheless, the little boy is unpredictable, he can dig his heels in very easily. Lislei asked him the name of his tribe. In fact, it was a way of getting him to name his father and mother. The question seemed to terrify him to the highest degree. Not annoy, but terrify! Shaking his head and with a stubborn look in his eyes, he refused to pursue the conversation any further. He continues to believe that he is in Tasmania. Kader has come to realise, in the course of these days, that he is more than a little afraid of this child.

"Don't make him any more confused and miserable," Lislei raised her spiteful, angry voice, "he's a lad like all the others. There is no end to his misfortune, it's true, but he is only a nice little kid struggling not to drown in a sea of sorrow."

Perhaps, but sometimes Lislei also looks, with disbelieving eyes, at the child whose skull has been so badly shaved . . . Kader can guess at what she is pondering: how to behave towards someone who is living out "the end of the world"? And her incredulity changes into terror in a few seconds, without her realising it. Tridarir seems to be aware of the emotions he is provoking, and Kader senses that he is often on the brink of tears.

"I should never have run across you, lad," the fugitive reflects often enough, "I would be free to move around, perhaps I'd already be on the ship, on the way back! The policeman was probably right: leave you by the roadside and take off without further ado . . ."

When it comes down to it, in whose eyes would he be "recognised" as cowardly? This black sparrow exhausted by suffering? But what difference would one misfortune more or less make for this little savage? In Algeria, his family had certainly bought black slaves from the Sudan, and no-one, Kader as much as the others, had ever cared what they thought about them.

Cowardly in the eyes of this Frenchwoman, almost a prostitute? But that one, fatigue playing its part, should regret only one thing: to have crossed the path of this brat whose very presence brings them ineluctably closer to the hour of their arrest. The proof: hadn't she agreed, for the first time, that the lad should spend the night in the stable while she and Kader would have the privilege of sleeping in a real room! Certainly, he himself wasn't against her choice. ". . . Yes, to leave you by the roadside and take off without further ado . . ."

These spineless thoughts make him want to vomit, but, equally, they make his heart beat with desire: one act of cowardice now, only one, though enormous it is true, yet one that would be rewarded with so much happiness later on . . .

He toys with this idea as he is climbing the rickety stairs leading to

163

the upper floor of the inn. Lislei is already in the room. The furnishings are rudimentary, a shutter is missing from the window. The bed is enormous. Their eyes avoid each other. They pretend to themselves that their embarrassment arose because they are about to sleep together in the same room. In truth, each knows that their agreeing to separate themselves from the child is its source. Lislei unpacks the meagre possessions the sheep farmer sold them at an exorbitant price. In a piping voice, she whispers:

"I like Trid very much . . . Don't you?"

Kader does not reply, puts a blanket on the floor. He can feel her eyes following his every movement. He sighs. Without getting undressed, he lies down and wraps himself in the blanket.

When Lislei puts out the lamp, the silence that falls on the room illuminated by a shaft of moonlight is too profound. Breathing is controlled, on his part and hers, devoid of the usual noises made by sleepers who shuffle a little in their beds before finding a more comfortable position. Kader snorts to himself: the young woman must have her eyes wide open and be on the look-out for the least suspicious rustling at the foot of the bed. You think I'm going to leap on your backside, little goat. But his amusement is tinged with embarrassment, for a slight tingling, less and less ambiguous, comes to agitate the lower part of his body: after all, you're not so mistaken, perhaps . . .

This is, strictly speaking, the first time that he finds himself truly alone with Lislei. On the ship, there were enough moments of isolation, but disgust and fear were the best protectors of his fellow fugitive's "virtue". The captain must have noticed it; he had sniggered: "Hey, halfwit, don't pretend to be squeamish, you can climb on her, the Parisienne, I've no objection so long as you don't give me the clap!" And then Tridarir provided relief by sleeping between them after they caught up with him at the farm.

"Miserable prick!" he ruminates, irritated by the desire which made his penis grow incongruously erect.

He forces himself to think about something else. Tridarir, to be exact. How would he manage on his own, if they left him there, tomorrow, without further ado? Kader grimaces in amusement: he imagines how he would get undressed straight away, set about fashioning a new spear, as ridiculous as the first, then, teeth clenched, set off to hunt awe-inspiring sheep . . .

Obviously, he'll get himself slaughtered quickly enough, the little hunter, naked as a grub. Kader's body is besieged by two independent impulses: on the one side, his member has risen in an almighty erection, hurting him in the kidneys and the balls; on the other, his mind is captive to a staggering realisation: it's up to him to choose whether Tridarir will live or not! Left on his own, the lad will die, that is a certainty in this land of madmen; if he takes him along, Tridarir would have at least the same chance of surviving as they. And it's truly up to him to decide, and not to Lislei, because the money is in his own pocket . . .

"Bastard, God's crap!"

The oath, in Arabic, rings out around the room. Kader has got up. His exasperation is such that he had trouble extricating himself from the blanket. Lislei stifles a cry as, side-on to her, he crosses the narrow space between the frame of the bed and the window. Glancing at the wall makes him almost burst out laughing: the shadow he cast has increased immeasurably the size of the "lump" between his legs!

But irritation seizes him. A second later, he no longer has any wish to laugh:

"It's no use barricading yourself behind your sheets, I'm not about to eat you up, idiot!" he growls as he leaves the room.

The innkeeper cleared his throat ("Who's there?") and, recognising his guest, shut his door. Outside, the night is brisk. The landscape stretching out in front of him seems too vast. When Kader looks up, the anger choking him gives way, little by little, to anguish. Yes, he really is at the other end of the world, even the sky and its constellations are unknown to him. Who will restore to him his own firmament with its old pole star, its beloved Altair and Deneb?

Distant, ill-tempered barking breaks out, stops abruptly: some dingos must have caught one of those reddish-brown kangaroos which bound along with such comic grace. Kader urinates against a eucalypt. The "muk

165

muk" of a night bird perched on a high branch grows more agitated, as if it were protesting against the intrusion.

"Excuse me," Kader sighs, "I know nothing of the customs of the country. But look, I've asked no-one to make me the guardian of that child. If I don't clear out straight away, I'm going to get caught because of him."

The "muk muk" grows more hectic.

"All right, I've understood, you want me to leave you in peace. But, I assure you, they're not going to let me get away if they collar me."

His steps take him to the side of the cart. His shadow leaves a weird image on the stable wall. Kader smiles, then he is shaking with truly insane laughter. The more he thinks about Lislei's terrified expression, the more the muscles in his belly jump up and down. He wipes his moist eyes, and breaks out laughing again, slapping his sex through the cloth of his trousers:

"You frighten young ladies, friend, be more discreet next time."

A dust-cloud has risen. Kader is shivering from fatigue. The day had been exhausting, and tomorrow promises to be no better. To go to sleep straight away; in any case, it's not healthy, he considers, to be doubled up, splitting your sides with laughter in the dead of night, like a madman. He opens one wing of the stable door, looks for the small slumbering body of the Aborigine. The horses snort, then calm down rapidly as the Arab strokes them.

The innkeeper had found a place for the child in the dampest corner of the stable. "It smells too much of nag's piss over here, son," Kader whispers, picking up the sleeping lad. The other looks vacantly at him, a little stunned, then straight away shuts his eyes again. Because of the cold, he snuggles up against the adult's chest. Tridarir is so light that Kader feels a lump in his throat.

"What has stirred you so much, have you been befuddled by these idiot balls of mine," the man reproaches himself inwardly, "because you've said 'son', eh?" With his feet, he tests the condition of the straw. When he considers it sufficiently dry, he puts Tridarir down and stretches out beside him.

"Isn't the straw softer than the floor, Trid?"

The child, as if he were answering him, moans in his sleep. Kader yawns. A few steps in fresh air were not enough to calm him down. He turns over the same question again and again: "What are we going to do with you, little one? Some would give their eye teeth for you, for others you are not even worth a scrap. Neither one nor the other wishes you well, that's the least that can be said. And me? As for me, I'm afraid to help you. I may be the nephew of the Emir Abd El Kader, but that doesn't stop fear from giving me a belly-ache. You, you must also be very frightened . . ."

The fugitive stretches, his body extended and his heart distraught.

"Go on, little hunter, me too, I'm going to walk around in my dreams. Tomorrow will be soon enough to choose between cowardice and courage!"

Kader has started to snore when a creaking noise startles him. Someone has opened the door. Blood rushing to his temples, he makes ready to defend himself. Before recognising the intruder.

"I . . . I was anxious about him," Lislei murmurs, pointing to Tridarir.

She lies down at the other side of the child, after whispering "goodnight". A moment later, she spits at him with muffled hostility:

"I will not allow you to call me an idiot. You must not insult me!"

Taken aback, Kader stammers out a vague excuse. The reference to the shadow in the room in the inn has rekindled his desire. But it is more gentle now, a tepid stream trickling inside his belly. To disarm Lislei's aggressiveness, he ventures:

"May I ask you one question: why did you choose to make us pass as Hungarians?"

Lislei coughs lightly. She baulks at losing her bad temper.

"It's . . . it's a story my mother used to tell us before we went to bed, my brother and I . . . It took place in Hungary . . ."

Lislei chuckles:

"In the story, everything worked out well. It's foolish, I thought that it might bring us luck."

"Can you teach me something about . . . my new country?"

"No . . . apart from what it said in the story. I haven't the least idea what a Hungarian name sounds like! Nor of the language, what's more . . . Guess what he asked me, the farmer?"

"Yes?"

"The swine wanted to know what language you cursed him in. He seemed dubious when I assured him that it was indeed Hungarian. He snorted: does it sound so peculiar, Hungarian? I made it clear to him that he had heard nothing yet, that such was the case with all the languages of that part of Europe!"

The "Arab Hungarian" breaks into resounding laughter, which he stifles when he hears Lislei's indignant "hush". It is now the middle of the night. A horse snorts, another answers, then silence falls again. Kader makes up his mind to go to sleep again. He has time, however, to experience a distracting sense of gratitude towards this outlandish *gaouria* whom chance had imposed on him.

Tridarir daren't pluck the sleeve of the man driving the cart. His temper is so changeable, and it rubs off on the woman. This morning, the man was almost perky. Then, as the road stretched on, he retreated into himself and only reacted to things with grunts.

Tridarir would like, however, to know what all this is about. What the man drew on the beach, was that the truth? Had they really left the island, could there really be other lands as vast, no . . . vaster than his parents' land? The child is dying to question that mute individual, but he is afraid of one thing only: to read in his eyes confirmation of what he suspects.

Tridarir does not recognise Tya, the Earth. Worse still, Tya does not recognise Tridarir. He can sense that she is hostile, dry, wholly indifferent. Nothing he has seen until now bears the mark of the people of the Dreaming. So where are they going in this cart? He has a strange taste in his mouth, not of fear nor of sorrow. Perhaps of horror and incomprehension.

Lislei has put her hand on Tridarir's shoulder. "Trid" is the name she has given him. Tridarir is hard put to understand why she does not use all of the sounds that make up his name. He repeated "Tridarir" several times, making an effort to pronounce it carefully. She seems determined to injure his name. To make her understand the outrage she is doing to his name, he does the same with hers: "Li" instead of Lislei. She was not annoyed. Rather, she seemed overjoyed: "That's it, Trid, it will be Li if you like!" she replied, affectionately stroking the top of his head. Tridarir did not dare contradict her any further. He lowered his head as a sign of dejection in the face of so much stupidity.

They are peculiar, these two adults! They saved his life and asked for nothing in return. At least until now. They do not give the impression of being disgusted by his presence. So many others of their kind take care, on the contrary, to display their revulsion when chance brings them into contact with Aborigines. But mightn't this be a trick perhaps, wouldn't it be better after all to remain on his guard?

The man "Kad" seems only to understand the language "Li" speaks. They are probably of the same tribe or clan. But in front of the other *Ludawini*, it's always the woman who speaks. She does not belong to the tribe of the Whites of these parts. She and "Kad" are obviously afraid of all the *Ludawini* they come across. Just as he is.

These blasted *Ludawini*! White, why do they call themselves white since they are light brown, beige, like the stuff you shit out after eating vegetables, or pink like certain kinds of puke, but never white? And besides, what is so extraordinary about calling themselves white: isn't white the dullest pigment in the forest? Insect larvae, they are really whitish, but they don't claim, just because of that, to be superior to birds of many colours!

Nothing good has ever come to him from the *Ludawini*. Even that depraved old sheep farmer did not hesitate to flourish his penis in front of him. He wanted to force him into doing something with him that only a man and a woman do between themselves. There was an ugly smile on his face as he fingered his crooked little snake. Tridarir could not understand straight away much of what seemed to him so unimaginable. He struggled and scratched the man's face with all his might when the latter managed to sit him on his knees. Mad with rage, the farmer whistled to his horrible dog and locked him in the barn with it. Luckily he found that shelf! Otherwise the mastiff would have torn out his guts as if he'd been a common bush rat.

His mother Walya once heard Truganini insist that she had discovered, in the course of a two-day sleep, the true name, *the hidden name*, of these invaders from every corner of the world, who hated each other, but were in agreement over one thing alone: to massacre, without pity, all their people. That infamous name was the tribe of the "Cruel Hunters"!

The killers themselves did not know that their race had been given that name by the Dreaming that had created everything; they would have been horrified by the curse that name contains. The Dream had revealed to Truganini that one day the turn of the Cruel Hunters would likewise come and that it would no longer do them any good to lament their former misdeeds. Then Truganini asked her Dream whether the children of the Ancient People would at length disappear.

Tridarir's nostrils are pinched in distress when he remembers that moment in his mother's tale. It was at the beginning of their flight into the forest. Walya had come to a dead halt, she started rubbing strands of hair between the palms of her hands, she snatched up a length of twine to unwind, then threw it away almost immediately. Her actions signified nothing, except for Tridarir: she was struggling against the desire to weep. Above all, it was necessary for her not to weep, because the father would have struck her, perhaps. She gasped: "The Dream admitted to Truganini that it did not know! A Dream that does not know, my son, that was the first time I heard anyone speak of such an abomination! Even the Dreams are going to die . . ." She began sobbing and the father moved away.

The way the cart is jolting, more bumpy now, brings the child out of his bitter reverie. "Kad" swore. He got down to check the rear wheel. "Li", her eyes like slits, is gazing straight in front of her, attentively. Her face lights up. She shouts joyfully to her companion, pointing her arm towards the hill.

*   *   *

"It's Jackson Town!" The innkeeper's wife hadn't lied.

Kader asks her what the name means.

"That, that is a town?" is his astonished reply.

The track enters the "town" directly, without any change of appearance. It is, perhaps, more rutted. On both sides of the main street, wooden structures lean haphazardly against each other. A tiny post office attached to the police station is followed by a church, recognisable only because of the cross embellishing its front. A water tank and a large enclosure, with slumbering cattle inside it, interrupt the alignment. One or two peppercorn trees provide meagre shade. There are few people out and about, on account, probably, of the sun and the dust. No-one pays them any attention.

"Where did she say we could find him, that fellow?"

"There's a tavern in the middle of Jackson Town. That Sam Baker is very easy to recognise, she assured me. He has the brightest ginger hair of any man she'd ever seen."

Kader cracks his knuckles with irritation. The two of them talked things over for a long while this morning. At the time, it seemed a good idea. It would allow them to avoid, at least for the moment, two immediate threats: their excessive "visibility" and their almost total lack of knowledge of the country. In any case, better to get away from the coast and, for a week or two, bypass the large centres of population. Staying together (in any event for Lislei and him . . .) is the only sensible choice for the moment: Lislei speaks English but has no money, Kader possesses money but can speak nary a miserable word of English. As for the child . . . Kader feels a leaden weight oppressing his chest when, for the hundredth time this morning, he runs up against the same iron-clad conclusion: either they get rid of him *now*, or the child will stay with them one day too many and it's certain they'll be arrested!

When they got up in the morning, Lislei decided to wheedle two or three bits of information out of the innkeeper's wife. The latter, after a little hesitation, realised that it was delightful to be nattering with another woman. "In this inn, miles from anywhere," she complained, "we don't have anybody come by except stockmen looking for drink, or troopers, and they're even greater louts." Lislei trotted out once more the story of the emigrant couple searching for gold. The publican's wife looked her up and down with a pitying expression, assuring her that that was no task for honest people, but rather for fools or for barefoot foreigners, saving her presence. But if she and her husband had really made up their minds, she advised them to join an expedition of hardy people. The country wasn't safe, full of former convicts, swagmen who'd gone mad from too much sun, or hostile Aborigines. As it happened, she breathed even more softly in Lislei's ear, she knew a guide looking for companions to make up a journey of that kind.

Lislei was surprised by the confidential tone of the woman who wore her hair in a tight bun. From her moist eyes, she understood that something had occurred between her and that "gentleman":

"He's not a common tramp. He's very brave, you know. And a fine man at that! He is thinking of going into the north-eastern parts . . ."

"This is the end of Jackson Town. We must have missed the tavern."

In front of them, the thoroughfare had regained the appearance of a reddish track clinging to the foot of a hill. They made their way back as far as the enclosure. The manoeuvre of driving the cart backwards proved difficult. The driver's face is running with sweat.

"What would I give for a turban!" he sighs. "As for the joint, we may have to ask a local. Will you take care of it?"

He turns his head to his companion, astonished that she does not reply. Lislei, dumbfounded, watches Tridarir as he jumps off the back of the cart and starts running towards a group of people sitting on the ground.

"By the Devil's arse! What's taken hold of him, that ass? Now we're in for a to-do!"

Kader is seething. "That, that takes the cake!" He lashes the mare with a brutal stroke of his stick. It almost trips over, so burning is the pain. Perhaps he'll catch the lad before he is set upon.

"My God . . ."

It is Lislei who has uttered the cry, but Kader could have taken it up on his own account: the two people towards whom Tridarir is hurrying are black! The two Aborigines, a man and woman, both elderly, are sitting cross-legged right in the middle of the main street. The man is bald, with a bushy, almost completely white beard. The woman is fat, with flaccid breasts covering all of her chest. The two Aborigines are naked, grey with dust, and, Kader notices with a curious anguish, do nothing to conceal their intimate parts: the penis of one and the other's vulva are only partially obscured by pubic hair. Lislei has turned crimson. The tranquil obscenity of the scene has made her lose countenance. She does not know if she can look at them. The couple in their incredible indifference suddenly call to mind her parents' listless, placid ways.

"Lislei," Kader whispers softly, "look at the boy."

Kader's eyes are shining. Still under the sway of her recollections, Lislei is astonished: why is her companion so relieved? And why does that taste of bitter joy foul her own mouth as soon as the reason for Kader's sense of relief seeps into her?

Timidly, Tridarir waddles over to them. He knows what the customs are, even though he's only a child. His father taught him that whenever you approach strangers who have found a camping place, it is necessary to drive a spear into the ground to show that you do not have hostile intentions, to sit down and wait patiently to be invited to join them. Tridarir is not armed, he mimes the action of thrusting a spear into the ground, crouches at a respectful distance from the couple. A wave of happiness unfurls in the child's heart. His face tries to maintain an impersonal expression, it is the polite thing to do when speaking to older people, but that proves beyond Tridarir's capacity. His muscles are twitching in exultation.

The eyes of the two strangers betray no astonishment. At the very most, their gaze turns a little more good-natured. Flies are swarming all over their faces, but they do nothing to chase them away. Tridarir is aware of his insolence when he is the first to break the silence:

"Forgive me, Uncle, forgive me, Aunt, if my mouth speaks without your permission. Overlook my discourtesy in presenting myself to you

173

with my body burdened with these rags of the *Ludawini*. So many suns have risen since I have seen other kinsfolk of the Nation of the Ancient People. My joy knows no bounds. I am Tridarir, son of . . . and of . . . I cannot speak their names because they are dead. But you must have known them, they were valiant and beloved by all. They were killed by white hunters. I . . . I have seen what should not be seen . . . my father's entrails and my mother's . . . I have not understood clearly why the killers did that. I believe that they want to eat them. Me, I only just escaped . . . Oh, Aunt and Uncle, why are they so strong and we so powerless?"

Tridarir drops his head. To resist the ravishing hunger for consolation which is urging him to bury his face in this woman's bosom and to catch an odour similar to his mother's. To control his voice, not to allow it to turn into the whines of a suckling infant.

"Beloved sisters and brothers of my parents, I have need of you. I am so exhausted, my head is filled with quagmires, my fists are clenched in tears. I have been lacking in respect for the Dreams of the Emu and the Monitor Lizard, I have been lacking in respect for the Dream of the Honey Ant. My knowledge of the Songs of our Ancestors is so poor, I do not know which lines to follow. My father . . . and my mother . . . began to teach me how to sing our Earth so that it would not die. But they taught me so little, they were not given enough time before their hearts were torn to shreds! What is the good of my wandering like this, if no-one will reveal to me what remains to be known? They told me each day that I was one of the . . . perhaps the . . ."

Tridarir is unable to finish. He crosses and uncrosses his hands. Every time, those words fill him with terror: "the last"! So he makes up an excuse. He will not speak the words out loud, for it would be unseemly to remind the two Elders of their advanced age and, therefore, of their closeness to death. He suddenly wants very much to ask them their names. When they fled from the station to the jungle, his mother fell into the habit of regularly reciting the names of all the Aborigines who were still living on the island. "There are so few of them now, they are the last offspring of your people, those old people! Never forget their names, the names of their tribes, the names of their Dreams. This is all that is left,

Tridarir!" She did not need all the fingers of her two hands to count them. So he knows them, without the least doubt, that man and that woman staring at him, as still as lizards, except when their heads tremble now and then with a slight twitch.

"Uncle, Aunt, these two Whites saved my life, they are the first *Ludawini* who have done me no harm, but they lied to me. They tried to convince me that I am no longer in my own land. How could that be possible since I am looking at you, dearest kinsfolk?"

His voice has cracked. The elderly man batted his eyelids quickly, his deeply lined face seemed to grow larger. A tremor rises at the corner of his mouth, spreads almost to the eye, distorting his features. The old Aboriginal woman has burst out laughing, without the least sound passing her lips! Her companion nods his head, as if she had reproved him for his lack of seriousness. Abruptly, she launches into a long tirade, broken by splutters, fixing with her eyes, by turns, the child and the man. She stands up, staggers two, three unsteady steps, collapses, though she does not stop grumbling.

Appalled, Tridarir realises that the two old people are dead drunk. But, and this is what chokes his heart to the point of suffocation, the woman is not expressing herself in his parents' language. Nor in any of the languages of the station at Oyster Cove. Even when he sharpens his ears to catch the woman's fuzzy harangue, he cannot recognise one word he had already heard at the station.

So he has spoken for nothing! And they listened to him as you listen to a fool of a parrot! His eyes grow misty. He puts his hands in front of his face, so as no longer to see the face of the old woman in the grip of that hideous cackling. The woman has succeeded in regaining her composure, she is staring at a white man who has just come out of a shed with a flag flying above it. When the *Ludawini* reaches her, she grabs his sleeve, whispering to him in an imploring voice. The man pushes her away violently, without managing to break free of her grasp. The drunkard, her face besmirched with dust and sweat, redoubles her insistence. Out of all patience, the man frees himself with a swift kick to the lower part of her body.

The howl of pain drags Tridarir out of his despondency. As in a night-mare, his eye first catches sight, through his fingers, of the woman as she is crawling away; then the old man slinking off, squealing ridiculously, to avoid a kick; finally, at the corner where the enclosure and the main street meet, four trotting horses, a white man in a red uniform on the first, followed by blacks in green and scarlet uniforms . . .

Riding past their cart, the horseman in red uniform raised an astonished eyebrow at Lislei. As for the three Aborigines escorting him, they only have eyes for the scene which has just unfolded in front of them: the white man who struck the drunk woman is already smiling at the trooper, while the whining old man has let his arms fall to the sides of his filthy body. He has lowered his neck. Tottering on his feet, he adopts an osten-tatiously submissive attitude. The woman has noticed nothing, she is still on her knees, absorbed in her pain.

Curious spectators have come out of the pub and look on, in silence, as the sergeant leans down and exchanges a few words with the indiv-idual who is adjusting the sleeve of his shirt. Lislei can make out nothing of their conversation, she simply sees the militiaman straightening up, reflect for a second or two – at the centre of general attention – before making a sign to the three black troopers.

The trooper closest to him forages in a bag and pulls out a whip. He goes nonchalantly in the direction of the naked old man, calls out to him in a way that sounds friendly enough to Lislei. Then, without any change of expression, he lashes the drunkard's face. The onlookers burst out laughing because the old blackfellow crashes to the ground, then springs up like a puppet on a string under the impact of a second blow of the whip. Someone shouts an insult in which Lislei can only make out the word riff-raff.

Her heart in her mouth, she sees the second horseman going over to the kneeling woman. She, her eyes closed, has clearly resigned herself to the blow she is about to receive. Throwing her head back, she raises her voice in complaint, without making the least show of protecting herself. Lislei's muscles grow tense. She would like to cry out when the thong etches a brown gash across the woman's breasts. The latter is writhing with the same disjointed movements as her companion. Her pleas have turned into an inhuman squealing.

Kader's face is ashen: the third Aboriginal trooper has noticed the crouching boy. The horseman laughs because the child gives the impression of wanting to hide behind the hands clamped over his eyelids. The Aborigine in uniform hesitates for a moment, he is looking for permission from his superior, who remains impassive. The trooper, brandishing his crop, makes for his prey. Tridarir has seen him; his only reaction is to throw his arms in front of himself.

"No!"

Lislei's scream ringing in his ear, Kader has jumped from the wagon. If he could, he would vomit from fear. The damned child is just in front of the rider with the crop. At that exact moment, the Algerian fugitive hates, with all his might, that stinking kid, that howling whore: why in the name of Satan, did he lack the courage to be cowardly precisely when he needed it so much? The woman's hysterical cry made the black trooper turn around. He fixes a furious look on the individual who has violently grabbed the child by the shoulders.

"Tell them that the lad's our servant! The proof, he has clothes on! He's disobeyed us by talking to the two drunks! Tell them, quickly!"

Kader's voice is hoarse, broken by rapid breathing. The onlookers gaze at him, not disguising their hostility mixed with incomprehension: how dare he interrupt such a captivating spectacle?

The horse's nares are level with his face. The animal, nervous, exhales it moist breath, with a foetid stench, all over him. Seeing the trooper's indecision, Kader raises his voice. He knows that if he spoke any more softly his teeth would chatter.

"Lislei, explain to their leader that we will punish the lad. Severely!"

The sergeant with the air of a well brought-up young man listens attentively to the confused explanations of the stranger in the cart. He leans down stiffly, commenting that it is rather dangerous to have degenerates like that in one's service. She and her husband are new to the country, they have no idea yet of how perverse Aborigines can be. If they insist on living in Australia, they should model their conduct on that of the true settlers, particularly the British.

"It would be better for you and your husband if you stopped setting yourself up against what the authorities in this country do and say. The next time, such imprudence could cost you very dearly. Tell your husband that he was lucky enough today."

Menace and scorn are so flagrant that Lislei's smile of gratitude freezes into a frown. The man pulls on the bridle, barks a short order to his men, and makes for the pub.

A murmur of approbation rises when the black troopers set to work with their whips once more. Surrounded by the horsemen, the two terrified Aborigines skip in front of them, sometimes collapsing, and immediately starting to walk again under a fresh shower of blows.

Without a word, Kader helps Tridarir get into the back of the cart. He avoids the child's wide-eyed look of gratitude. Ignores Lislei's stifled "Thanks." Experiencing only intense nausea, linked with shame, his hand trembles while grabbing hold of the halter. The two old people, driven on with whips, are now beyond the corner of the street, but their pitiful "Ow . . . Ow . . ." can still be heard

An individual with flaming red hair has left the group of spectators. He observes Lislei with interest. He is very tall and he strokes the tips of his moustache like a connoisseur, a man who appreciates the finer things of life.

When his eyes meet the woman's, he calls out:

"It's the black police, Abos enlisted to track down other Abos. They are incredibly skilled and without any pity for people of their own race. That . . . that's a little surprising at first, but you'll see, one quickly becomes . . . Your husband doesn't speak English, you're very new arrivals, aren't you? You are thinking of going on an expedition? You have money?"

Lislei responds each time with her head, too shattered to be annoyed by the insolence in his voice. His accent is drawling, mocking. But his hair is such a bright ginger that there can be no doubt that he is none other than the man the innkeeper's lovelorn wife mentioned to her.

"What are they going to do to them?" she asks with difficulty.

"Bah, have a little fun with them. And then finish them off somewhere in the bush . . ."

He shrugs his shoulders:

"Good riddance, if only they'd eat each other. After all, they're nothing but animals. They look a little like us, it's true, and they are fond of drink, just as we are, for example. But it won't do to exaggerate. Saving your presence, would you, yourself, go around stark naked, in public? No. So?"

He pulls a long face, drained of expression, as he whispers:

"Perhaps, dear lady, we can do business together?"

Her cheeks red, Lislei realises that he knowingly used an ambiguous expression. The way he said "we" could have implied all three of them – or just herself and the ginger-haired dandy.

"Speak to my husband, Harry Sutherland," she answers dryly, pointing to the sallow-complexioned person busying himself with the horse.

16

"Lislei!"

He got it wrong again. He called her by her real name. She corrects him harshly:

"Not Lislei, but Elizabeth . . . And you, Harry . . . Harry Sutherland! For goodness' sake, be more careful! After a month with these people, you should be much more on your guard!"

"Right," he grimaces. "I'll try not to forget any more."

"You'd do well. Baker suspects something."

"Oh, that one! I believe we've made a serious mistake putting ourselves in the hands of that incompetent. I'm not even sure he knows where he's taking us. We've lost our way twice, we almost got drowned in a marsh that shouldn't have been there. The only thing he's brilliant at is squeezing money out of us to be our guide. Just take a look at those snooping eyes of his. He's pretending to be checking the shoes on his horse, but he always has an eye on us . . ."

Kader sniggers maliciously:

"And on you above all!"

Before Lislei is able to reply, he addresses himself once more to the daily task of inspecting the fastenings on the tarpaulin. If he weren't so disagreeable, she would believe that he is jealous! That simple likelihood makes her uneasy, so much has she grown accustomed to their shared hostility. Up till now, he has observed his part of the contract: a more or less dutiful "husband" in front of others, he has not tried to profit from it by pushing his advantage, from the outset he has slept at the foot of the cart. Once or twice, however, she has dreamt about him. She woke up, exasperated by the foul stench of desire, and disgusted by the coarseness of her imagination. A near-prostitute who allows herself to be enthralled by someone who has already committed a murder, there, that is how her brother's wife would have made fun of her . . .

"Bloody axles," Kader swears, wiping his face. "At the first rut, the whole thing will fall apart."

On Baker's instructions, he had hoops and a large oil-coated cotton cloth fitted in Jackson Town. Baker muttered that their cart wouldn't last long. For once, that swindler was right, for, on the previous day, the framework at the front cracked.

Kader raises his arms in a gesture of impatience.

"We'll have to come to a decision. We are getting too far away from the coast and from the bigger towns."

"But that's exactly what you wanted, isn't it?"

"Yes, but this shouldn't go on too long. This is too much. How are we going to get back? Look around you, the further we travel the more like a desert it becomes. I don't like this desert. The horses will croak before long. And these devilish flies that come swarming from nowhere, they'd eat us alive if we let them!"

Lislei, disheartened, whispers: "Keep your voice down." She clasps the top of her arm with her other hand. The same anxiety seizes her again: as far as her eyes can travel, this accursed bush is stifled by heat and desolation. You'd say it was like the time-ravaged face of a grumpy old man. Here and there, its ochre monotony is broken by clumps of stunted eucalypts or sparse patches of spinifex which, if you're not careful, lacerate the horses' hocks until they bleed.

"What exactly did Baker say?"

Lislei first casts a precautionary eye over the half-dozen men scattered around the fire. A short while ago they finished drinking a foul concoction as they listened, with devoted attention, to Baker's homilies about what was waiting for them, and them alone, to the north. None of them has any experience of the bush, nor, for that reason, of the desert. The one thing that unites them is the quasi-religious hope of enriching themselves by grace of the "blood of the sun", as Baker calls it. One of them is a grocer, another a salesman in a Sydney shop, the youngest has abandoned an apprenticeship with a blacksmith. There is even a defrocked priest, who lets fly more oaths and curses than all the others combined. Baker claims to have worked with the mounted troopers, and that he has, therefore, travelled over a large part of Australia, but Lislei eventually came to realise that he had only been a cook. That does not prevent their guide from adopting the sharp tone a policeman uses to address civilians. Except with her . . . He shows great attentiveness towards her, a little too much at times, to the point of provoking sniggers from the other members of the party. For them, her husband is either blind or complaisant. The ambiguity and the ridiculousness of their situation make the Frenchwoman's eyes sparkle with a smile devoid of all gaiety: men, they are all the same, these asses.

"So, what does he want to know?"

"He asked me whether it was really because we want to look for gold that we decided to join them. According to him, as prospectors, we lack enthusiasm. He finds it strange that newcomers like us should be encumbered with a little Aborigine. It's plain to see, he added, that Trid is not our servant. The other men, particularly the ex-priest, don't like having him in their company. They are afraid that he will bring them bad luck. They have started insisting that we must get rid of him as quickly as possible, otherwise things could go badly wrong. Besides, they grumble about my presence. A woman on a journey like this, that's bound to cause trouble . . ."

"Perhaps they're not so wrong, after all."

Lislei shrugs when she notices her companion's mocking expression. Her face is careworn. Trid is squatting on a little mound at the edge of the encampment. With his vacant gaze, he will spend, as is his custom, all of the halt without betraying the least movement, not even to shield himself from the flies. A rock of sorrow baking in the sun. It is only in their presence that he forces himself into a semblance of life. Out of gratitude, probably. "An adult reaction" Lislei imagines, her heart contracting.

"What are we going to do with the boy, Kader?"

"Harry, not Kader, do you remember? . . . Trid? Everyone assures us that we should have already come across the first of the Aboriginal tribes that are still at large, more or less. We'll hand Trid over to whichever of them will agree to take care of him. Then we'll make for the coast. No-one along the way will remember the business on the boat or our escape."

He suddenly loses his composure.

"But how are we going to talk to them? Perhaps we won't see any of those desert-lovers? And if they refuse to take him? If they kill him . . . or kill us? Having him with us is even more of a prison than the clink."

His face growing haggard, he tries to make a joke:

"I've got nothing against the lad, but it's the work of a prophet, this, to be looking after a child who is the last of his people. Me, I don't ask that much for myself, I am not brave enough to turn myself into a messenger from on high! Either Christian or Muslim. An escapee from a chain-gang, that stinks more than rotten fish, and it certainly won't bring down the blessing of angels!"

His eyes – which are seeking her approbation – close with an unexpected blink:

"And besides, it was more fun for the real prophets, ours as much as yours. They watched over the *first* offspring instead . . ."

Lislei chuckles nervously. Anguished protest grips her throat:

"Stop, one should not laugh about such things!"

It was after the following day that things began to go wrong. First of all, that encounter with the horseman who was returning to the south. He had come from Rawlings, a township built by gold-diggers next to a dry river-bed, a day's journey to the west. He told them about a possible site, approximately mid-way, where they could make a halt, a group of huts put up by the troopers, now abandoned. The men wanted to speak with him about gold. He laughed at their insistence. He asked for some liquor, then told them that there was no more gold left in the district than lice on the head of a bald man. Voices were raised. Baker hissed that he was lying, but the horseman stuck to his story.

"If you push on to Rawlings, you'll see for yourselves. In a year or two there will be nothing left there except fly-blown ruins rotting in the sun. The seams have run out. Madmen are the only ones left looking for gold in that lousy hole. They dig, they dig, but it's their own graves they're digging. What's more, the Niggers are getting more and more restless. They are starving, they accuse us of hunting too many of their kangaroos and making them flee beyond their lands. Do what you like with you own skins, but believe me, a spear slips very easily into your belly-fat. Me, I'm going back to my old job: hunting dingos. Sheep farmers pay a few bits for a dozen ears. At least that way, while Australia's teeming with dingos, I'll be sure to stuff my face and get as much grog as I need!"

As he was about to leave, the horseman went over to Lislei. He greeted her with a finger to the brim of his hat:

"The little savage, he's not all alone, is he Missus?"

"No, he is with me. Why?" Lislei riposted dryly.

The man pulled a puzzled face.

"And you are with . . . with . . . that is . . . someone?"

"With my husband, that goes without saying!"

The dingo hunter snorted in an unpleasant way:

"So then!"

Lislei hunched her shoulders:

"What's got into you?"

A note of irony has slid into the man's obsequious tone:

"Nothing . . . An idea passed through my head . . . In any case, I never meddle in other people's business."

He got on his horse. Lislei's eyes followed him until he disappeared from view.

"Idiot!" she muttered, without throwing off an anxiety she did not want to share with Kader.

The dust settled, the atmosphere of the camp changed. The men threw hostile, suspicious glances at Baker. He gave the signal to depart, but Wallace, the defrocked priest, declared that there was no reason for them to obey him. The others agreed. The grocer grumbled: "We'll have to look to the money we've turned over to you . . . we're not halfwits." Baker was made to promise that they'd pass through Rawlings to find out whether the dingo hunter had told them the truth. Finally, they moved off, but their anger was palpable. Baker had lost his haughty pride. They could sense that he had shrunk into a humble cook again, someone humiliated by the arrogance of the police.

Afterwards, there was the theft of two horses. The caravan had reached the abandoned outpost, wattle and daub structures, in fact, some of them in ruins. The spring, which must have been abundant enough for a shelter to be set up there, hardly flowed at all, trickling drop by drop from a crevice. Magnificent birds in search of water – "mandarin diamonds" Baker remarked fatuously – were lapping up the miraculous liquid, without flying off when the group made its appearance in the yard.

The mood was morose. The guide launched into a tale of a gold mine, but the men gave him the cold shoulder. Kader, Lislei and Trid slept in an outhouse at some distance from the group. First, as had become their custom since they joined the caravan, Lislei gave Kader an English lesson. She had complained at the start that she was not his servant, but the Arab was insistent. In truth, the lesson boiled down to a list of words Kader gave her, for which she furnished, whenever she was able, the translation. Tridarir listened, with a faint smile playing around his lips, betraying no reaction. Eventually, he would end up by slumping between the two adults and falling into a troubled sleep. Kader and Lislei regularly put a hand on his shoulder to calm him.

In the morning, Wallace roused the camp with a volley of curses. Two packsaddle horses had disappeared, one of which was carrying the belongings of the former man of the cloth. Wallace bawled that only experienced thieves could have untied the horses without provoking a reaction.

"How could that happen without the horses neighing? By the Queen's cunt, I myself have lost everything because of this business! Things can't go on like this! I sold up everything I had, I did, to come into God's arse of desert!"

His fury grew and grew as he described the sacrifices he had made to come on the expedition. The other members of the party, fascinated, looked on in silence, somewhat horrified by this torrent of obscenities and blasphemies. Even the grocer, who had also lost his horse, stood by gaping. Wallace ordered Baker to saddle his horse.

"You say you know how to follow someone's trail? Now you're going to be able to prove it. I'm sure it's those bastard savages that have pulled this off. Get your weapons and follow me. They can't have got far. Come on, you blokes, what are you waiting for, for them to fleece all of us?"

"What are they up to?" Kader breathed softly, exasperated because he could not understand anything.

Lislei, unable to follow the rapid flow of words the man on horseback, who seemed to have become the new leader, was spitting out, translated almost nothing.

"They are going off to look for the thieves . . ."

It was at that moment that Tridarir appeared, his eyes puffy with sleep. He made for the cart, thinking that they were about to leave the camp.

"Ah, there he is, the grub! He's not going to wriggle out of this one so easily . . ."

A shower of saliva spurts out of Wallace's mouth. He tugs the bridle so fiercely that the horse stamps in pain.

"Son of a bitch!" he screams, hurling himself at Tridarir. When he reaches him, he leans from the saddle and strikes the child with the butt of his rifle. The Aborigine goes limp before falling over backwards, as slowly as a sack of sand.

No-one had time to intervene. Lislei was only aware of the thump of wood against bone. "Brr!" is the only sound, surging from the pit of her stomach, she is able to utter. Her fingers reach out for Kader's shoulder, brush against it, then let go. Kader strode over to Wallace. The Algerian fugitive is, in turn, speechless. He feels that his chest is harbouring an ignoble rat, which is devouring his flesh with its enormous teeth. His hand plunges into his pocket, searches for the revolver, grows stiff. My God, the revolver, why did he leave it in the bag?

"Don't move. Dingos'll soon be lapping up bits of your brain if you take another step. Ted, go through their things and take away their weapons!"

Turning to Lislei:

"Hey, crackpot, tell your fool of a husband that I won't think twice about killing him. Only your Nigger could have set the horses loose. That's why the nags didn't protest. He must have done a deal with some other Niggers, they're all the same, that rabble."

The former priest interrupts the men on horseback:

"You know, don't you, what he gets up to, that cockroach, when he leaves the camp?"

The grocer's face, which until now expressed disapproval of Wallace's cruelty, takes on a suspicious look:

"What you're saying, Wallace, is that possible?"

"Think about it a little, Cribb. If we let him run free, we'll be the ones to have spears sticking out of us the next time. Do you trust an Abo, do you? And his cronies? That couple there, ever since we set out I haven't much liked the look of them. We don't know where they've come from and why they're carting this brat around with them . . ."

He tapped the side of his nose with his index finger:

"Don't you think it all stinks a bit?"

Chattering female parrots are perched on a dead casuarina; their soft colours, green and yellow, explode over the surrounding dryness. Kader moved Tridarir into the room, where it is dark, Lislei bathed the wound at the base of the neck with water. A lot of blood has flowed. The adult's shirt the child is wearing has become sticky. Lislei, taking care how she does it, removes the shirt. At present they are waiting for the child to regain consciousness. They say little, both lost in their thoughts. At length, Lislei asked whether, in his opinion, the injury is serious. Kader assured her that it is not. His sombre look gives the lie to his diagnosis.

He has already seen, in Algeria, how his comrades lost their lives from this kind of a blow. Especially at the beginning of the uprising, when there was frequent hand-to-hand fighting. The death throes could last for days, men urinated and defecated in their coma.

"He needs a doctor, Kader," Lislei suddenly implores him. "He is not asleep, he is dying."

187

Kader stands up, restraining his rage:

"Lislei, those mongrels took all the horses, including the packsaddles! Even if we had a horse, how would we be able to get to Rawlings? We'd get lost in this damned desert!"

In the darkness, he can make out Wallace's belongings, and his followers': hides, food, bags of clothing. They took nothing except the horses, for fear that the couple might make off with them. They would be back by early or late afternoon, Baker informed them. Of all of them, he seemed to be the least excited by the chase.

Kader has cast another glance at Tridarir's gaunt features. His breathing is shallow, interspersed with moans. Kader avoids the eyes of the woman who, from time to time, strokes the lad's forehead. How is it possible to heap so much misery on such a small body? Who needs this kind of abominable display?

"Mother," he murmurs in Arabic, "explain it to me, I can no longer understand anything at all. *Yemma*, if you are still in this world, come to the aid of your stupid son . . ."

Without meaning to, he puts a hand on Tridarir's naked chest. It is hot, too hot even though they are in a shaded room. The skin has a fine texture, soft as satin. A sickening sense of compassion overwhelms Kader.

His voice husky, he says:

"Lislei, do you fear God? Your God?"

Because she has her back to the light, he cannot make out his companion's features. The question has taken her unawares. He realises that she is searching his face. At first she stammers:

"Well . . . yes . . . yes . . . I believe in a way . . . Everyone fears God . . ."

"Your God and mine, it's close to the same thing. Oh well, you see, God always makes me afraid, and He will certainly cause me to fear Him until the day the earth covers me, but . . ."

He paused. His mouth is set. He searches for the French words. How much more would he prefer to confess what is oppressing him in the only language that counts for him, the guttural tongue of his childhood, the unconditional tenderness of his father and mother . . .

". . . But that God, I no longer respect Him. I hold Him in contempt. He has set His pack of henchmen loose on . . ."

He pointed his chin towards Tridarir. The rancour in his breath is so fierce that it makes Lislei shudder, despite the sweat clinging to her temples.

They turned up again in the middle of the afternoon. The grocer, on horseback, leading another horse at the end of a long rope. Wallace came back empty-handed, but he is almost jaunty. The youngest, the apprentice blacksmith, flinches from the inquisitive looks Kader and Lislei give him. He blushes and snorts with laughter. An embarrassed laugh, menacing, which puts Kader on the alert. A nervous, disquieting gaiety reigns over the group, with the exception of Baker. The latter is pale, attempting several times to adjust the hat on his head. Kader tries to attract his attention, but Baker makes a pretence of busying himself with the pommel of his saddle.

Wallace, he is relaxed. More: serene. Nothing recalls this morning's individual maddened by rage. He calls out, with a broad smile:

"Perhaps the lady would make some tea? Good hot tea, there's nothing better for the heat!"

Catching sight of Lislei's flabbergasted face, he knits his brow:

"No hard feelings, I hope? This morning I got, let's say, carried away. Human beings are so fickle . . ."

"The little boy, he's dying . . ."

The ex-priest cuts her off dryly:

"These things happen. To everyone, besides . . ."

His voice is squeaking with menace. Kader tugs at the sleeve of Lislei's dress:

"What does he want from you?"

"He wants me to make tea."

Wallace's smile freezes slowly.

"Agree," Kader whispers, "it would be dangerous to refuse. Perhaps he'll give us our horse back?"

As she is pouring tea, Lislei is disconcerted by the excessive affability of the men around the fire. Each takes his mug, thanking her with a timid smile. An almost childish atmosphere hovers over the participants in the chase. Baker, for his part, mutters "No." His handsome face is creased with fatigue.

He raises his eyes to Lislei. Drops them immediately when they meet hers.

"He is ashamed . . . My God, him? What is he ashamed of?" The question has barely had time to form in her mind when Lislei's heart misses a beat. They have done something terrible, she is sure of that now. Her mother used to insist about their deceitful neighbours that even their friendly ways made them reek. Lislei sniffs involuntarily: Wallace and his companions do *smell* bad.

"Baker?" she whispers in a quivering voice. She walks away with her kettle, then makes a half-turn, and stands in front of the guide.

The other ignores her. Ted, the apprentice blacksmith, taps him on the shoulder:

"Hey Baker, wake up, someone's asking for you."

The young man chuckles for the benefit of his comrades:

"Perhaps he'll manage better than before. Good . . ."

Lislei does not even have the courage to blush. She hears the ribald "Good Luck", but the man who has stood up to join her under the casuarina with its peeling trunk is so downcast that she understands that the worst has come about. But what *worst*?

"Baker . . . Baker . . . what happened?"

"Nothing."

"Baker, did something dreadful go on?"

"Nothing, I am telling you."

An ugly crease appears, pulling down the corners of his mouth. Lislei is still holding the kettle. She would like to put it down because her arm is shaking.

"Baker, if you don't tell me what you have been up to, I'll start screaming . . . screaming like a madwoman until you tell me the truth."

The guide stares at her. Lassitude seeps out of his eyes.

"All right," he mumbles, "you asked for it."

His large hands are fiddling with the brim of his hat, pulling it out of shape. He clears his throat.

"We spotted them quickly, the thieves. Because of the smoke. There was an old man and two women. Wallace's horse had already been cut up and bits of it were roasting on the fire. But, instead of taking off straight away, the Niggers first waited for us to reach them before they ran away. The old man was in a bad way, he was limping, it was a clear sign that it'd been the women who'd stolen the two horses . . ."

He falls silent, shrugging his shoulders.

"Wallace was the first to fire. He picked off the old man. That wasn't difficult. Then everyone got down to it. The women gave us more trouble because there was scrub everywhere. It pricks the horses, you see! But we brought all of them down. Just like you do in a drill. Me too, I did some of the killing, I can't deny it . . ."

Lislei has put the kettle down. She is no longer shaking. Because an invisible snake is twining around her legs and breast. The sun in her face has grown into a great red ball which is about to set the sparse vegetation on fire. She gets ready to go back to Kader and Trid. Quickly, before bursting into tears in front of this creature.

"Wait . . . that's not all. Ah, if only it was . . . Wallace was still furious. His horse had been butchered while Cribb's was in excellent condition. He had a peculiar look on his face. He went back to the fire, poked around in it a little. He looked at the ground, followed the footprints."

Baker clicks his tongue:

"He's smart, that Wallace! He flushed them out soon enough: five little girls, stark naked, huddling behind the bushes, they were shivering in terror. So we understood why the Abos waited until we were upon them before they made themselves scarce. By leading us in the opposite direction, they hoped to protect the children. Wallace . . ."

Lislei recoils with horror:

"You killed them?"

"No . . . Do you want to know everything? Wallace undid his belt. He grabbed the first one he could reach and raped her in front of our eyes. We were thunderstruck . . . A priest . . . at least an ex-priest, but all the same! He yelled that no-one would ever find out anything about it . . . and that he, in any case, was giving us permission. You understand: permission! That was the madness: Ted, Cribb, the bugger from Sydney, everyone, yet they're not bad blokes, they're pretty decent. Oh well, everyone followed his example, as if they really believed they'd been absolved by goodness knows who. The little girls screamed, the others formed a circle and rounded them up with the horses. Cribb, the respectable good daddy who, every night, bores us stiff with his stories about his brats . . . he was over the moon: 'I didn't think it would be so good . . . like poking into butter' . . ."

"Stop" Lislei begs, "stop . . ."

"Oh no," Baker growls, "you'll have to put up with this right to the end. Me, they insulted me, called me impotent, but I just couldn't. I've killed Abos, and several times rather than once, it's true. That's what goes on in this nook of the world. But to attack little girls like that . . . Wallace reckoned I wasn't a man . . . So there, we went away, they weren't killed. That's worse perhaps."

Lislei's mouth is parched. In her head, there is a vast void. With one sole certainty: these men drinking their tea are savage beasts, this Baker, who's trying to make excuses for himself, is one as well. She must quickly go back to protect Trid and Kader. For the first time, she is thinking Trid *and* Kader, and that is a sure sign that something has changed.

". . . I am not like them, do you believe me?"

"Yes, yes," she burbles. She has not listened to the beginning of what he was saying. She is frightened. The guide is still fiddling with his hat.

"We'll have to leave now. The Abos will be looking for revenge. When the men find their . . . well . . . You can't stay here."

"We'll take the little boy with us. He'll die if he is left here."

Baker shakes his head.

"No, Wallace would never allow that. In any event, you should leave your wagon behind. It's slowing us up too much. Wallace is the leader now. Moreover, after all that's happened . . ."

"Then we, we'll stay here."

Lislei has dropped her voice. The guide is examining, with sustained interest, this beautiful woman whose chin is trembling from indignation and sorrow.

"Why do you say we? This Harry . . . he's not you husband."

"But he is," she splutters. "Who . . . who gave you permission to insult me?"

"You don't act like husband and wife. I've been observing you for a month now . . . It's easy to recognise a man and his wife. And sometimes you mix your names up . . ."

"You are wrong, Harry *is* my husband and . . ."

"So you love him?"

"Oh, you!"

Lislei has picked up her kettle. Her steps are unsteady, her head aches. This man has just killed human beings, he has allowed little girls to be raped. And here, without any more ceremony, he is talking like an ordinary man about ordinary things of life.

Baker sniggers bitterly behind her back.

"You won't answer my question?"

17

You have to follow the dry river-bed, the dingo hunter had advised, then fork to the left as soon as an outcrop of rock resembling the head of a lizard comes into view. Kader is breathing through his teeth, whistling to quell the anxiety tormenting him. How can you go on following a river-bed when you can no longer see any of it?

Night fell in a flash. Like a sabre over the head of a man condemned to death, he remarks with a joyless little laugh. For three hours, he has been making his way, arduously, across this sinister valley with its treacherous tufts of grass. On top of all that, his horse tripped over a rodent's burrow and has a limp now. Kader had to dismount. At this rate, one day more would not be enough, he muttered in his horse's ear, could Tridarir wait that long?

There is a dark mass rising on the horizon. Would he be right to think that he has caught sight of the perching-place of that celebrated lizard-head rock?

"Stop idiot, you'll get lost!" Kader berates himself at the top of his voice.

His voice is ridiculously shrill. "It's the anger of impotence. You don't know how to get angry," his mother used to reproach him, "it is easy to see that you are frightened."

"All this, it's all the fault of that shit of a preacher!"

He lets fly a cartload of curses, one more obscene than the other, until his throat aches. On account of the low contours of the landscape, there is no echo. The man is entirely out of breath, a little ashamed of himself.

Because this devilish fear has not faded in the outburst of anger.

"Even when you're on your own, you are scared out of your wits," the man grumbles, trudging along. "You've not changed much since that oasis of yours in Biskra, you rabbit of the Sahara . . ."

But is he all alone? He will have to sleep in the desert. The only luggage he brought with him is a waterbag and a little food. He strokes the unfortunate horse's neck. The beast is shivering from fatigue. Needle-like thorns in the undergrowth have made its hocks bleed.

"Graze a little, my friend, chew on the scrub if you dare. I really don't have anything to give you."

Kader searches for a crevice in the rock where he would have at least the impression of shelter. He does not entertain many illusions. He is unarmed; if an Aborigine chose to attack him with a spear, he'd probably have no trouble running him through with it.

"Damned Australia." He ponders as he tries to find a comfortable way of leaning against a rock. "If I die here, no-one will know anything about it. Not my mother, not my father, not . . ."

He thinks: not Trid, not . . . Wanting to take up the thread of his thoughts:

". . . not Lislei . . ."

Downcast, he chuckles silently: thoughts, lustrous fish slipping between your fingers! Kader is not duped: the laugh came only in order to mask his confusion: his life, why has it shrunk itself into only four people? Certainly, his father and mother. But these strangers, that lad and that woman he hardly knows at all?

"Hey, horse, help to blow the fog out of the brain of this mule, your brother. What possesses him to prattle on like this?"

The horse snorts through its nares. The animal has resigned itself to having next to nothing to eat, but it has not decided to put a distance between itself and its human tormentor. The sky sparkles with its thousands of incomprehensible stars. Kader pushes his knees up against his body. His stomach is in knots, he forces himself to remember Algeria. Fragments return, sparse, without connections. The smell of couscous, his mother reprimanding him. And, insistently, a story his grandmother, the second of his grandfather's two wives, used to tell. He no longer remembers the old woman's face, whom he nevertheless adored. The City of Brass, she used to insist, had been raised in the desert of Sijilmassa. The city had really existed. Everything there was made of brass, walls, roofs, fountains . . . The wall around it had no gate; you could get into the city only by climbing over the rampart. Whoever reached the summit would clap his hands (the grandmother had a curious way of slapping one palm against the other) then leap in. The traveller would never emerge again.

The man leaning against the rock is breathing heavily. In the distance, a dingo howls insistently. The animal breaks off, just long enough to get its breath back, then takes up its horrible lamentation again with the same intensity, as if it had been made desperate because there was no reply. Kader's eyes have grown used to the darkness. How desolate this landscape is!

"You were right, Grandmother, the City of Brass does exist. Except, for me, it is a large heap of stones and sand. Will I get away from it one day?"

He picks up a few pebbles, and whiles away the time playing jacks. When he has five stones on the back of his hand, he lets a sigh escape:

"Hey, Trid, and what if I can't manage to unearth a doctor? Would you dare to give us the slip? Just like that, without further ado? You'd join the ranks of your own people and the world would slam the door on you as if you had never existed? Is it possible, that kind of bastardy? And me, would I have played a part in that too?"

He clutches the pebbles. Such remnants of his childhood games. The velvety light caressing the landscape is too beautiful for thoughts as black as his. His lungs swell in rancour:

"Human beings are filth!"

Everything that happened during the day comes back to him: the killings, the blow to Trid's head, the rapes, his own panic. And that woman.

"Lislei . . ."

He curls his lips in puzzlement. She did not reveal to him what fate

196

had been set aside for the little girls until after the troop rode off. Wallace refused to allow the three to join them, arguing that the wagon was too slow and that, in any case, he and his companions would not put their lives in danger on account of Abo vermin, a thief what's more. All were of the same opinion, even Baker. When they went away, they left behind no more than two days' provisions. Lislei put Trid in the back of the wagon, then they set out on what they took to be the way to Rawlings. To cap their bad luck, the axle broke while crossing the river-bed. They made their way back to the refuge, by foot and in the sun. Kader carried Tridarir, making sure he avoided looking at the red-stained bandage around the nape of the neck and over the face. The child half-opened his dazed eyes before sinking into unconsciousness again.

"You have to bring a doctor back," Lislei decided. "I don't know how to ride a horse. Trid and I, we will stay here."

The expression on her face grew hard:

"Get going quickly. The boy won't last long. He relies on you. Wholly."

A shadow veiled her face.

"And me too, besides."

Kader, taken aback, stayed right where he was. Lislei eyed him scornfully, her chin held high. Very softly, she whispered:

"So, don't forget to come back."

She turned away, pretending to be busy harnessing the horse. The curious gleam in her eyes had been enough for Kader. Strangely moved, he thought: little *gaouria*, you are really scared stiff of dying in this desert!

It is the dead of night. From where she is, Lislei can make out a slice of a milky moon. She senses, more than sees, the light bathing the refuge and its surroundings. Now and then, bats with heads like foxes slash across the brightness flooding through the doorway; you could mistake them for leaves carried on the wind. Lislei has almost grown used to them, but she cannot stop herself from listening intently to every sound. From somewhere, an insomniac bird interrogates the surrounding wilderness with insistent recriminations. There are all the other night noises too, the kind to which one pays attention only when afraid.

And Lislei is very afraid. To the point of not having enough saliva in her mouth. When Kader left, everything was still more or less in order. She found a way of keeping herself busy. Making up a place for Trid to lie on, removing the bandages, cleaning the wound, putting the bandages on again, fetching water from the tiny spring. And also, the absurdity of panic, sweeping the room and a part of the yard.

Then there were no more chores. She sat down beside the child. Her own makeshift mattress was ready, but she did not have the courage to stretch out on it. She would have felt more exposed. The child's face was calmer, rigid perhaps; his breathing more even, also less laboured. Should she be glad or was it that Trid's body was preparing itself for the final defeat?

She nibbled on some dried meat, so tough that she had the sensation of chewing on leather. And if Kader did not come back? And if the others came? Baker tried, one last time, to persuade her to join Wallace's troop without the man or the child. Despairing of his cause, he flourished in front of her the menace of the Aborigines.

"You don't know what they subject women to before they kill them," he spat viciously. "They are real savages, cruel and lacking all humanity!"

Stupefied, Lislei protested:

"And the little girls? And the women this morning?"

He complained that she was mixing everything up, they were nothing but lubras, Aboriginal women. Even with the young girls, she shouldn't exaggerate things. Certainly, he was very troubled at the time, it made him indignant, and he told them as much. But all the same, with those blacks, little girls are raped by their fathers, brothers and all the men of their tribe from a very early age.

"They go around naked, so that's normal. It's a little bit their fault too if Wallace and the others . . . I don't want to make excuses for them, but it's been a long time since . . . It's different," he ended peremptorily. "Come with us. Afterwards, it will be too late to be sorry."

"You're no longer disgusted by your companions, as far I can see," she hissed. "What difference is there between the savagery of black people and theirs?"

He reflected, screwing up his face in an effort to convince her:

"We, we are only savage by accident. They are by nature. You've become attached to your little Nigger in the way that people grow attached to a puppy. You aren't going to sacrifice your life for that, are you?"

She shrugged her shoulders, turned her back on him, her heart crushed by incredible hatred. What objection could she have made, except an insult, to that face so assured of its clear conscience?

Towards four or five in the morning, Lislei woke with a start. From fear, then from joy. Yes, she certainly felt Trid's hand searching for hers. She had stretched out beside the lifeless body, promising herself that she would resist falling asleep. Exhaustion was stronger than terror. Snuggling up against the child, she quickly shut her eyes.

It is well after dawn. The child has a vacant look in his eyes. He hasn't really woken up. His eyelids are blinking.

"Are you dreaming?" Lislei murmurs. She feels foolish: she almost asked him: "you haven't died?"

She takes the little fingers in her hand, strokes them. Tridarir, calm again, closes his eyes. A moment later, his breathing indicates that he has fallen asleep again. His shoulder is out of the blanket. The scar on the wound is ugly.

"Snooze as much as you can, little man. So many people would squash you like a fly!"

She puts her lips to his face. Trid is still feverish. The bandages smell bad.

"What is going to become of you? Your maman and your papa, it would be better if they were looking after you. Not two good-for-nothings like us, fleeing like hares chased by wolves."

A louder snore from the child brings a smile to her face:

"They must have loved you very much, your poor parents. Of that I am certain. I have known you for such a short time and, with nothing but your interminable silence and the way you mimic this and that, you have already given me two or three happy memories which aren't going to leave me easily!"

Her hands stray into his thick hair. The frightful hair-do has disappeared. Inexplicably, she wonders:

"Are you handsome or ugly? I'm a fool, aren't I? Look, I'm going to marry you to Camille. She is pretty, my niece, you'll see. You'll make a splendid couple. You so black, she so pink. And me, I'll be carrying an armful of lilac. It smells so sweet, lilac."

Sadness clasps the woman's shoulders like an icy fist:

"Lilac? What am I ranting on about? Camille, my little Camille, perhaps you are dead. Because of me. I did not know how to take care of you . . ."

A sob rises, it sticks in her throat. One more word and she will not be able to restrain it any longer. Forces herself to get up. Yes, to be busy, not to wallow in memories . . . Wash Trid's blood-stained shirt. Get him something to eat. She launches into a mute prayer: "My God, let Kader come back, let him not forget us! Make the Arab . . ."

When she is fully upright, she tries cynicism:

"The gaolbird . . . the fugitive . . . the mur . . ." Quickly, get rid, as well, of this idiotic emotion, which took hold of her when . . .

She is now on her feet. Her head turns towards the doorway. A brief instant, her heart, her lungs freeze.

Then, all of a sudden, she screams. With all the fibres of her being. The black-skinned individual staring at her is brandishing a spear. He is naked, his whole body streaked with white markings. His hair is dishevelled, hanging in filthy strands, the base of the nose pierced with a long spike. He is wearing a ring of ochre feathers around one of his arms.

While her mouth gasps desperately for another gulp of air, Lislei's eyes, popping out of their sockets, have time to register that the man's face, the most terrifying she has ever seen, is slowly dissolving in tears.

Not even in the open Sahara had the sun seemed so fiery to him. Or perhaps he has forgotten what the Sahara is like. Overcome by anger, Kader pulls his hat down over his face. Even though he is melting in sweat, he knows that he is exaggerating. But his disappointment is so bitter that everything, in this half-deserted town, seems infernal to him.

When he reached Rawlings in the middle of the morning, he was still full of hope, despite his exhaustion, the pitiful state of his boots and the limping horse he was dragging behind him. Yesterday's rocky outcrop did indeed take on the appearance of a lizard in the dawn light. All he had to do was to go around it to find himself, at mid-morning, on the outskirts of a large settlement. A good many of the buildings had been abandoned. Some roofs had caved in, doors and shutters were missing. Idle men watched with curiosity as the miserable procession of the newcomer and his lame horse went past. Among them, Kader noticed a sizeable proportion of Asians, probably Chinese. He had already heard about ships that arrive from China and unload their clandestine human cargo in the southern parts of Australia; from there, prospectors, wretched peasants without any equipment, do not hesitate to set out, making their way across bush and desert on foot, for months, to reach the districts which are supposed to bear gold. Many among them do not make it. The survivors are obliged, by contract, to put aside the yield of their first year of prospecting for the benefit of the shipowners. The families of the unlucky ones – those who cannot find enough gold to discharge their debt – become veritable slaves to their creditors in China . . .

At first, luck smiled on Kader. A faded sign allowed him to discover quickly enough the doctor's "consulting rooms", in fact a house with rickety stairs and broken railing which had not been repaired. He held out a piece of paper to the ill-shaved character who opened the door. On it, Lislei beseeched that a "Mister the Physician" should come as quickly as possible to save the life of a gravely injured child. The man guffawed as he gave him back the piece of paper. Despite his impoverished vocabulary, Kader managed to grasp that the doctor had left, more than two months earlier, for lack of paying patients. Not having enough money, the assistant had not been able to follow his employer. "No gold, no money, no life," he sighed nostalgically. He was no more than the practitioner's jack-of-all-trades. He had acquired some experience just by observing the doctor, but he would not risk his life venturing beyond the town without an escort. The district is dangerous: "Abos!", the flunkey explained, making a gesture of running someone through with an imaginary spear. The sombre thought struck Kader: "What would you have said, idiot, if I'd informed you that the child is himself Aboriginal!" Kader left the dusty surgery in despair, carrying a foul-smelling bottle the assistant had sold him, which was supposed to bring the fever down. The man added another piece of advice: clean the wound with rum or brandy.

"Buy a rifle too," he insisted, winking.

A rifle too . . . Kader exhausted by the effort of concentrating managed at last to work out what that meant. Before pushing him out, the fellow seemed to be jawing on about something else, something concerning the use of liquor. The man talked too quickly; Kader did not understand him straight away.

"Scum!" Kader hissed. It is only after a hundred paces that the words he is trying to piece together in his head become a little more intelligible for him. In short, the lackey suggested that he should get hold of plenty of good liquor because, if that does not save the child, it would at least give the parents a handy way of consoling themselves!

The man, walking away, wipes his face. He is overcome by giddiness. And by a need to urinate which he recognises well enough: the result of anguish. The child is going to have a thousand opportunities to die, Kader will never arrive in time! He is a good-for-nothing, a foetus aborted by his mother!

He stops in front of a huge dilapidated building, formerly a bank judging by the imposing inscription. His horse lowers its head, searches in vain for grass to graze on, snorts in resignation. An Asian leaning against the hoarding is placidly examining the passer-by, all the while cutting, with a knife, rounds from a plug of tobacco. He explodes in nasal laughter when the passer-by mumbles:

"Horse . . . Where change . . .? Horse sick . . ."

"You not Engliss! Not Engliss!"

This simple observation plunges him into extraordinary hilarity. "You, Australia's eaten up your brain," the fugitive says to himself, feeling ill at ease. The Chinaman spits into his hand, crumbling the rounds of tobacco into the spittle.

"*You* . . . need not hooose . . . camel . . . not hooose . . . camel . . ."

The Chinaman kneads the tobacco-mixture into a lump which he puts under his tongue. His voice a little less sharp, he continues chuckling:

"Camel good . . . hooose not good . . . go there!" His pigtail, powdered with dust, is flapping against his shoulder. He points his hand towards a group of buildings. Kader cannot understand a word of what the creature is yelling about.

"There!"

"Your laugh's like a bark, that God would sort your head out, you nitwit!" Kader curses him in Arabic.

His interlocutor, thinking that Kader was thanking him, tilts his head forward, unfurls a ribbon of loud trills, punctuated with "not Engliss!"

Everyone takes him for a halfwit, even the halfwitted! Kader, piqued, comes to realise. He ventures, in any event to follow the baccy-chewer's directions. His hand grows weary from chasing away the flies which, by their dozens, swarm around any living thing. Flies, madmen and murderers, that's the most precise way to describe this continent, is his mocking, angry thought.

His first impression was that the sun and fatigue were playing tricks on him.

"It's not possible! . . ."

A dromedary, then a second dromedary came into view as soon as he turned the corner formed by a group of buildings, a few feet away from what seems to be an eating house or a general store. The animals are shut in a pen in full sunshine. The largest of them has just regurgitated, with great concentration, a sticky green lump, which – Kader knows from experience – gives off a remarkably a foetid stink if you get near it.

The fugitive feels a lump forming in his throat as he catches sight of the ungainly appearance of these dromedaries. How long has it been since he mounted one of these fine old beasts, "which display on their back the one ball they're blessed with", as his cousin Hassan used to jest? He has an absurd desire to weep: throughout his childhood, Hassan and he were rivals in daring and in rushing along at breakneck pace on these capricious and grumpy beasts, just managing to avoid the bites they usually deserved!

"And you, are you rotting in the earth, my good Hassan? Ah, you would be astonished by all this, just as I am! But what would you do in my place, you who could never say no to a headlong race or an heroic impulse?"

Lassitude has worn out the fugitive from the chain-gang:

"Hassan, I am an overcharged beast of burden. Any moment now, my back is going to break. Tell me what to do . . ." This impatience to let go of everything, he had already plumbed its depths when the French army drove the last warriors of his group into a blind ravine. "Close off the accounts," Hassan said, "certainly, but not just in any fashion! We always lose, Cousin Kader, but it all depends on the way we accept defeat."

"Do you still believe that, son of my uncle?" Kader grumbles, tapping his fingers on the railing separating him from the dromedaries. "With the French, you did not surrender, and their soldiers put you to death on the spot. Me, I gave myself up and they executed me in another way. So in that case, courage and cowardice, aren't they the same at heart?"

A sigh makes the Algerian's breast heave:

"Ah, Hassan, my friend! How I yearn to bicker with you! As before: you, you were always wrong and I, I was never right . . ."

A humming sound reaches his ears, indistinct at first, then . . .

"What's happening to me today? Am I losing my reason?"

His fingers stop drumming. He crosses the space in front of the slop-house, feeling that he is changing countries and time within a few paces.

On a tiny rug, a prostrate man is at his prayers. He's a Muslim: he has just pronounced the *basmallah* – "In the name of God the Merciful" – in Arabic, before bowing low once more.

The man deep in prayer shudders. He casts an anxious glance at the visitor but remains prostrate. Kader's heart is pounding like a drum. He thinks: "My God, wouldst Thou grant such a gift to one who is no longer Thy servant?"

Without giving it a thought, he kneels down at the side of the other, whose body stiffens. Face turned to the east, Kader listens attentively,

trying to recognise the verse. The accent is strange, he has trouble understanding the voice, which begins to stammer:

"... *God will say: How long tarried ye in the earth, counting by years?
They will say* ..."

Kader takes it up:

"... *We tarried by a day or part of a day Ask of those who keep count!
They will say* ..."

The man's disquiet turns into stupefaction, then into a smile of incred-
ulous joy:

"... *Ye tarried but a little if ye only knew!* ..."

"... *Deemed ye then that We had created you for naught* ..."

The two voices are now in accord, two strings of a lute:

"... *And that ye would be raised towards your Creator?*"

The man on the mat is visibly moved. His pupils sparkle with gratitude. He launches into a new verse:

"... *Say: I seek refuge in the Lord of the Daybreak from the evil of that
which He created* ..."

Eyelids lowered, the former student in the Great Mosque of Damascus
takes up the strain without hesitation – and each word has a sharp sweetness, born from the heart of enchanted days:

"... *From the evil of darkness when it is intense* ..."

When they pronounce the absolving "*Amen*", they remain silent for a
few seconds, neither daring to look at the other. Kader is the first to rise
to his feet. A strange thought has sprouted in his mind: "O my God, in
whom I no longer believe, this, all of this is nothing but inconsequen-
tial words! Thanks be to Thee, none the less, for reminding me of the
time when I could be happy without malice!"

The man who has just blasphemed bitterly, in his secret soul, offers
his hand to his companion in prayer. The other stays on his knees, shivering from the ardour of his appeal to his God. Eyes dazed with gratefulness,
he seizes the hand held out to him and kisses it. A frog in his throat,
Kader bows ceremoniously:

"*Assalam Alaykum!*"

"*Alaykum Assalam!*"

They confine themselves to exchanging greetings of peace in Arabic. His interlocutor cannot speak the language. Like most Muslims who are not Arab, he prays in the language of the Koran, but does not understand it. Disappointment and joy are simultaneously inscribed on the features of the owner of the slop-house.

"Who are you? . . . Me Afghan . . . Afghan, you know . . . Pashtun? You from?"

Damned English! Kader fulminates. What does he have to do to explain that he comes from a country called Algeria and that, well . . . Annoyed, suddenly impatient, he points his finger at the pen:

"I want . . . I want . . ."

"You want . . . what?"

The camel-driver's features contract. He has very brown skin, it looks like leather. Because of his lined face, he seems to be very old, just like those merchants in the souk in Damascus who are able to spend hours in the sun spying out for potential customers. Lizards with turbans is what the urchins of Damascus called them. What coincidence was it – whether driven by it or not, Kader asks himself almost with a sense of affection – that has led him into this blind alley at the end of the world, flanked by a slop-house and two dromedaries? "What are we doing here here, you and I, eh?"

For the moment, the Afghan does not disguise his displeasure at the newcomer's unseemly behaviour. How is it possible to share a prayer without sharing a conversation?

"You . . . want camel?"

"Yes . . . camel!"

Doubtful pupils size up the man, young despite his exhausted look and the several days' growth of beard on his face. Is he really a Muslim, this coxcomb, with his light-coloured skin and the face of a Christian? Nevertheless, the stranger can recite the Koran so well! What if this imbecile had received a Sign from On High? . . .

Kader realises that he has robbed the merchant of a great joy. He flourishes his banknotes, repeating stupidly:

"Camel . . . Yes!"

As the fugitive leaves the Afghan's place, he is perched on a dromedary, the less vigorous of the two, what is more. The camel-driver, out
of sorts, refused to sell him a second beast, despite a fresh display of
banknotes. There was a look of hatred in his eyes when Kader asked
whether he sold liquor.

When he emerges into the open space in front of the Bank of London,
the rider is still trying to balance, between the saddle and the animal's
neck, the sack of beans he had obtained in exchange for the horse.
Sniggering, the owner of the slop-house had made clear, with his fingers
bunched at his mouth, what fate he had in store for the limping mount.
Kader frowned, ill at ease:

"You poor bag of bones, in the hours to follow, when you come to
think of me, you'll hate me as the king of all false friends."

The Chinaman is still standing in the sun. A group of men, several with
horses, are in a heated discussion in middle of the open space. As soon as
the Asian notices Kader swaying on his dromedary, he breaks into strident
cackling. Kader forces himself to look the other way, but the Chinaman
keeps chirping excitedly, wagging his finger: "Camel, camel!" With a mixture
of pity and irritation, the fugitive mutters between his teeth:

"Shut up, idiot! What's buggered you up so much, something you left
behind there in China you can't do without?"

He has now reached the group of men. The inn is on the other side
of the street. He is running out of time, perhaps they'll let him have a
bottle of something. A horse neighs, its curiosity aroused when the
dromedary comes into its field of vision. Lost in his thoughts, Kader has
failed to look at the people around him.

"Hey?"

The brutal exclamation makes him start. He puts his hand to his eyes,
shading them from the sun.

"You!"

Kader's body grows stiff from disgust: it's Cribb, the daddy-rapist of
the little girls. Clearly, there's nothing surprising about that: he and his
stooges could only have reached the town the previous day. There is Ted
too, the youngest. The other two are unknown to him.

Cribb is beaming. With a yelp of joy, he turns to the man standing next to him:

"It's him! Him, I'm telling you!"

A man of some forty years is examining him attentively. Anxiety comes crashing down over Kader: that set expression, those neat features, despite the dust and heat, remind him of another face. Where has he seen it before? And why is he already so afraid of it?

The features of the man next to Cribb relax. He is exultant:

"Bastard, do you recognise me?"

The same cutting voice, the same pupils surrounded by that strange washed-out blue. He caught a brief glimpse of him only once, in the hold of the ship and in semi-darkness. But the resemblance to the seaman, who was drowned while tied to his mast, cuts off any doubt.

Kader's body rears in terror. He kicks the dromedary's neck in a violent effort to force it to go forward. The animal, taken by surprise, snorts. Despite the beast's braying, Kader can make out the click of a rifle as it is cocked. His dejection is mingled with a kind of icy relief: does it come as easy as this, then, the end of the world? Is he going to be discharged, once and for all, from the duty to live courageously?

His hands are shaking like two enraged beasts; his spirit is preoccupied, however, with calling to mind once more a verse from the *Book of Songs*: "*the world is a rose, breathe in its perfume and give it to your friend*".

"Trid . . . Lislei, I have never given you a rose," he mutters, turning to face the group of men.

Thinking of that rose has made him feel stupid. He thinks about nothing at present. Filthy terror creeps up his spine. He wonders how is he going to behave if he is not struck down straight away. Fear must have made him look hideous. A heartbreaking desire surges within him, lending him the last few ounces of courage: if he could go back, a handful of minutes only, and change direction . . . Oh, not to have strayed into this place . . .

"Down!" the hunter of Aborigines barks.

And Ted, with an artless laugh, tips the rider off his mount by pulling on the leg of his trousers.

18

The dark-skinned man stared at her in incredible distress. From the way he stood there, he must have been looking at her for a good while. He wiped, with rage, the tears flowing out of his eyes, smudging the traces of white pigment on his cheeks. He turned to the woman, spear still held high. At first Lislei thought that she was going to die. She put her hand in front of her in a risible gesture of shielding herself.

The naked man struck her with the flat of his hand. He knelt down and examined the sleeping child. With a light touch, he brushed his fingers over the head then the red-stained bandage.

He stood up. His face, lined deep with sorrow, spoke just as much of surprise. Because of the design daubed on his face, he resembled, for an instant, a terrifying moon-struck Pierrot. He murmured something. The peeping or the chirping of strange birds.

He had, in fact, asked her a question. He fixed his gaze firmly in the woman's eyes. Lislei glimpsed – she lowered her head quickly – one eye aflame with suffering and the other with anger.

He left the room with an abrupt bark. Of despair, probably. Lislei then spent the whole night waiting for Kader to return, losing hope little by little, ceaselessly going back to the image of that terrible warrior who had wept in front of her, filling her all along with such great dread. Certainty, hesitantly sprouting at first, then irrefutable, overwhelmed her in the course of the afternoon. A man weeps like that only when losing . . . no . . . not his wife, no . . . not even his father or mother . . . no, only when a horrible fate has overtaken his child!

"Yes, the father of one, maybe several, of the little girls who'd been raped . . . And perhaps, the height of misfortune . . . the husband of one of the slaughtered women as well . . . He came for revenge . . ."

Trid woke only once during the course of that interminable day. He fell asleep again, exhausted, after taking a little nourishment. The relief of knowing him to be getting better was not enough to allow Lislei to master her fear. That feeling came to resemble a persistent nausea, so diffuse that the woman even asked herself, on two or three occasions, what its source might be. The answer struck her in the face, her heart started to beat like a drum. And the wish to crawl into the deepest burrow.

"Kader, I implore you, come back . . ."

While she was praying, Lislei dreamt of snow, of the fragrant Sunday *Kugelhopf* her mother used to get ready on Fridays, and of wolves howling in the forests around her native Rhineland.

The warriors turned up at dusk. Bringing with them a strong smell of damp dogs. And a compact, violent hostility, lacking all expressive gestures. Five men, stark naked, all armed with spears, their bodies scored with the same white tracings. The warrior she had seen that morning accompanied them, followed by an old man with satchels around his neck.

Without a word, without glancing at the petrified woman, the old man hurried to the child stretched out on the floor.

A little time has passed. Lislei has lit a candle. In the room, apart from the woman, there is no-one except the old medicine man, and the man she saw in the morning. The others have dispersed around the refuge, lying in ambush probably.

All act as if Lislei does not exist. Wanting to get something warm to drink, she went out into the yard to set a fire. But one of the Aborigines, raising his spear to make his intention clear, forced her inside. He was afraid, no doubt, that the fire would attract others.

Lislei is huddling in the darkest corner. She cannot see what the old man is doing to Trid. All she could hear was the little boy waking up, spluttering like someone being made to drink, crying out in surprise and then soothed with some kind of a chant. Trid asked, in a faint, anxious voice: "Li, here?"

"I am here, Trid, don't be afraid!" she replied, forcing herself to keep an even tone.

The woman no longer knows whether she has been more frightened, or less, since these men appeared. She has grown accustomed to the suffocating fog clouding her brain, the inability to grasp that she herself might be put to death. Overcome by the need to urinate, she is almost grateful to her body because it has contrived to occupy her mind with that.

Without a sound, one of the men has come into the room. Out of breath, he leans down to the old man's ear. The medicine man and the two warriors rush outside. There is a whispered exchange, then nothing more.

The silence is total, apart from Tridarir's gentle snoring. No, they could not have gone away again just like that! Lislei, on her knees, creeps to the door. Her ears are buzzing from stress.

At last, rising above the noise in her ears, the sound, more and more distinct, of horses' hoofs in the yard. An uproar, a torch thrust through the door, guffawing men pushing someone else in front of them. Whose arms are tied. And face all swollen.

In his sleep, Tridarir is luxuriating in his dream: it is a *good* dream and he does not believe that any better will come to him. Be careful, above all, not to hurry the dream along. The dream could get annoyed, change its mind. It is his most precious possession, this dream. His only treasure, what is more, since . . . Since.

The sleeper's heart is overflowing with happiness because this is the favourite among all the dreams that have deigned to keep him company: the child is young, much younger than now. He is in his mother's arms. His father is sitting on a tree trunk; he has put aside his customary anger, that beast devouring his head. His eyes are almost smiling. As he observes the two of them, his fingers trace, with a melancholy gesture, the lines of the raised skin on his chest, which had been left behind by the scarring of his initiation. They are somewhere in the rainforest, they have eaten well. The mother purses her lips to blow a kiss on Tridarir's mouth. The boy whoops with joy. He knows that his mother and father love him more than their own life. His tender-hearted mother gathers up the most beautiful stones of the forest and clicks them in her hand to make him laugh. His father lifts him with one hand and . . .

. . . Drops of water fall on his face. The child opens his eyelids slowly. It requires incredible exertion. Never has he had so much sleep. Just above him, there is a terrifying face which he instantly recognises. Which he would recognise whatever the circumstances. The leader of the band of killers on the island with his enormous leer. Tridarir goes back to sleep with an easy mind. It is a dream within the dream. An evil dream which only wants room to grow, to kill the good dream. That can happen, the venomous snake-dream; it is possible, however, to frustrate that abortion of a reptile by treating it with resolute disdain . . .

So the father scratches his nose and growls; he has been moved more than he would care to admit:

"One day, my son, I will initiate you. One day you too, will have children, and you will initiate them . . ."

That is the part Tridarir likes best: *you too, you will have children*. That must mean that he is not the last. Father, say it again! And the resplendent warrior, as grand as the finest tree in the forest, continues, in a way so docile and gentle that he is sure his tears are going to flow: *you too, will have . . .*

A veritable flood breaks over the child's face, getting into his nose, choking him, making him groan in pain.

His eyes are now wide open. And only one wish: to scream like the wombat when the thylacine wolf has it by the throat!

Lislei snarls:

"Why did you do that? He's been seriously injured . . ."

She is still in fear of her own life. But she can no longer bear Trid's terror-stricken imploring: no sound emerges from the lad's lips, but he cranes his head as if he were being strangled. She has recognised, sure enough, the captain's brother: the physical likeness is astonishing. Her heart ready to burst, the same face comes back to her, the same body, in someone a little older, a little more pasty-faced, that used to heave beside her whispering obscenities . . .

O'Hara closes his waterbag. He is no longer smiling. Four men, weapons in hand, crowd behind him. Two are familiar: Ted and Cribb! On the floor, Kader. He has been beaten black and blue. He is conscious. He lifts his head to her, his eyes cloud over.

The leader of the gang cuts her off curtly:

"Little slut, look at what we've found! It needed patience to find you, you and your filthy . . ." – he pauses sarcastically – "husband!"

He clicks his tongue in satisfaction.

"All the same, you made the task easier for me. What a funny idea to hang on to the little Nigger! Wherever you'd planted your filthy paws, people remembered very clearly that you'd been by. This may be an empty land, but we get to find out about everything that goes on in this little corner of Australia."

Lislei tries to moisten her lips. But her tongue is dry.

"What are you going to do with the boy?"

"For the moment, he is in no danger. This is valuable merchandise for me. I am going to get a very high price for him. Especially because I need it very much. And my men too."

"The . . . the purchasers, what are they going to do with him?"

"That's not my business or yours. They can dissect him, pickle him, put him in a zoo, I won't give a damn as soon as someone pays me a good price!"

"But he's a child, have some pity for him!"

"This isn't a child, it is a little ape, an aborted animal! No-one pities a lamb when it's led to the slaughter, as far as I know. Not even you!"

O'Hara is amused by the look on his captive's face. For a foreigner, she speaks good English! Perhaps she hasn't understood yet that she is going to die?

"You know very well that he is a human being, don't you?"

"You can't be a human being with skin as black as that and with such a mug."

"But it's not his fault that he was born an Aborigine!"

"Oh well, all he had to do was not to get born."

Revulsion makes the woman gasp:

"You . . . you are saying . . . you are going to kill him . . . simply because he was born?"

"I don't want to kill him, I want to sell him."

"But you didn't hesitate doing that to his parents and the others. You are a . . . you are a . . ."

Lislei does not finish, but a whole world of contempt flushed through her stammering words.

"Let's get back to the point. Of the two of us, I am not the most inhumane. With your accomplice, you killed my brother even though he helped you escape. All that just to fleece him!"

Lislei opens her mouth, but the man stifles her:

"Shut your mouth you filthy whore. This is what you stole!"

He hurls to the ground a thin wad of money fastened with a length of thread.

"I found this in the pocket of that crook . . ."

With brutal force, he kicks the dark shape on the ground. A faint "argh!" is the only reaction. Horrified, Lislei thinks: they are going to do the same to me!

O'Hara, short of breath, struggling to calm himself, continues:

"In this little wad, there's all my brother's savings and a part of mine. Him, you've killed; me, you've ruined."

O'Hara's voice breaks:

"It so happens, you know, that I loved him, my brother. And he loved me too. He was a father to me. We used to say: we are a pair of twins, though we weren't born at the same time . . ."

Lislei screws up her eyes to hide her astonishment: this murderer, who seems so moved, is being sincere! Cribb nods his head, fawningly: "What misfortune, such ingratitude."

Frozen with fear, Lislei manages to ask:

"What are you going to do with us?"

O'Hara pulls a sarcastic face:

"You mean, am I going to kill you, you and your fucker?"

Panic overcoming her, Lislei begins to implore:

"That cannot be your . . . your intention, I am sure!"

O'Hara licks his lips before pursing them:

"But of course I'm going to kill you. And no later than straight away. You, all the time you've got left is however long it takes you to count on your fingers the number of years you lived . . ."

His "conceit" has pleased him. He gives a little laugh, filled with hatred and contempt:

". . . up to the damned day we first met. Off you go, trollop!"

He points his pistol at Lislei. The other has only one wish: "My God, let me not urinate in front of these men!"

"Count, or I'll fire straight away!"

Her mind numb with terror, Lislei begins to count quickly: "one . . . two . . . three", slows down, increases the pace because the barrel is now closer to her. O'Hara grins in commiseration:

"You can make yourself a bit older than you are. I'd understand, it goes without saying. But don't overdo it."

The men chuckle. Ted's laugh is the most penetrating. Lislei's abrupt scream turns into a squeal as a sob rises in her breast:

"All the same, you wouldn't dare to kill us in front of witnesses, would you?"

O'Hara arches his eyebrows and examines her with intense astonishment. Lislei is gnawed by an insane, animal hope. O'Hara has turned to the group of men:

"Lawson, Flynn, do you see any witnesses?"

There is, at first, a gleam of incomprehension in the eyes of the two henchmen. O'Hara asks again, with an even broader smile:

"Well, boys?"

"No, boss, we can see no witnesses."

There is a note of joyous expectation in Flynn's reply. Ted bursts out laughing, without really knowing why.

"Shitty little Frenchie, do you see any witnesses? There're none."

"And . . .?" Lislei makes a final imploring attempt.

"Them, the old bloke and the young 'un? One as greedy as the other.

But these idiots are already as good as dead. They swallowed my story about sharing the money with them if they showed me where to find you. Me, I only wanted one of them for a guide, but the young fellow insisted on tagging along."

Ted still has the trace of a smile on his face. His lower lip droops, he is flabbergasted by the outrageousness of what his new leader has just said. With a moan of despair, Cribb tries to load his rifle, but Flynn has already shoved a barrel against his temple.

"Outside," O'Hara orders. "Do it properly."

The candle is the only light in the room. Outside, Cribb can be heard begging: "Have pity on my children, they still need me!", Ted's astonished protests: "But you're out of your mind, you can trust me, I'm honest!" followed by the first shot, a scream of terror, a second shot. And silence punctuated by the raucous trills of a night bird.

Like two useless flies . . . And now it is going to be my turn . . . Me I'm a fly too. And I've come as far as this only to die like a fly! This thought, like a screech inside her head, makes the woman's body, limbs, brain shrivel. She feels ready to endure any vileness just to live one day longer. Lislei manages to whimper:

"Is it so easy, then, for you to be cruel?"

O'Hara knits his brow with a smug look on his face. He is agreeably surprised at having such a question put to him. As if she, whom he is about to kill, had, nevertheless, found time to be interested in him. The pretence of a smile breaks over his face.

"Don't fool yourself. Nothing's easier than killing someone. It's a most ordinary task. If you've never done it, you believe that it requires an effort to be, as you say, cruel. Cruelty, you see, is oppressive, unpleasant, it harms those who experience it. An indigestion of the emotions, in sum."

His articulation is less dry. As if he were grateful to her for furnishing him with an opportunity to show off.

"There wouldn't be so many deaths in this world if it were necessary each time to have feelings as excessive as cruelty or hate, for example."

He takes the pistol in his other hand. His posture, head cocked and turned towards the door, reveals that he is waiting for his two henchmen to return.

"Wiping out Abos, that's my trade. A popular trade in this country, thank God. And I get paid for it. In Tasmania there's nothing left for our kind to do, but not on the mainland! We're going to clean out Australia, get rid of all the parasites, dingos and Niggers above all. Those two kinds of bastards don't make good bedfellows with the people who are really going to make this country grow, the farmers and miners. When I pick off a family of Niggers, believe me, my beauty, I'm doing something altogether normal. If you were to tell me some story or other for children, I'd feel, I know it myself, a few pin-pricks of tender-heartedness . . ."

Nevertheless, O'Hara is already uneasy. The blue slits of his eyes have trouble masking their impatience.

"You see, the two characters who thought that they'd been recruited, I didn't need to make any special arrangements for them. Professional necessity, let's say. With you, there is something special: there's revenge. And hate, because I have been thinking about it for so long. And inevitably, it's more nerve-racking for me . . . Less than for you, I realise," he has just enough time to add.

A scream cuts through the silence. Explosions. Oaths. Another outcry. Made more jerky by pain. The noise of panic-stricken flight. A dull thud against the outer wall of the room.

"Put out the candle," O'Hara barks. He jumps to the side of the room opposite the door to look for cover, trips over the fettered prisoner.

"Mongrel . . ."

Lislei grabbed hold of O'Hara's arm but the man did not drop his pistol. Despite losing his balance, his free arm raises the gun. Lislei shuts her eyes, only waiting for the horrible bullet to strike.

O'Hara's hand has grown rigid. A strong, familiar smell penetrates the woman's nostrils. Her first thought: "I am not yet dead"; her second: "I want so much to have a piss."

A black man is leaning over them. In his hand a spear, its tip pressing against O'Hara's throat. By light of the moon, Lislei notices that droplets of blood are forming at the point of contact. But the captain's brother is alive. He is breathing with great care, to limit the in-and-out motion of his larynx, which is hard up against the tip of the spear. The warrior, the one who had wept, is using his spear only to pin the man to the ground.

The warrior picks up the pistol. He calls out something. Suddenly, the room fills with Aborigines. One of them lights a torch from the candle.

Lislei is trembling. These naked men with tangled hair and beard, whose genitals hang between their legs, are better dressed than she is. A garment of sorrow. And of hatred. Suddenly one of them brandishes a club in her face while the other sets about kicking Kader and O'Hara.

Lislei hasn't enough strength to defend herself. Her last instinct is to make herself crouch, so that the club strikes her on the head, rather than the face. Not to die disfigured.

A whining, strident sound rings out. Abruptly, little arms grasp Lislei's trunk, then let go. Without interrupting the flow of his aggressive moans, Tridarir hurls himself at the legs of the man who is showering Kader with blows. The child shields the pinioned prisoner's head with his hands. More and more enraged, he asks a question, and grows impatient at the silence of the adults with the spears.

Tridarir bursts out sobbing. Because he has come to realise that these men, essentially indistinguishable from his father, cannot, however, understand him. Because the pain in his neck has become unbearable.

He sobs silently, in front of the frozen adults. One of them coughs. The old medicine man is leaning over the child. He strokes his face, murmuring something. Without any result. Lislei, her heart shattered, tries to go over to Trid. The warrior nearest to her, more puzzled than hostile, blocks her way.

"But he's my . . . he's my . . ."

Lislei falls silent: *her* little fellow is weeping all by himself, he tried to save her life and she can do nothing to comfort him. A spasm of distress rises in her stomach. Never has an instant seemed so unjust to her.

The man who seems to be the leader of the group (the one whom Lislei called the warrior-of-tears) points to the yard. Four bodies are piled near the horses. Corpses, with the exception of old Cribb, who is only wounded and moans when catching sight of the Aborigines' torch.

The warrior-of-tears addresses Lislei with a grunt. His face taut, he embarks on some kind of a mime: the palm of the hand indicates height, someone bending down, other incomprehensible gestures. The Aborigine's breathing grows shorter, he repeats his weird gestures, at present explicitly obscene. He points to the corpses, one by one, with an questioning posture of the head . . .

Lislei has understood. The man, pointing to his penis, weeps once more. The warrior-of-tears is merely asking her whether one of the men had taken part in the murders and the rape of the little girls.

With Cribb's cries of protest when one of the Aborigines grabbed him by the hair still ringing in her ears, Lislei has come back inside. The warrior-of-tears touches Kader lightly with his spear, the woman says no with her head.

"What are you plotting?" O'Hara growls when Lislei extends her arm in his direction.

"He ordered me to point out to him those who, the day before yesterday, killed their women and raped their little girls. I think his daughter was one of them."

"What are you ranting on about? I've never touched any Nigger woman. It would disgust me too much!"

Lislei gazes at him, with a faint smile. Once again she points her index finger. An Aborigine has grabbed the hunter from behind, holding him by the waist . . .

"Do you see my finger? I am about to tell the father that you abused his little girl . . ."

"But you are a lying whore," O'Hara turns red with rage as he struggles to free himself from the Aborigine's restraint. One of the warriors makes him kneel, with blows of the club to the calf.

Lislei is as white as a sheet. She casts a glance at Trid, whom the medicine man has forced to lie down again. Squatting, the old man intones a chant or a prayer. The woman's heart is throbbing with hatred:

"I hope they will make you pay very dearly. And that they'll take their time over it!"

O'Hara is dragged into the yard by the man with the club. His back bumps against the two outside steps.

"You've no right to accuse me. Tell them that you are lying, slut . . . Ah!"

He receives a fresh blow of the club. Lislei goes out into the yard. Never has someone's suffering been a matter of such indifference for her. Cruelty is not necessary, that murderer had said with irony in his voice.

"Help, he's broken my leg . . ."

The voice is stifled:

"Tell them, I beg you. They are going to torture me for days! We belong to the same race . . . In the name of Christ save me!"

Another scream. Blows. The sound of bones breaking. An Aborigine ties his feet and hands.

"You don't have the right . . . You are white, like me . . . These are blacks . . . you haven't . . ."

A fist in the face silences the man, who is thrown, like a sack, on the back of a horse.

The moon is shining brightly above the deserted yard. As long as she is urinating, Lislei can allow herself not to cry. *They took Trid.*

She watches as the liquid traces a channel, quickly sucked up by the dusty ground. She has the impression that her kidneys are weeping out the tears in her head. That they may never exhaust the brine of her grief.

"I didn't tell him that I loved him. And he needs me!"

Camille first, then Trid.

A flying fox glides past her, looking like a stiff rag. The woman's body is heavy, filled with sorrow. Her breath scant, she makes for the shelter. For the first time, she realises that staying alive can be degrading.

Inside the room, the candle has gone out. The man, still bound, murmurs: "Is that you Lislei? Trid, where is he?" She unties him without saying a word. She would have too much trouble keeping her voice level. The man can barely stir.

She helps him move over to the couch where the child had been. Lights the candle, undresses her companion, cleans the many wounds with water.

She takes off her clothes and lies down beside him. "Oh Lislei . . ." the Algerian's breath is almost a plea.

Strange celebration of despair. The man lying on the pile of blankets reaches out, hesitates, strokes a shoulder. He would like to caress his companion's soul and haunches, to remove the oppressive poison of her pain. To cover her gently with bruises until she is no longer able to hear, in this time of pleasure, the sound of the missing child.

She is rigid all over. He leans towards her, whispers:

"One day, Lislei, I will give you fruit and snow."

A moment of silence. He can sense astonishment in her accelerated breathing. Then he places his lips on the nape of the neck.

19

She has turned crimson. He just had time to glimpse the lower part of her body. She got dressed quickly and went out into the yard. He closed his eyes to savour this birth of a memory.

The sun has resumed its brutal toil. Kader finds it difficult to get up. All of his body hurts. When she was on top of him, and he on top of her, the wounds and contusions were so painful that he could have bellowed. But the softness of the woman's hands, her thighs and her breasts encircled him, then quelled the urge to groan, relegating it to the background for the time being. He ejaculated inside her and cried out when she clamped her legs around his, with force. He choked with laughter, moaned in pain: it was on his backside that the riders' boots had been the most relentless . . .

She did not laugh. Her breathing hoarse, she kept moving her pelvis around. There was, already, sperm between her legs when, with a violent jerk, she grasped his shoulders, then snuggled up against him.

"Kader, I want to find Trid."

The whole morning went by waiting for these words, each hoping that the other would raise the subject. Hobbling, Kader caught the dromedary on which O'Hara and his band had brought him there. The beast had been nibbling, without much conviction, on the bark of the casuarina. The Aborigines had taken everything away: horses, prisoners and corpses. The dromedary must have seemed too ludicrous to them.

They ate poorly. There was little food left. Their eyes avoided each other's, they did not speak about the previous night, neither about the killings, nor about love. Kader pulled out the wad of notes he had discovered in a corner of the room. The Aborigines had not seen it or had ignored it. Because he thought it was time, he started dividing up the money.

"Why are you only making two piles?"

Lislei, shattered, stared at him. It took Kader several seconds to understand. He blushes.

"Kader, I want to find Trid."

She grasps his hand, lets it go. Her voice is like a dirge:

"I miss him . . . he is so little . . ."

She bends down, fiddles with some twigs.

"I am not very proud of myself . . ."

He notices that the sides of her nose are pearly with tiny drops of sweat. She lifts her head, wants to take up the conversation, gives up. Filled with resentment.

So, without really setting their minds to it, they settled down to wait. Waiting for the child, obviously. At first, they did not talk about it like that. To speak about it directly would have been foolish, you cannot talk sensibly about impossible hopes. To talk about it could even have lessened the chance of realising that hope. No, they decided that they must stay at the shelter, until Kader regained his strength and things "settled down".

"We have nowhere to go at present," Lislei declared in an ardent voice. "We'll stay here a week or two, there's as much water as we need and we can buy food in Rawlings. That's the best solution, I am sure."

"What hypocrisy!" Kader sniggered to himself, without allowing any of his anxiety to show. It was plain to see that the best thing would be, on the contrary, to leave straight away: the Aborigines could return with much more aggressive intentions towards them, O'Hara's companions, or perhaps Ted's and Cribb's, are about to set out in search of them.

Kader got on the dromedary again. He needed less time than on the first occasion to find Rawlings. Clenching his teeth because his buttocks were tormenting him, he crossed the open space without running up against any opposition, and startled the astonished Afghan out of his afternoon nap.

On his return, loaded with foodstuff, he grumbled, as soon as the cylindrical shapes of the termite mounds around the shelter came into view:

"You'd think I've come home . . ."

That "home" alarms him. How could he have thought that? It had at first put him in a good mood: Lislei would agree, perhaps, to tend his wounds once more and . . . His mood changed almost immediately: what would become of him if he took so easily to trampling on the most sacred of his memories, those which gave him the strength not to succumb to the madness of New Caledonia? "Home", that could only be Biskra, the mauve and green oasis of his parents, of his childhood, not this Australia of madmen where everything is out of kilter, both nature and cruelty. Returning to Algeria, or at least to Damascus, isn't that the only way of recovering at least a part of that sweet "home"?

And then what should he do about that woman? And that lad, whose misfortune is so horrible that it passes all understanding. Why that tenacious sense of being accountable – and before whom? – for the fortunes of both one and the other? Had he escaped just to fall, feet shackled, into the trap of other people's fate?

The first true question, poor idiot, is why your heart beats so fast when your eyes meet hers? The second, Trid, that little black boy who rose up from the pit of time, isn't it merely the case that you have taken to loving him and that you can't do anything about that? Without taking into account, ha ha, that he had, moreover, saved – and without shilly-shallying like you – your mediocre and insignificant life . . .

Night began to swallow up the outline of the shelter. Kader unsaddled his dromedary. Lislei ran up to him. She stammered out: "Did it go all right?" as if she had been afraid that he might not come back. Kader answered her greeting with a grunt. His ill humour was worse. He turned his back on the woman.

*   *   *

224

They settled into this bitter expectation, all the more painful because they never mentioned either its object or what limit they had set on it. They spent the first days jumping at the least suspicious noise and, above all, avoiding each other, by a tacit agreement which ensured that they were never both in the same place for long. At night they slept in the usual room, but separated by as great a distance as possible. As soon as they woke up and for as long as the sun allowed them, they prowled around the shelter on their own, among the termite mounds and the thorny scrub, turning gloomy questions over in their minds, without finding any answers. They met up again at meal times, exchanging a few sharp words, always on the brink of quarrelling. Both realised that they could not sustain indefinitely that kind of guard-duty in the desert, and each resented – perhaps on account of that celebrated night which was never mentioned, however – that the other was in just as much despair. On one sole occasion, on the third or fourth day, Kader ventured:

"What are you going to do *after*?"

"After what?"

He himself did not know what he had meant by that "*after*". She blushed, as if someone had asked her an indecent question.

"Lislei, we can't stay here for ever!"

"Oh, you!" she burst out. "You only think of your own skin! And the little boy?"

"Do you really believe that they are going to give him back to us? What would we do with him then? Isn't he better off with them?"

She stood up abruptly and went outside to seek refuge behind one of the mounds. Kader did not see her again until nightfall. Her eyelids were puffy. She muttered a vague "Excuse me," and went to bed without food. That night, Kader felt miserable.

The next day, she asked:

"Would you show me, please, how to get on the camel?"

"What?"

"Have I said or done something inappropriate?"

A mulish look broke over her face. Kader retorted, with good humour:

"In the first place, it's not a camel but a dromedary!"

Lislei smiled:

"And how do you say that in Arabic, a dromedary?"

Cheered by that smile, Kader suddenly thought: "Kohl would suit you, Miss Hoity-Toity, stubborn as a 100-year-old goat!"

He spent the whole day showing her how to manage a dromedary:

"Getting off a dromedary, that's nothing. It's climbing on its back that's hardest: you turn your head towards your mount, you hook your fingers in its nares, you immobilise the dromedary that way. And then you leap as quickly as possible into the saddle. Be sure not to get your feet caught up in your dress. If you are too slow to jump, it could get annoyed and bite you!"

Lislei, docile and attentive, listened to her companion's explanations. They were both delighted to have found an occupation which made possible a less tense relationship. She was willing to copy Kader's actions ceaselessly, failing on several occasions, even falling off the dromedary, which began to show signs of impatience.

"Your feet, you place them on the neck . . . No, not like that!"

In the evening, aching, scratches all over her body, covered in dust, she inquired:

"Do you think I'll manage to do it?"

In her voice, an excessive anxiety, out of all proportion to the mere feat of learning or failing to learn how to ride a dromedary. Kader, embarrassed, cracked a joke:

"One more week at this rate and you'll be going on *meharis* across the Sahara, if you don't break your neck first."

It was only on the following day that he came to appreciate the reason for her rage to learn to ride a dromedary. When he woke at dawn, she had already disappeared. He thought at first that she had gone for a walk around the termite mounds. But the dromedary was no longer where he had tethered it. He spent the morning cursing her at first, then eating his heart out with worry. She had no experience of the desert, nor did she know how to take bearings in a featureless landscape. She risked falling from her mount, no longer able to find her way back to the shelter, dying of thirst, what else?

He climbed on the roof and stayed there looking out for her. Baking in the sun, he tried to gather his thoughts, confused as he was by the extent of his own panic, by his inner turmoil. The bottom of the human heart is farther than the end of the earth, his mother used to claim.

That feeling that he was harbouring a hedgehog in his breast, which kept extending and retracting its quills, stayed with him until, in the middle of the afternoon, the shape of the dromedary came into view. He climbed down from the roof and pretended to be busy getting the meal ready. When she came towards him, he was seething with anger and happiness.

She had an exhausted look. Suddenly, he noticed her cracked lips.

"I wanted to go over that way . . ."

Her voice was veiled, hoarse. Kader almost suggested that she should drink a little water first. But she had caused him so much anxiety . . . Raising her arm, she pointed into the distance. Kader's features remained set.

"When they took Trid away, they went that way. I simply thought I'd go along in that direction. Perhaps to show them, too, that we were still in these parts. I told myself . . ."

Her arm fell.

"And then, very quickly, I got lost. I'd taken nothing with me . . . I had the fright of my life . . ."

Pointing to the dromedary, which was grazing on some scrawny mulga berries, she gave a miserable little laugh:

"That is what brought me back here."

He offered her some water. She took the bowl. The rolled-back sleeve of her dress revealed some ugly scratches on her forearm.

"Were you worried?"

He scowled in irritation:

"No. Why, should I have been?"

Then, frowning as he saw her face cloud over:

"Yes, I was worried. A little."

*   *   *

Throughout the following days, they were occupied in exploring the countryside around the shelter. One in the saddle, the other on foot, changing places regularly, they took a different direction each morning, not returning to the shelter until the end of the day. Both lost in their thoughts, they travelled in silence for the most part, hoping and dreading at the same time that they would come across those naked men of the desert. Occasionally Kader felt that he was back again in the Sahara of his adolescence, at the time when he used to set out to hunt ostriches with his cousin. With the same terrors and the same constraints: fix firmly in his head the tiny details of the landscape, stay alert in spite of the monotony, restrict his movements and rein in his imagination . . . That was easier to say than to do, especially when it was Lislei's turn to walk on foot. Kader, on his *rahla*, could not stop himself from gazing at the determined figure which kept going without complaint, despite the blisters on her feet, the heat, and those clouds of flies swarming from nowhere . . . There was no repetition of that first night, each locked within an almost hostile reserve, with a vague understanding that the nature of their relationship had changed, that they had reached the edge of a chasm where they had to make a choice which would prove costly, perhaps irremissible. On two or three occasions, however, Kader forced himself to remember, with painful precision, that moment when his sex buried itself in his companion's moist vulva. Drink from the woman's cup and thirst for ever . . . Eventually, unable to bear it any longer, Kader dismounted; claiming an urgent need, he hid behind a clump of wattle amd caressed himself. As he was readjusting his clothing, he noticed that a frilled lizard was gazing at him with great curiosity. Kader, ill at ease, chuckled:

"Hey, don't denounce me! Fortunately, neighbour, you can't speak."

The lizard flashed the bright pink border around its gaping mouth, hissing furiously before disappearing beneath a rock. Kader went back to Lislei, feeling out of sorts. She was leaning against a mound, wiping away the rust-coloured dust staining her face. His voice was tart as he growled:

"It's your turn to get on this humpy ass."

It was not true. She should have kept walking for a good hour more. Lislei cast him a grateful glance.

That evening, they are exhausted when they return from their expedition. Their clothes hang heavily on them. The mud that covers them almost to the waist has dried into large foul-smelling patches. They had been trapped in a salt lake, the crust of which turned out to be fragile. The dromedary panicked when it felt the ground giving way beneath its hoofs. Under the noonday sun, they wore themselves out extracting the animal from the viscous, mustard-coloured dough.

Kader was the first to enter the yard, dragging the dromedary behind him; it is in poor shape. The man lowered his head, turning cantankerous and mulish thoughts over in his mind. This evening, all this'll have to stop. This evening, they must have it out. This evening, they must put an end to this folly . . .

It was Lislei who whispered:

"They're here!"

"Who?" Kader grumbled, before noticing them himself.

There are three of them, the old medicine man, the warrior-of-tears and a third man, who is wearing a filthy hat. Silent, armed with spears. Though they are all naked, the only one who really looks naked is the man in the hat. Kader forces the muscles of his legs to go tense to stop them from trembling.

Lislei has gone over to the warrior-of-tears. Wide-eyed, she stares at him inquisitively. Without uttering the least sound, the man points towards the interior of the shelter. The woman ran into the room. Kader heard Lislei's stifled cry. She reappeared in the doorway, holding Trid by the hand. She is beaming while the child looks straight ahead with an expressionless face. He is no longer wearing a bandage, but a large cicatrice still disfigures the base of the neck.

The three warriors have sat down in the middle of the yard, in the full sun. Kader understands that they are waiting for them to do the same. He lets go of the dromedary's bridle. His heart is pounding like a drum. Lislei is already squatting; Trid is a little way behind her. The child is appallingly thin. Here it is, "the decisive moment for those who are indecisive", the Arab realises with an onrush of anguish.

The man in the hat is supposed to act as interpreter. Lislei has great difficulty understanding him. He tells her that he was a stockman with a grazier, but ran away because they treated him so harshly. The translator spat on the ground. He fixes his hate-filled eyes on Lislei then on Kader:

"Damned whites, damned whites!"

Is he speaking about his former employers or does he have the occupants of the shelter in his sight? For a brief instant, Lislei shudders at the thought of the fate that must have been set aside for O'Hara and Wallace. The old medicine-man has started speaking, expressing himself in peeping little snatches in a language that seems to consist only of vowels. In the tone of his voice, it is possible to discern a mixture of hostility and good will. He points to the child, his inflection passes from incomprehension to contempt, to fury.

"What is he saying?" Kader whispers.

"Wait."

Lislei, her features taut, listens to the intepreter. She makes him say it again. The man, with a faint touch of irony, does so. He screws up his nose, revealing clearly enough that he does not appreciate the smell of mud.

"They knew that we hadn't left the shelter. They kept watch over us all along. He says that they are amazed, the words the child uses do not belong to any language they have ever heard, in any place where their steps have taken them in the bush. Apart from English words, it goes without saying. Trid wept all the time. The man insists that Trid asked them to let him go home. They do not understand where that is, that place beyond the Great Water . . ."

She hesitates. Her voice is expressionless:

"The old man is furious because the child has refused to eat for some days. They have . . . they have beaten him several times, but they could not manage to make him change his mind. They are afraid that he will die. They say that it will bring them misfortune, a child who no longer wishes to live. The old man says that sorrow is even more greedy than scabies. When it bites one, it bites all. They want nothing of this disease. Their own people have enough of their own misfortunes. Already, he insists, it is difficult enough to keep up the strength they need to survive the hunters' and the land-snatchers' rifles."

The three Aborigines embark on a discussion among themselves. The old man's eyes grow narrow with discontent. The man in the hat raises his voice, as if he were disputing some point. He brandishes his spear, clears his throat. The warrior-of-tears comes between them, touching the stockman's shoulder as if to console him, and whispers something while he looks at Lislei. The interpreter seems to have grown resigned and, with a sullen look, addresses her.

Then she turns to Kader. Her hand wipes away the sweat running down her face, leaving behind long salty streaks. She swallows hard:

"They have made up their mind to leave Trid with us, at least for the time being. The medicine man is of the opinion that the child is insane because he claims that we are members of his family . . ."

"Why did you tell them that we are related?"

She stroked the child's hair. Lislei and Tridarir stayed squatting in the dust until the three warriors reached the other side of the dry river-bed. Kader followed them as far as the casuarina trunk.

"Kad threw my father and mother in the Great Water . . . *Oyb!* And he spoke some words to console them for having been ill-treated while they were alive."

He has trouble getting his breath back. At no time does a smile break over his emaciated face. The child must have turned all this over in his mind hundreds of times.

"Li, you looked after me . . . *Oyb!* you hugged me while I slept . . . Only my mother . . . You . . . him . . . You protected me once, twice, three times . . ."

He held up all the fingers of his hand and counted again: "*marrawah . . . piawah . . . luwah . . .*". Trid's voice is shrill. He goes on, more softly:

"So . . . so you . . . you are . . . became my aunt and my uncle . . . my sister and my brother . . . And . . . you are going to take me back to the other side . . . aren't you?"

Lislei has stood up. She murmurs, forgetting the stinking mud on her dress:

"Get up Trid, we'll get filthy if we leave our bottoms stuck in the dirt!"

There is a sudden pang in her breast. The woman is shaken by a fit of coughing, she is like someone drunk on sorrow.

"*Drink from the cup of destiny when it serves you that which resembles happiness.*" Kader has put his hand in his pocket and touches the *Book of Songs*. Are you still there, little book, so how does the rest of the poem go? "*But for that cup where you will only find deadly calamity perhaps, would you be prepared to pay the asked-for price?*"

Lislei told him what Trid said. Without comment. Kader sighs. He is unable to remember the other verses any more accurately. Throughout his captivity, he dreamed intensely, passionately only of one thing. If he was able to escape, if he was able to kill, it was for that. And is this the *cost* of that cup?

Lislei turns her back to him. She is busying herself with Trid. The child has not spoken another word. She prepared some food for him and feeds him mouth-to-mouth, like a bird. "*He was and he was not, in the very ancient time both the Lily and the Basil . . .*" His throat tight, Kader thinks: if you knew, Lislei, how beautiful Algeria is, if you knew what a terrible price you are asking me to pay for loving you, Trid and you . . .

From her taut shoulders, Kader realises that she is waiting for a reply to the question she has not put.

He lit a fire. Twilight settles gently over the bush. A battered pot is at the centre of the fireplace. A stew of beans is cooking slowly in it. Soon, it will be necessary to go to see the Afghan again.

The dying sun brushes the scrub and the prickly pear. Kader's eyes follow the flight of an eagle slashing its lust for life across the sky. Lislei and Trid have joined him around the fire. The child is still naked because there are no clothes to fit him. No-one speaks.

Only the birds remain as the last witnesses of what is rising on the surface of the earth. So, today, there is just this bird of prey . . . To mask his joy, Kader knits his brow. He bends over the fire, pulls a lump of coal out with a stick. He waits for it to cool before breaking off a clump of cinders. Lislei and Trid watch, with astonished eyes, as he gets up and pretends to go into the room. Lislei shrugs, sinking again into her sullen thoughts. Her heart is heavy with contempt for Kader, for his silent rebuff. Oh, he did not say anything, but that is worse, perhaps.

Only the child continues to observe what the man is doing. Coming back, he signals to Tridarir to stay silent. When he is just behind Lislei, Kader takes, with his right hand, a fistful of ash from the palm of the left.

Lislei notices a change in Trid's attitude. She turns around abruptly, but cannot evade the hand smearing her cheeks with ash.

"What's got into you? I have just washed myself . . ."

She chokes with indignation:

"I . . ."

She has understood. Kader's smile is well on the way to turning into a laugh. He holds out the ash-covered palm of his hand.

"It's your turn, Lislei. Trid, come, you too . . ."

He closes his eyes. Feels the woman's fingers then the child's as, turn by turn, they spread the black powder meticulously over his face, his cheeks, his chin. Of a sudden, Lislei bursts out laughing. *Who loves woman is a cousin of the sun.*

Kader murmurs softly:

"Honey is concealed beneath your tongue, Lislei."

Lislei, taken by surprise, stops. She must have grown pale. Or blushed. But nothing shines through the clown's face apart from sparkling eyes and a slight tremor of the lips. To hide his feelings, Kader grabs the child by the shoulders:

"Up, kangaroo! Do you think you're going to get off lightly?"

He has lifted the little Aborigine by the waist. Trid struggles, giggling as Kader and Lislei daub him with ash.

There's a short whistling cry, perhaps the call of the eagles still circling around and around. The night is dark in the yard, apart from the ring of light illuminating, for the moment, the sooty faces of two adults and a child, all of whom are shouting with laughter as they chase each other.

The woman and the man brush against each other. Then touch. The Arab is out of breath:

"You see, Lislei . . . Trid is laughing! For the first time . . . You, me, we're not worth a scrap . . . It's even worse for Trid . . . Perhaps . . . we can . . . only be whole when there's three of us? But that, that means too much misfortune and, if we are lucky, just a little happiness. Could we bear that for ever?"

Lislei puts on her girlish, pouting face, which, every time, gives Kader a mad desire to embrace her, to fornicate with her and to protect her. Forcing herself to seem more perky than she is, she raises a hand, the index finger and the middle forked to conjure fate.

She puts her arms around Kader and Trid. And the man, more moved than he has ever been, feels the soft silky touch of the woman's hair against his cheek and neck.

EPILOGUE

Queensland, North-East Australia, January 1919

There, so it's done. The coffin has been lowered into the ground. The preacher intoned a few grandiloquent words, I threw the *Book of Songs* on top of the coffin, someone gave a little cry, thinking it was a Bible.

Lislei had begged me: "When they begin throwing earth over me, think about my breasts, about what they were like when we first met, and about what you called the little willow weeping between my thighs; that way, perhaps, I won't be quite so dead for you. Swear that you'll do it!" She laughed and coughed violently, what is more – that was two days before her death – insisting that she could see me with a black band around my erect sex. In this cemetery, less than a metre from the man of God preaching about heaven and the might of the Lord, I tried to think about my wife's lower parts because I had sworn to. And about the daisy I once placed along her vagina. But I could not do it, because I was sure I would weep. There were a few clods of earth. And then, nothing more.

I went home, supported by Trid. I could feel the censorious looks on the faces of those who had come to the funeral; on such a day, you should be surrounded by your own people, and not by someone half-human, an Aborigine, no matter how close he might be to the family. Even Joseph, my son, seemed embarrassed. Perhaps because of his wife Margaret's attitude. She is always on her high horse about what's proper and what isn't in a little town like Allisson. He poked his chin in his wife's direction, probably meaning to say: excuse him, it's his grief, he is no longer in his right mind. Margaret pulled a long face, she has always thought that Trid took up too much space in the life of the household. "And then who knows where he'll be dawdling when he disappears from the farm for days and months? He comes back filthy, exhausted, his clothes in tatters, he is going to pick up all sorts of diseases from those blacks and he'll bring them back with him!" she grumbled one day, thinking that I was out of earshot.

I stretched out on the bed where Lislei and I have slept all these last years. For several days now, I can only think of her by calling her Lislei. My granddaughter looked at me with pity in her eyes when I forgot myself and spoke to her about her grandmother Lislei. "What does that mean, that peculiar name, Granddad? My grandmother's called Elizabeth . . . Elizabeth!" Caught out, I nodded my head in docile agreement and said nothing to my darling Joan.

I am freezing, even though the heat is stifling. Trid has tucked me in like a child. He got a chair and put it down next to the bed. A little hesitant, he settled down at the bedside. Always the lowered eyes, that timid deportment, essential everywhere in this country where any white man would react violently if a blackfellow dared to look him straight in the eye.

"Kad . . ."

Trid never called us anything other than Kad and Li. He is now over fifty and I am almost eighty. He never got used to those disguise-names, Harry and Elizabeth. He cleared his throat, stayed silent for a good while.

"Li, Kad, *mena loyetea nena* . . ."

I know almost nothing of Trid's language. His true language, the language of the island of his childhood. Perhaps the oldest language on earth. But those words, I could never forget them: "Li, Kad, I love you." Ah yes, how many times have we not heard it!

When Trid was a child, he was always afraid that we would abandon him. At night, when his anguish became unbearable, he used to creep furtively into our room, kneel down in front of our bed and murmur, like a song or a prayer, *mena loyetea nena . . . mena loyetea nena . . .* until we would let him get into bed with us. In time that turned into a game and the words "*mena . . .*" became synonymous with "can I get into bed with you?"

Now it is a man with grey hair and a grey beard who is whispering: "Li, Kad, I love you . . ."

I take his hand. He has been speaking about Lislei as if she were still alive. I lift my head, try to make a joke. I control my breathing, I whisper: "Trid, my little boy, you can still get in bed with us . . ." but sorrow overwhelms me.

"Trid, I miss her so much!"

The Aborigine has let his head drop, he crosses his two hands on his knees. His shoulders shake. I am certain that his grief is even greater than mine. For all that, he will not weep in front of my eyes.

The sun has just risen. We, Trid and I, took the horses out with as little noise as possible. A week has gone by since my wife was buried. I feel that I have an open wound, a stabbing pain which never leaves me. All the time, I want to howl but I dare not because everyone around me seems to have come to terms with Lislei's death. Even Joseph, although he was very close to her . . . "But you loved her, all the same!" I almost protested in the middle of dinner yesterday; Margaret had burst into peals of laughter at some story or other about cattle and Joseph joined in. I rose from the table, terrified that I would start sobbing and furious because no-one noticed it. No-one paid attention to me. In the evening I overheard a woman of the neighbourhood insisting that Mrs Sutherland had died a beautiful death, surrounded by her husband, her son and his family. In this time of war, she'd been devilishly lucky, she remarked and added: "and then she was so old, it's better this way, isn't it?" A terrible rage shook me, I wanted to hurl insults at our neighbour. Courage deserted me at the last moment, but a mute sense of shame stayed with me, as if I had allowed Lislei to be maligned without intervening.

The horses are picking their way along the rutted track. The railway station is some twenty miles away. Trid has not yet revealed to me why he wanted me to come along. "Bring clothes for a long journey", was all he let on. I had a pang in my heart because he also asked me to give him his share of "the captain's money". It has been almost fifty years now that I have been looking after Trid's portion and made it grow. Despite our insistence, he never wanted to use it. I had explained to him that a third of everything we had, Lislei and I, the house, the land, the livestock, would come to him by law. He shrugged in silent reprobation. He once said to me, in that gentle way he has of bringing a discussion to a definitive close, that he only had one possible use for that money. Without divulging it. He kept his teeth clenched to prevent them from chattering, and I recognised that the most peaceable man on earth it has been my good fortune to know had bottled up an unquenchable hatred, always accompanied by that boundless incomprehension at its heart: "*Why did they do it to us? Why did they wipe us out?*"

The child has grown old. I have grown old. The little naked child and the runaway gaolbird are still together, their figures a little more bent, however. Neither of us has forgotten those years when we wandered all over Australia, the constant danger, the fear of being turned in, the moments of happiness we snatched and defended in total secrecy behind a fortress of lies. The taciturn Aborigine pacing beside me is probably one of the most wonderful things that have happened to me. The most devious, certainly. I loved him – I love him – more than my son. Perhaps as much as I could love – and loved – Lislei. I can feel my heart beating faster because of this ridiculous way of reckoning love. I have often asked myself whether, in the final count, Lislei had stayed with me only because of her affection for the child she'd seen put to such torture on the ship. It is possible. For me, however, it is an additional reason why I am so attached to Trid.

We left the horses with a farrier. I had to beg the station-master to let Tridarir board the train. There was such distaste in the Queenslander's eyes that at first I thought he would refuse, despite the money I slipped surreptitiously into the palm of his hand. I claimed that the Aborigine was my servant and that, at my age, I could not travel without someone to look after me. The station-master muttered that it was a peculiar idea to have Nigger vermin for a manservant.

"Get into the rear carriage, and don't leave it," he finally gave permission. "I don't want to have trouble with the other passengers."

As we were about to board the train, the station-master pulled me by the sleeve:

"You're sure your Abo has the right to go wherever you are going? Everyone's seen me talking to you, I don't want to get mixed up in any infringement."

I replied emphatically that I was certainly sure, though, in reality, I know nothing about such things. Regulations concerning Aborigines vary from state to state, and whoever can tell exactly what a *native* is still entitled to do in Australia would need to be pretty knowledgeable.

When the train moved off, we found ourselves sitting on crates near the lavatories. Trid made no comment. He sighed, no more than that. He has learned to live with this endless humiliation, his face and body locked into an exhausted impassiveness. Looking through the window, he gazed at the landscape of Australia Felix, which has been so cruel to its first inhabitants, as it unrolled.

Ah, Trid, my own . . . Nothing has changed in Australia in the course of these last years. The massacre of the Aborigines has not stopped, it has been aggravated by greedy farmers eyeing the pastureland of the reservation-prisons set up by Christian missionaries. In the course of a dozen years now, all the state parliaments have passed, one after the other, laws allowing the separation of black children from their families in order to raise them in institutions run by the churches. For the officially declared purpose of saving these children from the vicious influence of their mothers and fathers. The government of Queensland has even looked into the possibility of deporting all of the state's Aborigines to Palm Island, more than a thousand miles from Brisbane and thirty miles from the coast . . . At heart, all white Australians of the mainland envy – and copy – more or less overtly the bloody practices that went on in Tasmania, the one state which succeeded, in so short a time, in cleansing the whole of its territory of Aboriginal defilement . . .

I now know where Trid wants us to go. It will take us a week, perhaps two. We must cross Queensland and a part of New South Wales to arrive in the neighbourhood of Melbourne in Victoria.

"Why do you want to go so far?" I wondered with growing anxiety. I had warned no-one at home that I would be gone such a long time. My son Joseph and his wife would get alarmed, put my disappearance down to the way senile old men are apt to run off.

"I'll tell you later, Kad. Trust me."

"I will always trust you, Trid."

In fact, as I understood from the look of restrained triumph on his face, *we will not be going back*! I was so moved by this discovery that it filled me with fear. My companion knows that I also know now. He gives me a feeble smile:

"Forgive me, Kad."

"I have nothing to forgive you, Trid."

A painful pang shoots through my heart, an old man's heart. I close my eyes. I open them again. I closed my eyes because I can immediately conjure up images from the past: me, droning away at my English lessons, Lislei laughing, the little Trid fashioning wreaths from chicken feathers for us and, annoyed, protesting: "Not on the head, you wear them on the top of the arm!", our first house, my wife's saliva in my mouth, Trid weeping at night because he is calling for his mother . . .

I open my eyes because I am choking, so many of those things are still very close to me. And gone beyond recall. I am a donkey that wants to bray in distress.

The journey is difficult. No inn wants to take in an Aborigine. We have been reduced to sleeping in barns and, often enough, under the starry sky. I feel as if I am mortifying my flesh to sanctify a pilgrimage. Trid is in a singular mood. He gives me the impression, at one moment, that he is strangely happy, the next he seems to be afflicted with hideous sorrow, which makes him crumple like a piece of burnt paper.

We have not got as far as Melbourne. The wagon stopped for a moment in a little fishing village to give the horses a rest. Trid unloaded our luggage, and the wagon left without us. We paced up and down along the jetty of the little port, our hands shading our eyes, dazzled by the sunshine. The sea was beautiful, with rolling foam-fringed waves spilling their violent kisses over the rocks.

"It's because *it* is just over there, eh?" I asked.

He murmured, "Yes, it is . . .," but could not go on, his voice suddenly too husky. He stayed silent for a moment. Then he took out of his pocket a page of a book, carefully folded in four, and held it out to me.

"Do you remember? It's the very first book Li bought for me. There was a map of Australia . . . The one you're holding in your hand . . . I tore it out. Since then, it has never left me . . ."

He chuckles sadly:

"Li didn't know about it, it goes without saying. She did not like me to spoil the books she gave me."

I stood there speechless. Trid tapped me on the shoulder: "Don't pull such a face, Kad!" Abruptly quickening his pace, he went over to a fisherman sitting on an upturned boat who was mending his net. I saw the fisherman looking at him with amazement at first, then he raised his voice. I hurried over.

"Has he gone mad, your Abo? He's making fun of me, he wants to buy my boat!"

I managed to buy the boat – at a price – ("Use only the money from the ship, it's important for me," Trid insisted). I didn't ask any questions. We rowed the boat, clumsily, past the rocks for a good part of the afternoon. Trid seemed to be in excellent humour. He pealed with laughter when the waves sprayed over us. I came to suspect that here was a whole part of his life which had escaped us until then. Since his adolescence, he used to vanish without warning for a week at a time, sometimes for months. We came at length to discover that he went walkabout, that forlorn wandering from tribe to tribe across the whole of Australia. We realised that he was attempting to create new song-lines, but never managed to do it. We used to wait for his return, our stomachs tight with anxiety. He never wanted to take us into his confidence over any of his encounters with the Aborigines of the mainland, except once: "They are neighbours of mine, they are almost my people, but they are not mine. Time separates us." He said this in his usual voice, calm and careworn.

When the sun sank low on the horizon, we dragged the boat to the beach. From where we were standing, the village was hardly visible any more. Night fell. We ate, we stretched out on the sand, the boat sheltering us from the wind. The stars, assembled into those strange troops of light which I never had enough time to get to know, were sparkling in the night sky.

"Kad, the day Li decided to go back to her own country, do you remember it?"

"Yes, Trid . . ."

I waited for the rest, but Trid did not go on. Of course I remembered it! We were still in the Northern Territory, Trid was no more than fourteen, fifteen years old. One day I brought a bundle of old newspapers home, I'd bought them from a bankrupt bookseller. We had almost nothing to read, I thought that these would give us a little amusement, even though the news was very much out of date. The same evening, Lislei pushed under my eyes a paragraph about an amnesty for communards. For a whole a month, I observed Lislei closely. One morning, she announced her decision to return to France. "I must go to look for Camille . . . Do you understand?" No, I didn't understand. And Trid kept silent about it. We accompanied her as far as Sydney. We left before she went on board. We stopped for the night with the farmer who had put us up on the way. I wanted to console Trid, but I could not find the words. Lying on the straw, I had the terrifying sensation that little by little we would slide, the child and I, back into the abyss from which we, all three of us, had managed to escape. In the morning, Lislei rejoined us. How she had contrived, mediocre horsewoman that she was at the time, to find her way back there by night, she could not explain. More than a little panic-stricken, very pale, she behaved as if nothing miraculous had occurred. She gave us chocolates – they had melted in the heat – and we set out for home again, Trid clinging to her like a tick. That day, I had an inkling of the price she had to pay for staying with us.

Tridarir went on, as if our thoughts had been following the same course:

"And that little girl . . . Camille . . . Did you ever have news of her?"

"No . . . She was her brother's daughter . . . your cousin in a sense . . ."

Trid cleared his throat. He failed to reply. He said nothing else. There was nothing more than the incessant growling of the swell scraping against the reef.

I woke very early. But Trid was already on his feet. He was busying himself around the boat. He had managed to drag it almost to the water's edge. The sea is higher than yesterday. Trid has undressed completely. He came back to me, looked at me with compassion.

"It's time, Kader, the sea is about to rise, I'm going over there."

"You'll drown yourself, Tridarir (I did not dare call him Trid), you'll never make it to Tasmania. And besides, there's nothing left for you there . . ."

"I do not need to go as far as that. My parents are out there, in the middle of the water. I will simply join them."

My voice broke:

"Why? Has the Dreaming come to an end?"

He smiled:

"You are old, Kader. If I die after you, there will be no-one left to weep for me. I cannot imagine how there might be no-one, no human being, left to weep for the last, the very last of my people. They deserve that at least, those numbskull Niggers of Tasmania, too fuck-witted even to work out how to light a fire! You, on the other hand, you love me, so you will weep . . ."

"And me?" I shot back at him with cowardice.

"You, you have your son, your granddaughter . . ."

He clasped me in his arms.

"Have no fear for me, Kad. I'll quickly find my way again . . . I will pass on your greetings to my father and my mother. My mother always assured me that we would all meet again up there around a campfire . . . Perhaps, when we're together, we will be able to understand why we were booted in the arse until . . . These thousands of years we've survived, what was the use of that? We would've been no more than a grass fire for others to piss on. And doesn't anyone among those who killed us feel any remorse? To understand, yes . . . if there's a lousy explanation for that! . . . I want so much to snuggle up against my parents, to set their minds at rest about what became of me . . . I know what they were like, my old folks, they must have got themselves into such a state . . ."

He grasped my hand, then dropped it abruptly.

"Without you, without Lislei, I could not have endured waiting so long!"

His eyes suddenly misted over. He turned his head away. Because sobs were crowding in my throat, I wanted to interrupt him in anger and scream at him that it was idiocy, those old tales of campfires, that he himself didn't believe any of that, that when people died, everyone died only once, that I refused to let him snuff it, that I didn't give a damn whether he was the last of the Tasmanians, that for me he would always be the lad who saved our lives and the one I loved . . . Face to face with that naked man, I could only moan: "No, I beg you . . ."

The Aborigine cast a glance at the immense ocean. The wind had risen, puffed up by trade winds born high above the Indian Ocean. Trid shivered.

"I think that my father and mother would have been very happy to meet you, Li and you . . ."

He started to walk away from me, his body slightly bowed, his sex dangling between his thin thighs. Without looking back. Not without difficulty, he dragged the boat into the water. A wave overturned him, but he managed to heave himself into the craft. He screwed up his nose, because he must have swallowed a lot of water. He started rowing. He was doing it badly. He did not look at me a second time.

I followed his shape until it vanished in the troughs between the waves. I lifted my arm, still unable to believe my eyes. Bile began to flood into my throat.

"Bastard," I burped, "bastard!"

Peacefully, the rolling waves continued polishing the landscape with their foam. A somewhat stronger wave carried away the shoes which had been left lying on the sand. The shirt was still dry, a gull landed near it. One eye turned towards me, it gave the bundle a few greedy pecks. A supplication rose in me, brutal as a dagger: "Tell me, Trid, tell me at least that you've knocked up someone somewhere, eh? When you used to disappear, for a month, for a week, a black woman or a white, pretty or ugly, whatever kind you yearned for . . . It wouldn't make any sense for a young fellow like you to leave nothing behind! Trid, it's not fair, there are so many questions I haven't asked you yet . . ."

I caught sight of Joan before she noticed me. It was already dusk. She was hurtling down the narrow path like a mad thing. My granddaughter's joy was balm to my heart. At the same time, it did not touch me at all. I sighed. I couldn't give a damn now about Algeria, about France and about Australia. I stopped my horse. It was bathed in sweat. I patted it to calm it.

I thought of the two sweet savages of my tribe. Of Lislei. Of Tridarir. Of the ruin of our love now that they were both dead.

"Granddad, I am so happy to see you!" Joan called out.